Final Call

Alex Lake is a British novelist who was born in the North West of England. *After Anna*, the author's first novel written under this pseudonym, was a No.1 bestselling ebook sensation and a top-ten *Sunday Times* bestseller. The author now lives in the North East of the US.

 @AlexLakeAuthor

Also by Alex Lake

After Anna
Killing Kate
Copycat
The Last Lie
Seven Days
The Choice
Ready or Not

Final Call

Alex Lake

HarperCollins*Publishers*

HarperCollins*Publishers*
1 London Bridge Street,
London SE1 9GF

www.harpercollins.co.uk

HarperCollins*Publishers*
Macken House, 39/40 Mayor Street Upper,
Dublin 1, D01 C9W8, Ireland

First published by HarperCollins*Publishers* 2023
1

A catalogue record for this book is available from the British Library

ISBN: 978-0-00-853202-4 (PB b-format)
ISBN: 978-0-00-853203-1 (TPB)

Typeset in Sabon LT Std by Palimpsest Book Production Ltd, Falkirk, Stirlingshire

Printed and Bound in the UK using 100% Renewable Electricity at CPI Group (UK) Ltd

MIX
Paper | Supporting
responsible forestry
FSC
www.fsc.org   FSC™ C007454

To Sharad and Adam

PART ONE

The Pilot

The pre-flight checks were complete. Engine, hydraulics, fuel: all fine. The weather too was clear. No rain, no wind, no snow, despite the time of year. It would be a smooth flight.

In terms of turbulence, anyway.

She had flown aircraft hundreds of times, but her palms were as damp with sweat and her heart racing as fast as on her first flight.

Faster. This was the most important flight she would ever take. The rest of her life – and of her passengers – would be determined by what happened on this flight. How happy and fulfilled it was. How much meaning and purpose it had.

How long it would be. Decades? Years? Months?

Or hours.

To all external appearances – and to all the passengers – it was just another flight. Just a corporate jet shuttling some executives back home for Christmas.

But appearances can be deceptive. There was nothing normal about this flight, nothing at all. And it would not be long before everyone on board knew it.

Their lives were about to change forever.

A movement from the hangar caught her eye and she

glanced out of the cockpit window. The door to the office was open and a woman in a red wool overcoat and dark pants was walking toward the plane, her phone to her ear.

The pilot checked the manifest. She had counted six. This was the seventh, and last, to board.

She recognized her. Jill Stearns, CEO of one of the country's – the world's – largest food companies.

She spoke into her headset to let the tower know they were ready to depart. She made her voice low and deep and male with a drawling Southern accent. 'Fully boarded. Lemme know when you have a slot for takeoff.'

There was a burst of static, then a male voice, low and calm, replied, 'Whenever you're ready. Quiet day to day.'

It was usually quiet in these kind of airports. Small, local airfields used primarily for freight and private planes. There was no security, no baggage scans or ID checks. You just walked on to the plane like it was a chauffeur-driven car.

Which made this much easier. Made it possible at all.

She glanced at the empty seat next to her. She'd have to hope the tower didn't ask to speak to the pilot who was supposed to be there, or they'd figure out she was the only one on board and refuse her permission to depart.

Although this late in the game permission no longer mattered. She didn't need it. Once everyone was boarded, she would be taxiing the plane down the runway and into the winter sky. She hadn't come this far – all this way, after all these years – to turn back now.

Jill Stearns

Her phone rang just as she left the hangar. She looked at the screen. Mila, her daughter. Had it been anyone else – a board member, maybe, or a banker calling to wish her all the best for the holidays – she would have taken the call and boarded the plane as she spoke. It was fine for the other passengers – her staff – to hear that kind of conversation. In fact, it would help remind one or two of them that she was the boss.

But not a conversation with Mila. That was personal, and she did not mix personal with professional. Besides, she and Mila had not always got along that well. Things were better now that her daughter was out of college and starting her career, but the teenage years – that was how Jill thought of them, 'The Teenage Years', as though they were a discrete and distant event that had happened to someone else – had been a little challenging, if by 'a little challenging' you meant an out-and-out daily battle. At some point her daughter had transformed from a cute little friend who padded around beside her gazing – at least in Jill's memory – adoringly up at her, into a sullen, unsmiling adolescent who hated everything about her mother and disagreed with everything she said, on what seemed to be a point of principle.

I think I need to take the car in, she'd said once, listening to the brakes grind as they drove to Mila's soccer practice.

Why?

Because the brakes are worn.

No they aren't.

She pressed the brake pedal and the brakes groaned.

That's the sound of worn brakes.

No it isn't.

I was unaware you were an expert on cars.

Like you are?

Well, I'll take it in and see what they say.

They'll say it's not the brakes. It's obviously not the brakes.

So it just happens to occur when I brake?

Mila snorted, and didn't answer. When they arrived at the field, she glared at her mother. *I hate you. You're such a know-it-all, but you don't know* anything.

Jill wanted to reply, *Really? Odd, then, that I should be the multimillionaire CEO of a massive corporation, charged by the shareholders with making complex decisions that impact the lives of thousands and thousands of employees and customers and suppliers every single day. So maybe I know* something. *Maybe I know one little thing, after all.*

She didn't, though. She just watched her daughter walk to the field, where she fist-bumped the coach – Annette, her friend Fern's mom – then hugged her.

Hugged her. Jill would have given anything for such a warm, natural, hug from her daughter.

Then Annette laughed, broke the embrace and pointed to a pile of cones. Mila jogged over and started laying them out, a wide smile on her face.

It's just me she hates, Jill thought. *Which is really unfair. I'm her mom. I do everything for her, provide whatever she could want. And yet it's me she hates?*

She knew it was a childish and self-pitying response, and that her daughter was a typical teenager, but it didn't help. She felt rejected and unloved.

And now Mila was calling. Anxiety prickled her scalp. It could well be something simple – *What time will you be home, Mom?* – but Jill had plenty of scars from the trauma of previous phone calls with her daughter. Yes, they argued less now, but less was not never, and when it started it could escalate pretty quickly, especially if certain topics came up. And she did not need *anyone* to witness that.

She stopped halfway to the plane and answered the call.

'Hi,' she said. 'What's up?'

'Hi Mom. What time are you home?'

Jill glanced at her watch. 'I'm just about to board the plane. It's two now, so I should be back by four.'

'OK, great. Archie and I wanted to take you out to dinner.'

Them take *her*? That was a first. She wondered exactly what type of dinner it would be. McDonald's, maybe, or KFC?

But more, she wondered why.

'Really?' she said, allowing herself a little white lie. 'That's a nice surprise. What's the occasion?'

'Nothing.'

'Nothing? You just felt like buying me dinner?'

'There is something. We have some news.'

Jill turned and looked back at the hangar.

'What kind of news?'

The Pilot

She had stopped. The woman in the red coat, Jill Stearns, CEO, had come out of the hangar and started to make her way to the plane, but now she had stopped.

She turned around to face the hangar.

The pilot's stomach knotted. She had come to a halt when she had answered the phone. Why? Who was she talking to?

Why had they called? Did someone know what was about to happen? How *could* they?

It was impossible. No one knew.

She looked at the empty seat next to her.

Perhaps someone had noticed the absence of a copilot? Or perhaps he – and the pilot who should have been in her seat – had been found and released and sounded the alarm? She pictured them as she had left them: no, they were not out yet, she was sure of that.

But then why had the woman stopped? What was happening?

She got out of her seat and put her hand on the flight deck door. She hesitated; she had wanted to keep it closed so no one saw her, but she needed to take a closer look. Maybe she could hear what Stearns was saying.

She unlocked it and pushed it open, then stepped into the galley. She pulled it closed behind her so no one would notice the flight deck was now empty, and walked to the main door. To her left she could see into the main cabin. It was small; there were seven seats, all of which, excluding one, were taken.

She went out onto the top step and stared at Stearns, straining to hear what she was saying. She could not make it out.

Stearns was still facing the hangar. The pilot started down the stairs. Maybe she could ask what was going on, tell her that *they had a departure slot, so she was awfully sorry but if there was any way she could board shortly that would be much appreciated?*

And what if she said, *No, thank you, but I'm staying put?* What then?

Then this would all be over before it had even got started. Years of planning, gone in an instant.

That could not happen. She had to do something, now. Drag her onboard, lock the cockpit door, and take off.

She stepped out of the plane onto the tarmac, and started toward Stearns. When she was a few feet away, Stearns turned to face her. She had finished her call and let her hand drop to her side. She was frowning, a look of concern on her face.

She knows, the pilot thought. *Somehow, she knows.*

Then Stearns smiled, a forced, tight smile.

'Sorry,' she said. 'I had to take that one. We ready to go?'

The pilot nodded.

Stearns stared at her. 'Are you new?'

'I am.'

'I'm Jill.' She held out her hand. The pilot shook it briefly, aware of the dampness of her palm.

'Sarah Daniels,' she said.

'Nice to meet you.' Stearns headed toward the plane. The pilot followed, weak with relief. Her legs were shaking and she had to fight to maintain a calm demeanor.

Stearns climbed the stairs and turned right. The pilot looked around the airport, wondering whether there would be someone – a police officer, an official of some kind – sprinting toward them.

There was nothing.

She smiled, and entered the plane. She closed the main cabin door and stepped into the cockpit.

There was no turning back now.

Chip Markham

Charles – Chip – Markham looked up from his paper – he hated reading on a tablet or phone – as Jill Stearns put down her bag in the aisle. It was a sleek, multicolored backpack that said, *Look at me, I'm the CEO of a major food company but see how casual and modern I am*. He stifled a smile. It really was very transparent.

He sat back in his chair and tilted his neck, stretching it as far as he could. Something in it clicked and the tension in the back of his skull dissipated, leaving in its wake a sense of profound relief. He'd have to go and get it looked at; recently he'd been experiencing the build-up of an uncomfortable sensation at the back of his head, a kind of pressure, which could only be relieved by stretching his neck until it cracked.

At his age he hated going to the doctor with some odd complaint. The chance of the reply being *Oh, don't worry you'll be fine* was ever-dwindling, replaced by an increasing likelihood of tests and checks and scans and – in the worst case – diagnoses.

The pilot – he didn't recognize her – closed the main door and headed to the cockpit. They'd be airborne soon, and then he'd be home for a large Scotch and a few chapters of the book on General Patton he was reading. A two-hour flight, more or less, then thirty minutes to his house in Cape Elizabeth and a berth in his armchair by the window over-looking the ocean.

Thank God for the company jet.

The rest of the world was packed into a dirty, crowded airport, scrambling to get a slightly better seat, hoping that their flight wasn't delayed or canceled, choosing from a selection of greasy sandwiches and over-priced drinks. Life was dismal for most people, and especially during the last few years. Shuffling around in masks, terrified of catching some awful disease from the people around them, but unable to avoid them.

But here he was, on a plane almost his own. A plane that would take off on time and get him, and his colleagues, to their destination as fast as possible, and in as much comfort as possible.

There had been a review of expenses at the height of the COVID pandemic and the question of the corporate jet had come up. Was it really the best use of company funds? With people struggling to make ends meet, was a corporate jet really a good look (he hated the phrase *a good look* – fucking stupid consultant speak). And wasn't it kind of a disaster for the environment? He had clear ideas on the answer, but the question was out there: couldn't senior executives fly commercial?

They could, Chip said. And they would, if the review found that to be the best solution. Nothing was off the table; all options would be considered and weighed appropriately.

And they were. Thoroughly, and with all due diligence. The paper trail was clear: options had been reviewed, costs and benefits weighed and assessed, and the answer was in: the jet stayed. There were many good reasons and Chip could have quoted them all, but the real reason – and one he would never have mentioned – was more simple: there was no way he was flying commercial.

So the jet was wonderful and he loved it. There was one small aspect that he would have changed, that could have made it better. He could have been in the seat across the aisle.

There was a clear hierarchy in the allocation of seats. It was unspoken, and he and Jill would have denied it existed, but they got the seats at the front, the seats with more legroom and a table. Everyone else sat in the normal seats – good by commercial standards, but still a little cramped – behind them.

Of course, no one had a specific seat number on their ticket – there *were* no tickets, or boarding passes, so anyone could have taken any seat they wanted – but if you got on first and you were not Chip or Jill it was understood to be career-limiting if you did not sit in one of the five seats at the back of the plane, and leave the others free.

Jill looked over at him and raised an eyebrow. 'Sorry I'm late. Had to take a call.' She nodded at the flight deck. 'New pilot. I've not met her before.'

Chip paused. As CFO the aviation department was part of his remit, and he wondered whether Jill was hinting to him that he should have known about the new pilot. He gave a vague and noncommittal nod. He didn't remember anyone mentioning it to him. Perhaps they had, and he'd forgotten. He couldn't be expected to be on top of everything.

Either way, a pilot was a pilot, and all this one had to do was get them up and down safely.

The Pilot

She had wondered many times what would happen when this moment arrived. She had played it out in her mind's eye over and over and over. Would she be nervous, heart racing and palms damp? Would her voice crack and falter when she spoke to air traffic control? Would her mind be blank and unfocused, concentration hard to come by?

Perhaps she would crack under the pressure and walk away, leave the plane with a comment that she'd be back soon but vanish, never to return? Or maybe she would lose her nerve once they'd taken off and fly them safely home. In the days running up to the flight she had doubted – seriously – whether she could do this.

After all, she didn't have to go through with it. Nobody was making her. It was entirely her choice.

Except it wasn't. There was no choice, not really. She *had* to do this. She had to, or she would not be able to live with herself.

So the question was not whether she had to do it. It was whether she *could*.

Well, now she had her answer. As soon as Jill Stearns was

aboard and the door was locked the only sensation she felt was relief. No fear, no hesitation, no doubts.

Just relief.

In the quiet of the cockpit her heart rate slowed. Her breathing became calm and unhurried. Her mind focused.

She was here.

The time had come.

She put her hand on the throttle, feeling the hum of the engines in her hand. She pushed it gently forward and the plane began to move across the tarmac.

Behind her, seven passengers stretched out their legs or opened their books or looked at their phones. She wondered for a second what they were thinking about – their kids? Their Christmas plans? Their future career?

Whatever it was, none of them had any idea what was about to happen.

Marcia Fournier

The sudden thrust from the engines was like a hard shove at the base of her spine. She was always amazed by the sudden awareness of power that she had when the plane – any plane – started to gather speed on the runway. She had studied engineering at college and she understood the equations outlining how much horsepower was needed to overcome air resistance and gravity and send the plane shooting thirty thousand feet above the surface of the Earth. She could still recall the math, but the raw numbers didn't do it justice.

These two engines – basically some worked metal and a bag of fuel – were going to make this cigar tube with wings – and all its temporary inhabitants – fly. It was just physics, yes, but it was no less magical for that.

As the wheels left the tarmac she closed her eyes and drank in the momentary feeling of weightlessness. It was a ritual of hers to quietly experience the exact second when she ceased to be earthbound. It was still thrilling even after all the flights she had taken.

It was thrilling for another reason: it marked the moment when she could indulge in another ritual. In the old days it had been automatic: as soon as they were airborne the cabin crew would come down the aisle with a tray of white and red wine, which they would hand to the passengers – always white for her – before taking an order for another drink. Marcia flew often on the company jet and the cabin crew – Sharon, Wendy, Christi, and latterly, Patrick – knew her preference: a large vodka and soda with a slice of lemon.

Maybe another, half an hour later, with one more for the descent.

But that was all gone now. There was no alcohol on the company plane. There were no cabin crew either, just the pilots and a self-serve fridge with bottles of water and Diet Coke.

The pilot was new, she'd noticed, a woman she hadn't seen before. Normally the pilots left the door to the flight deck open, but not this one. Maybe it was a new regulation, or maybe she just preferred it that way.

Or maybe she and her copilot were having a secret drink up there. No: it was just her who did that kind of thing.

Because these days that was what she had to do. It made her feel slightly ashamed, but she did it anyway.

When they had stopped serving alcohol on the plane she had made it through a few flights without drinking. It was good: it proved she could, if she wanted to. Then one time she'd had a very tough day. A presentation to a client – she couldn't remember what about now – had gone wrong and Chip, who was then her boss, as well as, at that particular moment, her lover, had told her that if they lost the client as a result she'd pay with her job.

It was a double blow: the professional embarrassment and the personal betrayal. After he said it she couldn't shake the thought that, hours earlier, they had been in her hotel room sharing a bed. It had been an intimate moment, made more so by his request for her to make cat noises, a request to

17

which she agreed with some inward amusement, and now he was threatening her with losing her job.

So yes, it had gone wrong, but in large part that was because she was exhausted after the late-night meowing for Chip and the many drinks they'd had before that. She felt small and anxious and exposed, a feeling not helped by her hangover, and by the time the day was over and they were getting ready to go to the plane she needed a drink.

She *deserved* one.

So she ran out of the office and bought a bottle of vodka and two small bottles of sparkling water from a nearby liquor store, then emptied half of the water out and replaced it with the vodka.

And then, once the plane was airborne, she took one of the water bottles from her bag and drank it.

She knew it wasn't a good idea, but it was just this once. Just on this particular day when she really needed it.

Just this once quickly morphed into a ritual.

Two 12oz bottles of water, half vodka – although more, these days – on each flight.

But never before they were airborne. Never before that moment of weightlessness. That was her proof to herself that she was in control and that she could stop soon. And she was going to. Not just on the plane: she was going to stop drinking altogether. She had a grandchild now, Edie, and she wanted to be there to see her grow up. Not that her drinking was a problem. Yes, she drank most nights – every night, if she was honest – but it was only because her job was so *stressful*. Without the stress she wouldn't drink. So when she retired, maybe five years from now, the drinking would be retired too.

But five years was too long. She was going to quit sooner, much sooner.

Maybe today. Maybe she would leave the bottles she had prepared for this flight in her bag. She pictured herself pouring them out onto the floor by her car door, then starting the car and driving home, a proud non-drinker. Apart from anything else, she shouldn't drink and drive. She happened to be a good driver when she'd been drinking – not everyone was – but she was OK. Better, even. She felt more alert, sharper.

Forget that, though. Today was the day she quit.

She pushed her bag under the seat in front of her and looked out of the window. The ground fell away beneath the plane. She imagined Edie here, sitting on her lap, spellbound by the rapidly receding city.

She reached into her bag for her phone. She'd take a video for her granddaughter.

Her hand brushed the bottle top.

Her mouth dried up and her pulse quickened. She felt a bead of sweat form on her temple. *No*, she told herself, *not today. You made up your mind*.

She pulled her hand away. Her mouth dried up, her lips tingling. She was flooded with a sudden anxiety. Could she get through the flight without the alcohol? Was this who she was? Was there even any point in giving up? Had she already fucked up her health too much for it to matter?

And then there was Sylvia. A marketing director who was surplus to requirements. She was supposed to fire her but had decided to wait until the New Year. She hated firing people.

She took a deep breath. Her head spun. She took another, and another.

It made no difference. The panic would not go away. She felt like screaming and banging herself against the chair in front of her. Maybe that would help.

What would help was in her bag. An insidious inner voice taunted her. *You know it's there. All you have to do is have one little sip . . .*

She had to stop this feeling. She had no choice.

She glanced around to make sure no one was looking, then took the bottle from the bag. She twisted off the cap and lifted it to her lips.

One sip, that was all.

Then two, and three, and four.

Jill Stearns

What kind of news?

Mila had just laughed. *You'll find out at dinner.*

Is it good news?

Relax, Mom.

Relax? That means it's good news, right?

Mom, please. There was a familiar edge to her voice, an edge which was the precursor to an outburst about how her mom was too protective and treated her like a little girl. *It's nothing to worry about.*

Jill had wanted to ask for more details. She didn't want to wait. She wasn't used to waiting. But this was not the office, and Mila was not – as she often reminded her – one of her employees.

Besides, the pilot – someone new, which she hadn't expected – had come out onto the steps, so she had wrapped up the call.

OK, she said. *I'll see you in a couple of hours.*

Now, as she sat on the plane, her laptop open in front of her, she replayed the conversation. Mila had said *it's nothing to worry about,* and not *yes, it's good news.* They were very different things. What Mila thought was nothing to worry about encompassed many things that for other people – Jill being one of them – would be the cause of endless sleepless nights. Being thrown off the varsity soccer team for drinking when she was a junior, for example. For Jill that had been close to the end of the world, but Mila had shrugged it off.

Don't you want to play soccer?

Not really. I'll do something else.

She had taken up drama and got a minor part in the school play. That had ended equally badly when a group of them were found smoking weed before a performance. Again, she had laughed it off, seemingly unconcerned. Jill found her insouciance quite admirable, in a way, but not enough to overcome the anxiety it caused her.

So *it's nothing to worry about* was hardly reassuring, especially as there were only two options that qualified as news: she and Archie were engaged or she was pregnant.

She closed her eyes. Neither of them were *nothing to worry about*. She was too young and too irresponsible to have a baby. Jill would have to shoulder the burden, and that was *not* in her plan. As for engagement, Archie was a nice boy but . . . well, he was hardly what Jill had in mind for a son-in-law. He was friendly and polite, but there didn't seem to be much else going on in his head. He never challenged Mila, never argued with her. Once she had watched him suggest they go to a tapas bar for dinner; Mila had scrunched up her face and said *No, I was thinking of something more original*, and he had shrunk into himself and agreed. The relationship was unbalanced; he was no match for Mila and Jill did not hold out much hope for him.

Honestly – and she would not have said this out loud, not in the current climate – she sometimes wished he would grow some balls.

So she didn't want him as father of her grandchild, which meant she also didn't want him as husband to her daughter.

Shit. How was she going to respond when they told her? She'd have to find a way to look pleased, but Mila would know she was pretending. She could see right through her. Her colleagues would have been amazed. She was known as a great, tough negotiator, blessed with an inscrutable poker face, but in front of her daughter she was feeble, an open book. She could picture it: her forcing a smile onto her face, Mila noticing and her expression darkening.

Some people would let it pass and address it later.

Not Mila. She would frown, her lips would press into a thin line and her eyes would narrow. There would be a long pause.

Mom, you didn't seem that thrilled at our news?

I am, darling, really . . .

Thanks, Mom. A vicious, spitting tone.

Mila, I don't know what you're talking—

You've ruined it. We're giving you our news and you can't be happy for us. What's the problem? It's my life. Why can't you even pretend *to be happy for us?*

I am pretending. It's the best I can do.

No, she wouldn't say that. She'd want to, but she wouldn't. She would to a supplier or customer or banker: anyone who pushed her around at work would get nowhere.

But this was her daughter. She had never had any idea how to handle her. They were so different. Jill found it bizarre how different they were – she had talked to her therapist about it and he had reminded her that even though they are your kids, they are their own people. You had to let them find their own path.

You can't control the decisions they make. And if you try it'll only push them away.

Jill had managed to give Mila some space, but she couldn't stop herself being disappointed – with Archie, with her poor grades, with her apparent lack of ambition. She simply

23

couldn't stop feeling a kind of ownership of her daughter, but that was the next step: for now, if Mila and Archie were engaged, she would have to find a way to be happy for them. Be genuinely, sincerely happy.

But she couldn't. It was beyond her. And she wanted to avoid the big reveal as long as possible. In fact, she wanted to avoid it full stop.

Could she get out of it somehow? Invent a meeting, or go for a drink with someone? For a moment she imagined the plane crashing. She didn't want it to, but at least it would get her out of her daughter's announcement dinner.

Of course, it could be something else entirely. A change of job. A new car. A holiday.

But she knew it wasn't. She knew her daughter, and the thought of what was to come filled her with dread.

Marcia Fournier

The first sip burned, a little.

Then it hit her stomach and she felt a warm glow spread outwards. The tension in her throat fell away. Her thoughts slowed and her mind went blank. It was similar to the feeling of weightlessness when the plane first lifted off, but it was better, tinged with bliss, a portal to a better – or easier, at any rate – world.

But then came the regret. It happened more and more these days, in direct proportion to the number of times she told herself she was quitting before she inevitably had that first drink.

I've done it again. I've failed.

She wanted to throw up what she had drunk and start again. She wanted to throw up everything she had ever drunk and go back to who she was before she had ever had a drink at all.

Was that what drove her alcoholism? It was only at this exact moment that she used the word: when she was sober she pretended she had some control of her drinking; when she was drunk she didn't care. That was, after all, the point of being drunk. But now, one drink in, the anxiety was gone, the inebriation yet to come, and in the space between the two she had clarity.

She knew what she was. She was an alcoholic.

And the thought left her bereft. It gave her an overwhelming desire to go back and correct the mistake she had made by starting to drink in the first place, but she knew she couldn't.

She knew she had turned into someone who smuggled vodka onto a corporate jet and there was no turning back. There was no never having that first drink, however much she wished for it.

There was just more drinking and more promises to herself that she wouldn't.

She was weak. A loser. Pathetic.

She was consumed with shame and self-loathing and she wanted to throw herself from the plane. She wanted to tumble through the air, screaming, until it was all over.

But she wasn't going to do that. She was going to sit here quietly, her mind spinning in turmoil, aware that the only solution was what caused the problem in the first place.

She needed another drink.

Varun Miller

Varun Miller stared at his phone, his lips parted in shock. This was impossible.

The email had arrived as he took his seat behind Chip. He had only glanced at it and had assumed it was spam, but there must have been something about it that caught his eye, as it came to mind as the plane took off and he decided to take a second look.

It was the subject, he realized. He received hundreds of emails a day, most from people at the company, but a good proportion from circulars or salespeople or malicious actors trying to get him to click on some link that would infect his computer with whatever malware they were peddling. He never clicked on anything sent by someone he didn't know and trust. As general counsel of a major food business, he could do without his computer being hacked.

This one was different. It was more muted, calmer. There were no capital letters – at least, there were only the ones in the places they were supposed to be – and there were no exclamation marks. Just a few words in the subject line:

Attn: B. Miller. Legal Review Required

They had his name, which in itself was no big deal, as anyone could have found it out. What stuck out though, along with the lack of capitals and exclamation marks, was the absence of any product or invitation to a seminar.

Just a simple title.

So he'd decided to open it. If there was a link he would ignore it, for sure, but something suggested he should take a look.

He was glad he had, and he could not believe what he was reading.

Dear Mr. Miller

Your company is in dire legal trouble. I hope you read this email promptly, as the reasons will become clear shortly. Certainly before you land.

Yours

That was it. No signature. Just three sentences. Three shocking sentences.

Certainly before you land.

That was the most shocking of all. How could whoever sent this know he was on the plane? And they knew the time of the departure, too. It had come just before they took off, so it was clearly timed to coincide with the flight.

But who knew about the flight? And what was going to become clear before they landed?

He closed his eyes and took a deep breath. He wasn't the best of flyers in normal circumstances but now he felt a rising panic. He'd have to talk to Jill, but then what? How would she know what was going on, and what could she do?

He was suddenly very aware they were off the ground and rising fast. He – they – were trapped. There was no way off the plane.

And that made even the suggestion there was something amiss a terrifying prospect.

His phone buzzed.

It was another message, but this one had nothing to do with any legal trouble. It was from his wife. A photo of Ari, his three-month-old son, lying on his back. He was on a colorful blanket which had a frame over it, from which were suspended various toys. Some plastic shapes he could grab with his tiny, fat fingers. Some furry squares that squeaked when he held them, some beads on a wire he could spin around.

It was supposed to promote brain development; whether it did or not, Varun didn't know, but he did know Ari loved being in there. As soon as he was lying down a smile spread over his face and he squirmed in delight, his hands reaching for the toys and his legs kicking left and right.

God, he loved Ari. More than he had ever suspected was possible. Susheela and he had always planned to have children, but he had never really wanted them. He'd wanted them in the sense that he wanted to have a family with Susheela, but he didn't want the baby itself. He couldn't picture himself as a father. He had no experience with kids – especially not babies – and he assumed he'd be a total flop, at least until they were older.

The reality was like nothing he had ever – or could ever have – imagined. He *adored* Ari. From the moment he'd set eyes on his son he had been in love. It was the most all-consuming love he had ever known. He rejoiced in getting up at night to walk his son around and soothe him back to sleep; he delighted in every gurgle and giggle; he was thrilled by every soiled diaper he changed.

Before Ari, work – and Susheela, of course, but mainly work – was his life. He left early and came home late, then lay in bed thinking about whatever was happening at the office. He made no bones about it: he wanted to be legal head of a big

29

company by his mid-thirties, and he'd achieved it. The next stage was to start a law firm, then sit on boards and, eventually, run for public office.

The Attorney General's office, maybe.

All that had changed. Now Ari was his life. All he wanted was to get home and play with his son. There were moments when he didn't recognize himself. He wasn't who he thought he had been all these years. He was a dad, and that was all he wanted to be.

He's beautiful, he wrote. Kiss him for me!

Will do. What time are you back?

He paused. They had just taken off, so about another two hours to go, then he had a half-hour drive.

Two and a half hours. See you soon. Love you!

He sent the message, but when he glanced back at his phone there was a red exclamation mark in a circle next to it.

Message not sent.

Damn. He looked at the signal indicator. There was no service. One of the perks of flying on the company jet was inflight Wi-Fi. Commercial planes had it too nowadays, but it could be spotty.

It seemed this was too. He waited for it to come back online. It didn't.

His mouth dried up. It could be nothing, of course, but it was unusual, and then there was the email.

He looked at Jill. She was typing on her laptop.

'Jill,' he said. 'Could I have a word?'

Jill Stearns

The Wi-Fi was down. She had just finished editing the Christmas message that the communications team were going to send to the company the next day, but when she went to send it nothing happened. Hopefully the Wi-Fi would come back online, or she'd have to send it when she got home.

She didn't really need to edit it. It was pretty basic stuff – *Thanks for a great year in difficult circumstances, none of us expected such a challenging year when we entered 2021 – we thought 2020 was going to be the hard year! – but you all rose to the challenge, proving once again that our greatest strength is our people. Here's to a better 2022* – but she liked to put something of a personal spin on it – *as for me, well, like many families, we added a puppy, who has brought us great joy as well as some slightly messy moments!* It didn't matter that there was no puppy, or that there was no family for it to be added to. Mila lived away and her husband, Toby, had moved out in the summer of 2020, but no one needed to worry about that. It was the image that mattered.

They had gone to couples counseling to see if they could salvage their marriage, but it had become quite clear that neither of them wanted to. That, it turned out, was a prerequisite for successful relationship counseling.

We just spent too much time together during lockdown, Toby said. *And I guess it became obvious we don't have much in common.*

That was a generous interpretation. She couldn't stand the way he walked around in track pants and T-shirts, then pulled on a sweater for video calls. It worked, and he seemed to be productive, but it was so *sloppy*. And then there was the bread-making. All of a sudden he was fascinated by bread, in particular sourdough loaves. Someone had given him a starter – which he explained at length was some kind of live yeast – and he was always messing around with it. Periodically a misshapen loaf appeared, after what seemed like hours of work. She couldn't understand it. It didn't even taste good; there was far better bread, made by professionals, in the supermarket – Whole Foods were delivering – and it only cost a few dollars. At the hourly rate he charged his legal clients, his bread was coming in at hundreds of dollars per loaf.

And it went off. It kept for a day, two at most. He was proud of this: no preservatives, but it meant it was wasted. They couldn't eat a loaf of bread a day. She'd have a slice at most, so, apart from anything else it was a waste of time and flour. When she pointed this out he laughed and gave a small shake of the head.

There's more to it than that, he said. *There's more to life than that.*

Than what? she replied

You know.

She didn't know.

And then there were the evenings. Without late nights in the office they had to face each other over dinner. Even if she could claim she had work to do, there was no excuse for not sitting down for thirty minutes to eat the meals he had prepared – accompanied by the sourdough – and talking.

About what? Their day? They had spent it together.

So on top of it all, it turned out they had nothing to talk about. Thirty minutes is a long time when you're sitting in near silence with someone you're supposed to know well. One thousand, eight hundred seconds. Doesn't sound like much, but it lasted an eternity.

So yes, as he said, *I guess it became obvious we don't have much in common.*

She tried to send the email again, but there was still no connection. She opened another email and started to write a reply. She'd have to log on and send them all later.

'Jill.'

She looked up. It was Varun. He looked worried.

'Could I have a word?' he said.

She nodded. 'Of course.'

'Maybe in the galley? Or by the door. Whatever it's called.'

The galley? Why did he want to talk to her there? She studied his face to confirm whether her original assessment was correct. If anything, the look of worry had intensified.

She unclipped her seat belt. 'Of course.'

Kevin Anderson

Kevin Anderson's bag thudded into his calf. He turned to his right; Miller had got to his feet and must have kicked it into him.

'Sorry,' Miller said. 'I tripped. It's narrow.'

'No problem,' Kevin said. Miller looked worried. 'Everything OK?'

'Yes. Everything is fine.' He gave an unconvincing smile. 'Just need to talk to Jill.'

Of course he did. He was an ass-kisser. Always had been. That and he was good for the Diversity and Inclusivity statistics. Or Inclusivity and Diversity. Whichever way around the words went.

He couldn't believe how much they spent on that shit. It was important, for sure, he agreed with that as much as the next guy, but come on. An entire department to shove it down everyone's throats? Mandatory training on safe spaces and unconscious bias and privilege and whatever else they came up with to justify their existence? Yes, everyone should have a fair chance and equal opportunity but that was as far as it went. As soon as you took it further you were giving people jobs because they were black or gay or lesbian or

34

whatever the other initials stood for, and not because they were the most qualified candidate.

Not that he'd say that. It would be career suicide. He'd been to all the training sessions, declared his privileges, submitted himself to the public rituals of purification. It was like re-education sessions in some communist dictatorship where everyone professed their loyalty to the state when they didn't believe a word of it.

So he went along with it. He had to. But it rankled when he saw a guy like Miller in a job he didn't deserve.

It wasn't like Miller was *bad* at his job. He was fine; he'd been with the company for years and he was competent enough. He just wasn't the best guy for the position. The best guy was Chase Windrow. He and Kevin were schoolmates – not that that was the reason Kevin rated him – and he was by far the best lawyer at the company. When the position had come up he had expected to get it and when it had gone to Miller he had come to Kevin in a rage, demanding he do something about it.

It's totally unfair. Just a ridiculous decision. You know that.

Kevin did know it, but he couldn't say it. Chase was his friend, and he sympathized with the fact he had lost the prize because of some bullshit politics, but he was the chief operating officer and he could not say anything that could later be held against the company.

Miller is fully qualified, he said. *And legal recruitment is not an area I have much influence over.*

I'm fully qualified too, Chase said. More *than fully qualified.*

Kevin wasn't sure you could be more than fully qualified, but he accepted the point. It was the least he could do. Mainly he was just glad he had got his job when he did. Had Chase been general counsel they would have wanted more diversity at the top table, and he would never have become COO.

So there was that, at least.

35

And now Miller was taking Jill Stearns aside, giving her some important update on something, or an update designed to show how important he was. Just wait until we land, or call her later. Don't go off to the front of the plane and talk in whispers.

That was teacher's pet shit. It wasn't the way you did things.

He took out his phone. He needed to check on his plans for the night. He'd been seeing a woman, Laura, for a few weeks. She was in her mid-thirties and a lot of fun – good-looking, funny, smart – and he enjoyed spending time with her. She'd asked that morning if he was free later, and he had been about to say yes, but then he'd remembered Katie.

She was a triathlete, twenty-eight years old – so fully twenty years his junior – and an absolute knockout. He'd spotted her at the pool at his club and he had been unable to take his eyes off her. He'd timed his exit so she saw him drive away in his Audi R8, and then, the next time their paths had crossed, he'd suggested a coffee.

They met mid-afternoon; he'd been as charming as he knew how, and they ended up at Portland's most exclusive restaurant. When he asked if she wanted to eat there she'd pointed out that it could take weeks to get a table, but he smiled and said, *Let me see what I can do.*

They found him a table, of course, as they always did. People who left 100 percent tips were rare, and highly valued.

She hadn't invited him back to her place, though, despite his hints. It was a shame; he was desperate to fuck her. He didn't know when an opportunity as good would come round again and he didn't want to let this one slip.

Laura was great – guaranteed sex, and a good time – but Katie was the prize.

So he'd told Laura he wasn't sure – it paid to have a backup – and sent Katie a message asking if she wanted to get together that evening.

I'll be on the jet so you can contact me there.

She hadn't replied by the time they boarded, but he was hoping she would.

He checked his phone. There was one message, from Laura.

So? This evening.

There was nothing from Katie. He felt a surge of disappointment.

He typed a reply.

Not sure yet. Lots on at work. Is it OK if I don't give you much notice? Sorry!

The message didn't send. There was no Wi-Fi.

Which was good and bad. Bad because he couldn't get in touch with either Laura or Katie, but good because it meant the lack of a reply from Katie didn't mean she was out of the picture just yet.

He glanced up. Stearns was walking back to her seat.

She didn't look happy.

Jill Stearns

It was without doubt a very odd email. Troubling, even. As she sat down, she tried to decide what was more worrying: the threat of some kind of legal trouble, or the reference to it being clear what it was before they landed. It was such a specific, and such an *unusual*, timeframe.

What do you think? she asked Varun. *What kind of legal trouble?*

I have no idea. I'm not aware of anything. And we would not be notified like this. This is trying to make a point. Activists, maybe?

Activists made sense. It was a given when you worked for a major food company; despite the fact that your products provided nutrition to millions of people, there would always be some who complained about how you did it. Yes, there were ways in which they could do better. Manage their water usage better. Insist on improved standards of animal care in the supply chain. Label their products clearly so people knew how much sugar and fat and salt were in them. But in general, they were a force for good.

And besides, what did these people think the alternative was? Humanity needed food. The world needed calories. And someone had to provide them. That was the real story; the ability of millions of people to get the food they needed at prices they could afford. Not everyone could pay the price for organic produce and exotic grains, for hand-reared happy chickens and rainbow- and unicorn-flavored tea. Nor did they have the time to prepare meals from the over-priced ingredients they got at their local farmers market. The vast majority needed cheap, readily available calories, and this was one of the few periods of history when they could reliably get them.

And it was companies like hers that made that possible.

That was not the story the activists told the world, though. For them, Big Food was irredeemably evil and corrupt, a cynical force aimed at one thing only: profiting from addicting its customers to sugar and fat and whatever else they could manage. It was ludicrous. Of course they sought profits; that was what their shareholders expected, but they did it in a socially conscious way. They no more wanted mass obesity than anyone else.

Either way, the activists were not going to believe them, and were going to continue their attacks. This had all the hallmarks of one of them. An intimidating email designed to sow panic. Well, they were not going to get their way.

It probably is activists, she said. *Ignore it.*

What do you think they mean?

Nothing. There's no legal trouble. She flashed him a grin. *You'd know, right. That's your job!*

He wagged his head from side to side in a noncommittal gesture. *There could be something.*

Like you said. Nothing that would show up like this. If it was the regulators, or a class action suit of some kind, we'd hear formally. Not some weird threat.

I suppose. He paused and caught her eye. *But how do they know we're in the air?*

There are ways, I'm sure. Flight tracker, that kind of thing.

He didn't look convinced, but he accepted with a nod, and turned to his seat. *I guess we'll find out.*

They returned to their seats. Kevin Anderson was watching her, a thoughtful expression on his face. She didn't like him, much. He was polite and courteous – he was highly trained in that kind of thing, coming from his private school and liberal arts college – and he never gave any hint of anything but the utmost professionalism, but after every *Thank you for your time, Jill,* she heard a silent *you fucking stupid woman.*

And then there was the way he looked her up and down, assessing her body. He did it every time he looked at her, and she had seen him do it to every other woman he met. That afternoon, when they were returning from lunch, he'd studied Marcia's butt as she crossed the room. It was a nice butt, for a sixty-year-old, but she didn't think he was interested in her. It was just a reflex. She wasn't sure he even knew he was doing it – in fact, she was sure he didn't know – but it was so ingrained in him he had no idea, or ability to stop it.

She sat down and opened her laptop. After a moment, she pushed it away and looked out of the window. She wanted some time to think about the email Varun had shown her. It was probably nothing, but there was something about it, something that disturbed her.

It was the tone. It wasn't threatening, it wasn't triumphalist. It was matter-of-fact.

And that worried her.

Marcia Fournier

She slipped the empty plastic bottle into her bag and pulled out the second one. She had drunk quite a lot already – maybe a quarter of a bottle of vodka – but she was just getting started. She glanced around; across the aisle, Varun was typing something, a frown on his forehead. Jill Stearns was staring into the distance, lost in thought. There was a vulnerability about her which she worked hard to keep hidden; at least, that was what Marcia thought. It was possible she was as tough as she presented, which was not the case for Kevin Anderson. He was a lawyer, and full of bravado, but it was all front. It made him dangerous; his insecurity left him prone to lashing out if he felt threatened, which he often did.

Behind him was Jeff Ramos. He'd been around forever, held every job. He was a veteran – some kind of special forces – and it gave him an aura. People deferred to him, whether they were his senior or not. To his left was the nurse, Mary Jo. Marcia had no idea how and why she'd ended up on the company plane, but there she was.

And then there was Chip Markham, reading a newspaper, his legs crossed at the knee. Their affair had ended abruptly;

41

she was wounded by his sudden declaration that it was over and on many occasions she had imagined the revenges she could wreak upon him, but nothing had happened. It was imperative that the private and the professional were kept separate.

It still hurt, even though it was now a decade ago, back when her daughter was near college age and his son – who even then he rarely saw – was in his early twenties. They had both been focused on work, spending long hours in the office. It had begun when they were working on an acquisition, and, on a trip to New York, had gone out drinking after the deal was finally done.

They had drunk martinis, hers vodka, his gin. Looking back, it had been inevitable. They had both known they would end up in the same hotel room that evening, and so they had.

In a strange city, anonymous and on a high, they were different people for an evening, people who could do whatever they wanted, could allow all the anticipation and buildup to become what they had both known it would.

And then it had ended. It hadn't made any difference to their professional relationship; if office affairs did that then there wouldn't be many functional workplaces in the country.

Because – in her experience, at least – there were a *lot* of affairs. Take her, for example: she was happily married, had no intention of breaking up with Mike, but their sex life had dwindled to more or less nothing sometime in her mid-forties. She wasn't ready to give up sex altogether, so she had found it elsewhere.

Did he know? If he'd asked, she would have told him. She didn't want to lie, at least not about that. Drinking was another matter entirely.

But he'd never asked. And she'd never asked him.

She took the bottle from her bag and checked again to see if anyone was watching. The coast clear, she opened the second bottle, and took a sip, unseen.

That was the problem. She *wanted* someone to notice. She wanted someone to be watching, wanted someone to realize she had a problem, that she was drinking in secret. She had become too good at disguising it, too skilled at hiding the amount she drank. There was the bottle of vodka – pretty much odorless so perfect for secret swigs – she kept in the car. The bottle she kept in the basement. The bottle she kept in her office at home.

Mike – Marcia and Mike, M and M, always the life and soul of every party, known for the great bashes they put on every year in the run-up to Christmas – would see her settle down with a glass of white wine, sipping it slowly over an hour or two. What he didn't see was the gulp she took after she parked in the garage and before she got out, or the two nips she bought at the gas station, or the quick shot she inhaled when she went into her office for a few minutes to 'check on some things'. Had she told him, he wouldn't have believed her. He didn't drink much, so for him the idea that someone could drink a large glass of vodka – maybe a sixth of a bottle – in a minute or two, just because they needed it, would have been ludicrous. He sometimes commented on her drinking – *Do you think you should have a glass every night?* – but he had no idea what was really going on.

She wished he did. She wished he had worked it out, become suspicious and tracked what she was drinking. Then he could have confronted her and she could have found a way to stop. But how could he? She was far too good at hiding it. She'd had years of practice, after all.

So she was left like this. An old, hopeless drunk, who was desperate to stop but had no means of doing so.

She took another sip, then another. That was the thing with drinking: it made you hate yourself, and the only way you could get the self-loathing to stop was to drink it away.

43

She realized, with sudden horror, that she needed the bathroom. The jet had a small bathroom at the rear. It was cramped and not very private and people rarely used it. She could have used the bathroom in the hangar but hadn't thought she needed to. She should have, as there was now an insistent – and growing – pressure in her bladder. She looked out of the window. Below her, mountains sloped down to a sandy beach. They'd bank left shortly, and head for Portland, Maine. She knew the route; she'd flown it many times. There was about ninety minutes to go. She'd be fine, she thought, just about.

The beach veered away to the left. She waited for the plane to follow, to make the turn for home.

It did not. It headed out over the water.

She looked up, checking if anyone else had noticed. Everyone was staring at their phone or laptop or newspaper, everyone except the nurse, who turned to meet her gaze.

Marcia looked away. A nurse could probably see the glaze in her eyes and the flush in her neck and know exactly what was causing them.

She looked out of the window again.

They should not be going this way.

It was OK. She told herself there would be an explanation. A change in the flight plan.

But it didn't help. Even through the numbing fog of the alcohol, panic fluttered in her stomach. In a small metal cylinder thousands of feet above the Earth's surface, anything out of order, however small, was magnified.

They should be headed north, and they weren't.

Kevin Anderson

The nurse was sitting behind him. He could tell that at one point she'd been quite hot; the fact she was a nurse added to it. Nurse porn was one of his favorites; he'd watched so much of it that every time he was in a medical appointment he found himself fantasizing that it would end up in some kind of group sex with the nurses.

She'd come to the board meeting to pick up a check the company was donating to some hospital foundation. Stearns had made a speech about it, a look of fake concern on her face.

Our key workers were the front line in the struggle against COVID, a struggle that is ongoing, Stearns had told the assembled press, *and we want to make clear our gratitude. Our people – our greatest asset – have donated over a million dollars to support the efforts of our key workers, and we have matched their donation dollar for dollar. We are honored to have a nurse, Mary Jo Fernandez, with us today to accept the check on behalf of her colleagues.*

Then she had handed her the check, but Kevin could see she was not impressed, could see she was thinking if they could afford this why not thirty million? Or three hundred?

Or why not get their jet to fly her and her exhausted colleagues to a beach somewhere and let them rest for a week or two?

It was too obvious this was a token gesture, something to show how socially engaged the company was, so when he had bumped into her afterwards he had asked about her travel plans.

Four o'clock flight, she said. *Probably be delayed. It's chaos, these days.*

Why don't you come back on the jet?

It was meant to show that he was different, he was sincere in caring about others. He'd do something practical to help her. It was an added bonus that it felt good, that he got to be the medieval knight helping out the fair maiden, the wealthy Victorian gentleman bestowing a gift on a lowly maid.

She'd replied, *Is that OK?* and he'd nodded. *There's a spare seat. It's like a car. You just hop in.* And now here she was. On a private jet.

He'd tell Katie about it later. Make her see what a great guy he was – and give her a hint of what he could offer her, if she played the game. Another benefit.

He sat back and picked up his phone. Still no message; still no Wi-Fi. This was becoming annoying. The pilot had the cockpit door closed – normally it was open – but if it didn't come back soon he would head up there and find out what was going on. He needed to know if Katie was available; if not, he wanted to line Laura up. He intended to get laid that evening, and he wasn't about to let some dodgy Wi-Fi stop him.

Marcia Fournier half-stood in her seat, looking around the cabin. She peered out of her window, then looked past Kevin so she could see out of his.

'What is it?' he said. 'What's up?'

'Look,' she replied. Her face was strained and nervous.

46

He turned to the window. It took a few moments for him to understand what she was saying.

They were over the ocean. They should not have been.

He looked back. Behind him, Jeff Ramos was also looking out. He caught Anderson's eye.

'You thinking what I'm thinking?' he said.

'Yeah,' Anderson said, his voice rising. 'Are we going the right way?'

The Pilot

She listened to the man's question. She could hear everything they said, thanks to the microphone she had positioned above the door to the cockpit.

Are we going the right way?

So he had noticed something was wrong. It was quite obvious, really. They had no business heading east over the Atlantic. Soon they'd realize that the next stop was Portugal, or North Africa maybe, and that was not their destination. In any case, both those places were well out of their range. They'd run out of fuel well before they arrived. The engines would sip the last of the aviation fuel and sputter and die and the plane would glide, silently, onto the ocean.

It would not skip over the surface and slow to a halt, bobbing on the waves. They would not climb out onto a survival raft and await an unlikely rescue. If a plane hit the water at 200 miles per hour it might as well have hit concrete. It would disintegrate on impact.

She didn't need to tell them the answer to the question he had asked. They would figure it out for themselves.

No, they were not.

At least, not as far as they were concerned. This was going exactly the way she wanted.

Another voice spoke, a woman's voice strained with worry.

I don't think we are. What's going on?

Maybe she had noticed the Wi-Fi was down. Or been shown the email the pilot had sent to Miller. Or both. They would cause worry.

They were designed to.

Either way, it was time to up the ante.

It was time to introduce herself.

Chip Markham

Jeff Ramos's question – *are we going the right way?* – fell into an uneasy silence.

It was broken by Marcia.

'I don't think we are. What's going on?'

Chip looked at her. She was wide-eyed and nervous. He knew that expression, had seen it many times. He knew a lot about her, about how fragile and unpredictable and needy she was. It was the neediness that had turned him off in the end. He had been worried about how she would react, although he hadn't expected the drunken late-night visit and the threats to kill herself if he didn't reconsider.

You have a husband, and a family, he said. *Just accept it's over.*

I want you, Chip. You're everything to me.

This is crazy, Marcia. You have to move on.

No! We're meant to be! She had tried to force her way into his house. *Chip! We love each other. You know we do.*

He'd shaken his head, which was when the suicide threats had come. He hadn't been sure whether he would see her the following day at the office, but they had passed in the corridor, and she had nodded and smiled, as though it had never happened.

'Anyone?' she said. 'What's happening?'

She also looked drunk, although where she was getting the booze, he had no idea.

Ramos spoke first. 'It's unusual. There's no doubt about that.'

'What do you think it is?' Marcia said.

'Don't know,' he replied. 'Could be nothing.'

'Doesn't it seem *strange*?' Marcia said.

He tilted his head to the side. 'I guess it does.' Chip was surprised how calm he was. Too calm, almost. He'd been an Army Ranger, so maybe that was how they were trained to be. 'But there could be any number of explanations.'

'Like what?' Jill Stearns said. She was far less composed; there was an edge of tension bleeding into her voice.

Ramos shrugged.

'A problem at an airport meaning planes are stuck in a holding pattern and can't land. Or maybe Air Force One's in the area.'

Chip nodded. That had happened to him once. The president – it was Obama – had been flying into DC. Since it was the tenth anniversary of 9/11, security was tighter than usual and all planes in the vicinity had been grounded. His plane had spent two hours on some crumbling airstrip in the middle of nowhere.

'That sounds reasonable,' Chip said. 'I've had something like that happen before.'

'Except,' Marcia said, her voice thickening with fear, 'we're not in a holding pattern. We're heading over the ocean and there's no reason we should be.'

Chip's stomach stiffened. He felt an ache in his back. He looked at Jeff for reassurance, but Ramos's expression had tightened.

'This *is* weird,' he said. 'We shouldn't be going this way. There's no reason for it.'

Chip could feel the rising panic in the plane. That was not what they needed now. 'It's nothing,' he said. 'Just a different route.'

'Could be,' Jeff replied. 'But it feels odder than that.'

'And the Wi-Fi's not working,' Kevin said. 'Great flight. You need to get onto the aviation department, Chip.'

Chip glared at him. 'I'll bear that in mind.'

Varun coughed.

'There's something else,' he said. 'An email.'

Chip turned to him. He was wide-eyed with terror.

Jill Stearns looked from face to face. 'Varun just mentioned it to me. It's—'

She was interrupted by a crackle from the PA system.

'Hello,' a woman's voice said. 'This is your pilot. I hope you're enjoying the flight.' There was a long, heavy pause. 'As some of you have noticed, there's no inflight Wi-Fi. So no emails, news, text messages. I apologize for the inconvenience. I know you like to keep busy on these flights. As compensation, I'm going to help you pass the time.'

Ramos's spine pricked. Something was wrong here. Something was *very* wrong.

The pilot gave a laugh. 'I hope you don't mind,' she said, 'but we're going to play a little game.'

Barrow, Maine 2018

Stacy Evanston

The phone call – as she would come to think of it – came when Stacy Evanston was at work.

She was at her desk in a small Air Force recruiting station on a former base – the recruiting station was the last remaining military presence on it – in Barrow, Maine, where she lived with her husband, Dan and her daughter, Cherry. It was their last two weeks there; they were due to move to South Carolina next month, and she was going to miss Barrow. It was a small town, but it was lively and welcoming, with good schools and a thriving downtown. Dan had found a job he loved in construction management and he didn't want to give it up, but that was the military life.

At least she would have some news to share with Dan before they left. She had been due to get her period four days ago, but it had not arrived. They had been trying since Cherry was born for a brother or sister, and on a few occasions she had been late, but they had all been false alarms.

And each one had been a disappointment as painful as the last. It had been so easy with Cherry – she had stopped taking the pill, and, the next month, she was pregnant. The pregnancy had been a joy: some mild morning sickness, cravings for tomatoes with balsamic vinegar and feta cheese, which was weird as she didn't recall ever having eaten that in her life, but she just got this picture in her head of a plate of delicious red tomatoes swimming in dark balsamic with crisp white feta crumbled on top of them. She must have eaten this meal thirty or more times, but one day the craving had left her, and she had not eaten it since. In fact, the thought of it made her feel nauseous.

Once the cravings passed, she felt great. She felt complete, like she glowed. The birth itself was how she'd always dreamed it would be: hard, and painful, yes, but beautiful and rewarding in ways she still didn't understand.

So the years that followed – of periods that came like clockwork – were a shock. They tried everything: sex when she was supposedly most fertile, diets that promoted sperm health, a fertility charm they bought in New Mexico.

None of it had worked. Until, that was, now. This time felt different. This felt like it had with Cherry. She couldn't explain it – but a few days ago her period had not come and she had thought, *This is it, this is real.* Before that she couldn't have said how it had felt with Cherry, but now she had the feeling again she recognized it.

So she had bought a test that morning after driving Cherry to school, which she was going to take when she woke up the next day. That was when the hormones were strongest.

She knew what it would say, though, and she couldn't wait to share it with Dan. It had been a long time – they had both questioned whether it would ever happen – but finally it was here.

She lifted her phone from the desk. Normally she didn't answer personal calls at work. She and Dan had an agreement: anything non-urgent could be done by text. If it needed to be dealt with, they would call, hang up, and call again.

So this wasn't Dan.

Her eyes strayed to the screen.

It was Cherry's school.

It was probably nothing – Cherry was five and very shy, so it was unlikely she had been fighting or acting out – but when the school called you had to pick up. Most likely, Cherry had come down with a fever or a cough or some other minor illness which meant she had to be picked up and taken home. She'd had the call a few times.

Hi, this is the school nurse, is that Cherry's mom? She's not feeling too great, so I was wondering if you could come get her?

Stacy didn't like to leave the office in the day, but Dan had gone to Bangor to meet a client who wanted their camp remodeled for the summer, which was a good two hours away.

So it would be on her.

'Hello,' she said. 'This is Stacy.'

'Mrs. Evanston? This is Carol Smalling. The principal.'

Her tone was flat. There was a hint that she was struggling to control her voice. Stacy sat upright. It was rare for the principal to call, and she did not like the way she sounded. She thought about checking her computer – maybe there had been a shooting, or some other event that would be in the news, but it would come quickest from the principal.

'Is everything OK?'

There was a long pause.

'I'm afraid' – another pause – 'I'm afraid Cherry has been taken ill.'

Taken *ill*? Her throat constricted. 'What do you mean? She was fine this morning.'

'She started to feel unwell half an hour ago, so Ms. Jackson sent her to the nurse. She had a slight fever, but was otherwise OK. Then she started to vomit.'

'Oh my God,' Stacy said. 'What happened?'

'I'm not sure. But if you can, you might want to leave immediately.'

'I'll come and get her. I'm at work but I can go now.' She'd have to find someone to cover for her, or at least inform the CO she was going to have to hotfoot it. 'I'll be with you as soon as I can.'

'Mrs. Evanston,' the principal said. 'You shouldn't come here. We called an ambulance. Cherry's on her way to the hospital.'

2

'The hospital?' Stacy said. 'She's going to the *hospital*?'

'Yes. The ambulance left as I was calling you.'

'Why's she been sent to hospital?' Stacy said. 'Because she's vomiting?'

'No,' the principal said. 'I'm sorry to be the bearer of bad news, Mrs. Evanston, but Cherry is unconscious.'

It was as though she had been punched in the stomach. It was hard to draw a breath. 'Did you say unconscious?'

'I'm afraid so.'

'Why? What caused it?'

'I don't know. The nurse was alarmed at how quickly it progressed and decided to call an ambulance.'

'OK.' She fought to think clearly through the shock. It felt like her world had changed utterly in an instant. 'I'll be there as soon as I can.'

'Keep me posted. We're very fond of Cherry,' the principal said. 'And good luck, Mrs. Evanston.'

Stacy ended the call. She sent a message to her CO – *Got to go, Cherry's been taken ill, will fill you in later* – and ran out to her blue Honda Pilot.

She could not understand what was going on. Cherry was

in hospital? She had dropped her off at school that morning and she'd been totally fine. Was there something she'd missed? Had Cherry been off-color in some way? She tried to remember in detail how the morning had gone. They'd had waffles and blueberries and maple syrup – Cherry had eaten plenty so no lack of appetite – and then they'd read a book about a girl who survived in the wilderness for a week. It was something Dan had bought for her to try and inspire his daughter into the fishing and hunting lifestyle.

On the way to school she'd been laughing about her friend Ella's dog, Ruby, which kept eating Ella's socks. The two of them, who had been inseparable for the last two years, thought it was the most hilarious thing they had ever seen, so had kept feeding Ruby socks. Ella's mom, Stacy thought, probably found it less amusing.

She had seemed fine, her normal chatty self. It was a puzzle to Stacy that her daughter was so ebullient with her and Dan and Ella, but so shy as soon as anyone else was there.

Either way, there were no signs of anything wrong, so whatever it was had come on very suddenly. But what *could* come on that quickly, and lead to unconsciousness?

Nothing good, that was for sure.

She called Dan. His phone rang out to voicemail. She cut it off without leaving a message and called again.

Two calls. Their urgent signal.

'Hey,' he said. His voice went faint as though he was holding the phone away from his mouth. 'Sorry. I have to take this. It's my wife.' He came back on the line, full volume. 'What's up?'

'It's Cherry.'

'What about Cherry?'

'The school called. They sent her to hospital.'

'They sent her to what?'

'Hospital.'

'Jesus. Why?'

'I don't know.'

'Did something happen?'

'She felt sick, then started to vomit.' Stacy paused. 'And now she's unconscious.'

He did not reply for a long moment. 'OK,' he said eventually, the effort to stay calm clear in his voice. 'Do you know why?'

'No. I'm on my way to the hospital now. You should come.'

'I will. Of course.' She heard another voice – presumably his client asking what was going on – and Dan's voice went faint again. *Something came up. Family. I'll have to go.*

Then he was back.

'I'm leaving now. Call me as soon as you hear anything.'

3

Stacy held her warrant card up to the screen. The woman at reception studied it then gave a nod.

'How can I help?'

'My daughter was just admitted. Cherry Evanston. She came in an ambulance.'

The receptionist gave her a sympathetic smile. 'I'm sorry,' she said. 'Let me check.'

'She came from school,' Stacy said. 'She fell ill.' She realized she was babbling. The extra information would make no difference.

'Yes,' the receptionist said. 'I see her. She's in—' She stopped and gestured to a seat. 'Let me get someone to come and see you.'

Stacy's stomach lurched. Why would the receptionist not say where her daughter was? And why did she need to get someone to come and talk to her? The awful thought, the one she had been avoiding, forced its way into her head.

Was Cherry dead?

'Is she OK?' she said. 'What's happening?'

'Take a seat,' the receptionist replied. 'Someone will be right along.'

Stacy sat down, then, a second later, got up and walked to a window. She had too much nervous energy to stay seated for more than a second or two. She sent Dan a message.

Here now. Not seen Cherry yet. Waiting to find out more.

About two minutes later – two minutes that felt endless – a door to the right of the reception opened and a tall, thin man in his early forties walked out. He was wearing glasses, which he pushed up onto his forehead. He turned to the receptionist and she nodded at Stacy.

'Mrs. Evanston?' he said, as he walked over. 'I'm Dr. Neal Williams.'

She cut to the chase. 'How is she?'

He sucked in his top lip. 'It's a difficult situation,' he said. 'She's stable, but she's in a serious condition.'

She heard *stable*; that was good. She heard *serious*; that was not.

'In what way?'

'She's in a coma,' he said. 'And it seems she's suffering from liver damage.'

'*Liver* damage?' Stacy said. 'How can she be suffering from liver damage? She's five.'

'It's odd. But it certainly looks like it's the case.'

'But how?'

'I'm afraid I don't have the answer at the moment. For now we need to continue to keep her stable, and focus on helping her recover.'

Many questions swirled around her mind, but there was only one she really needed an answer to.

'Is she going to be OK?'

'I hope so, Mrs. Evanston. Whatever this is, we caught it early, which is good. But I have to be honest. I haven't seen anything quite like this. Not ever.'

'OK,' she said. 'I understand.' She didn't; she didn't understand any of this.

'You can stay here,' he said. 'And as soon as we can get her out of the intensive care unit and into a room we'll make up a bed for you.'

'When will that be?'

'I can't say. But I can say we're doing our best.'

'Thank you,' she said. 'That means a lot.'

He reached out and squeezed her shoulder, then turned and headed back to the door he'd come from.

The receptionist came over to Stacy. 'Would you like a coffee?' she said. 'Or something else to drink?'

Stacy shook her head. 'No thank you.' There was no way she could eat or drink at a time like this. If Cherry didn't recover, she wasn't sure she would ever eat or drink again.

'Let me know if you change your mind.'

'Thank you,' she said. 'I will.'

4

Was there anything worse than this? Than waiting, alone, in a hospital for news of your five-year-old daughter, who had slipped suddenly into a coma?

Was it a coma? Or was it just unconsciousness? Stacy realized she didn't know when one became the other. It wasn't something she had ever thought about.

It didn't change the question. Was there anything worse than this? Yes, there was. And that was hearing that – she shook her head to clear the thought. It made her legs weaken and her stomach shrink and her mind go blank.

It was not going to come to that. Something had happened to Cherry and the doctors would resolve it. They had to.

Because the alternative was – she tried again to push the thought away, but it was too insistent, too strong – the alternative was unthinkable. What would she do if Cherry died? What would she do if that door opened and a solemn Dr. Williams walked out and looked at her sadly and gave a shake of his head? What would happen then? She had no idea, but she had never been as scared of anything in her life.

Because it *could* happen. Cherry could die. People – children – did, and this was how it happened. A sudden, mysterious illness, intensive care, failed treatments. A serious, sorrowful, doctor.

Death.

She sat forward, curling around herself, her knees on her thighs and her face in her hands. She gave an involuntary whimper, and realized she was crying.

There was a touch on her shoulder and she looked up. The receptionist was standing next to her, holding a bottle of water.

'Here,' she said. 'I know it's hard, but if you want a sip, I brought this.'

Stacy started to sob, and the receptionist sat next to her, her arm around her shoulder.

'I'm Daniela,' she said. 'It'll be OK.'

'May—' She started to say *Maybe it won't*, but the words were stuck in her throat, and all that came out was a lurching sob.

'Shh. Just take a deep breath.'

'Hey.' It was a familiar, welcome voice. She glanced up. Dan was walking toward them, his face unsmiling. 'Did you – did you get some news?'

Stacy shook her head. She tried to speak but only a choked sob came out.

'Still waiting?' he said.

She nodded, and he sat next to her. Daniela took her arm from around her shoulders and Dan wrapped both his around her, hugging her tight.

'I'm here,' he said. 'I'm here now.'

She was glad. She was glad he was here and he was holding her, but glad meant nothing. She knew it made no difference. There was nothing he could do.

There was nothing either of them could do.

5

Dan could not stop moving. He paced from one window to another, to the door, to a noticeboard, to a fish tank. He spent a few seconds at each one, then moved to something new. He was clearly not taking anything in when he got there, but the constant movement must have soothed him.

I didn't know you were like this, she thought. To her, Dan was imperturbable, quiet and thoughtful. He was hard to rouse to anger, hard to rouse to any strong emotion. She could fly into a rage, especially when she felt something was unjust, but Dan would invariably remain calm. When Cherry was a baby, she had been misdiagnosed by her pediatrician, who had mistaken a dangerous sinus infection for a simple cold. The infection had migrated behind her eyes, which had meant a course of nasty antibiotics. Stacy had been all for marching into the office and handing the pediatrician a lawsuit, but Dan had smiled, and folded his arms.

She's OK, he said. *And people make mistakes. I'm not happy either, but this serves no purpose.*

But now he was a bundle of nerves. He folded his arms, put his hands in his pockets, looked around the room, stared at his feet. It was as though he was unable to find any position in which he was comfortable in his own body.

But whatever got you through. She'd paced at first, but now she was deflated, energy-less. The movement seemed to set her mind racing, so she'd slumped in a chair, trying to keep her mind as blank as possible.

He turned from a window and headed toward her. He took the seat to her left and looked up at the ceiling. She put a hand on his thigh.

'You OK?'

He shook his head. 'I'm a fucking mess. Why's there no news? What's going on?'

'I'll go and ask.'

She expected him to say, *No, don't bother them, they'll tell you if there's anything to tell* but he nodded.

'I'll come with you.'

Daniela was behind the reception. She looked up as they approached and smiled.

'We were wondering,' Stacy said. 'If there's any news? About Cherry?'

It was obvious there wasn't, but Daniela was too kind to say so. She tapped on her keyboard. 'Let me check.'

Before she had a chance to say anything further, the door to the waiting area opened and Dr. Williams came out. His face was lined, his eyes red and exhausted.

'Mrs. Evanston,' he said. He looked at Dan. 'And Mr. Evanston?'

'Yes,' Dan replied. 'How is she?'

Dr. Williams smiled, and Stacy felt her legs weaken in relief. He had *smiled*. She grabbed Dan's elbow.

'She's doing better. She's still unconscious, but she's stable now. We're moving her out of the ICU and into a room. You'll be able to see her in a few minutes.'

'Will she be OK?' Stacy said.

'I'm quietly confident,' Dr. Williams replied. 'Although we still don't know what caused this.'

'Does that mean it could happen again?' Dan said. 'Is that what you're saying?'

'Yes. Not that it *will*, but until we know the cause we have to accept that it might. Do you have any other questions?'

'You said we could see her?' Stacy asked.

'Yes. I'll send someone out as soon as she's ready. Anything else?' He held his hands out, palms up. 'Anything at all.'

Stacy shook her head and Dr. Williams headed for the door. As he reached it, Dan called out.

'Thank you,' he said.

Dr. Williams smiled. 'My pleasure,' he said.

Stacy hugged Dan. 'Thank God,' she said. 'Thank God she's going to be OK.'

'She's still unconscious,' Dan said.

'I know. But it's an improvement. And we can see her.'

'That's good news,' Daniela said.

'She's not out of the woods yet – but yes, it's good news.'

'I love it when it's good news. You want that coffee now?'

'Yes, please. If it's not too much trouble.'

'And one for your husband, too?'

Dan nodded. 'Thank you.'

Stacy sat, her head on Dan's shoulder, and took a long, deep breath. She blew out her cheeks.

'I need to stand up,' she said. 'Get some energy out.' She stood and walked over to the window. The hospital was surrounded by forest, a long driveway leading from the main road and branching off to the various car parks and departments.

She saw the lights of an ambulance through the trees and watched as it appeared and headed for the entrance to the emergency room.

It drew to a halt. The rear doors opened, and two paramedics jumped down, then pulled out a ramp. Two more pushed a stretcher onto the tarmac and into the hospital.

Someone else, she thought. *Someone else having the worst day of their lives.*

The paramedics were getting back into the ambulance, the patient no longer visible, already hustled into the hospital. They pulled away, and behind them a car slowed to a halt and the passenger door opened.

The car was a dark blue Toyota RAV4. It had roof bars and a Thule box on top.

She knew someone with a car like that.

Behind her a door opened.

'Mr. and Mrs. Evanston? You can come through now.'

She turned away from the window. A nurse was holding the door to the consulting rooms open. Dan was already by the door and he beckoned her to join him.

'One minute,' she said.

She recognized the car. But that didn't necessarily mean anything. There were a lot of dark blue RAV4s around. They were practical. Safe, and good in the snow.

Still, it was a coincidence.

A figure emerged from the passenger door and her blood ran cold.

'Stacy?' Dan said. 'Are you coming?'

She ignored him and leaned forward, peering out of the window, unable to believe what she was seeing.

A woman in dark jeans and a black quilted jacket got out of the car. It was a Patagonia jacket and it was only a few days old.

She knew it was a Patagonia jacket, and she knew it was new, because she had been with the woman when she bought it at a sale in Freeport.

The woman in the car – the woman behind the ambulance – was Nicole Farmer, the mom of Cherry's best friend, Ella.

Jill Stearns

She felt all eyes turn to her, felt the shock – and worry – at what they had heard.

That little laugh, then the pilot's soft voice.

I hope you don't mind, but we're going to play a little game.

What the hell did that mean? She felt a flare of anger. It was partly based in fear, but also indignation. She was not the kind of person who would have expected deference, but part of her was pissed that whoever this was thought they could treat her, Jill Stearns, like this. She was not someone who you played games with.

And what did she mean, a game?

Was this maybe some kind of Christmas joke, and after she and the others were caught in the trap the pilot would start playing a Christmas song, or open the door and come out in a Santa suit? If that did happen, she would not be very forgiving. The pilot was going to find herself out of a job. Not expecting deference was one thing, but there were limits.

And this was clearly one of them.

This was *not* funny. Nothing at this altitude was funny. Some people were nervous flyers, and this could tip them over the edge. It was downright irresponsible.

Although perhaps she was overreacting. She was on edge because of the email, but the two things were unlikely to be related. The email was almost certainly an attempt by some activist to provoke Varun and her, and maybe waste some of their time. This was something else.

Probably.

It better had be. If it wasn't – if they were related and the pilot was not joking around – well, that was something she did not want to contemplate.

She reached for her phone. It was a reflex reaction; a quick check to see if there were any notifications. She'd read that people checked their phones over a hundred times a day – when they got in an elevator, when they sat at their desk, when they stood up from their desk. All day long people were checking their phones, and most of the time there was nothing to see. But once they had picked it up, they started to scroll through their Facebook or Twitter or Instagram feed and before they knew it, five or ten or twenty minutes had disappeared. She had set her phone to lock when she reached fifty pickups; the first day it had locked by two in the afternoon. She was shocked – and appalled – so she had started to limit herself. When she reached for the phone she made herself pause and ask: *Do I really need to look at it now?*

Often enough, the answer was no, and she left it untouched.

It happened this time, too. She paused, and thought, *Do I really need to look at it now?*

And then she remembered. She couldn't.

There was no Wi-Fi.

Was that a coincidence, too? Or was it something else? She pictured the pilot, pressing some button or other in the cockpit to disable it, then speaking into the intercom.

I hope you don't mind, but we're going to play a little game.

The more she thought about it, the more concerned she

was. So it turned out she did need to look at her phone after all. She needed to check if the Wi-Fi was back. If it was, then it hadn't been disabled, which meant there weren't three weird things happening at the same time. If it wasn't back, then yes, it could be a coincidence, but it left open the possibility that it wasn't.

She checked her phone.

There were no notifications.

There was no Wi-Fi.

Everyone was still looking at her. She had to say something, but she had no idea what.

Jeff Ramos

Stearns was staring at them, open-mouthed. Ramos caught her eye.

'What the hell does she mean, we're going to play a game?' he said.

'I don't know,' Stearns said.

Jeff knew when something was amiss, and something was amiss now. They were flying the wrong route, the Wi-Fi was down – both of which *may* have been nothing other than unusual coincidences – and now the pilot had said they were going to play a game.

Pilots didn't play games.

They didn't change routes. And they didn't switch off the Wi-Fi, which was what he was now sure had happened.

'I don't know either,' Chip Markham said. 'But whatever it is, it's going to stop.'

'Damn right it is,' Jeff said, aware, even as he spoke, of the hollowness of his words. What he – or anyone else – said made no difference. They were in the pilot's hands. The truth was that she could do whatever she liked.

The thought gave him a chill. He had never stopped to think about it before, but there were some situations in which you put your life in someone else's hands. Not many, but there were some. When you were under a general anesthetic, for example, you were completely powerless. The surgeon might be struck off or prosecuted if they deliberately harmed you, but they could. They could do whatever they wanted.

Likewise on a plane. The pilot had total control over your fate for the duration of the flight. If they decided to fly into the side of a mountain or East over the ocean they could. You had trusted them to take you safely to your destination, but they didn't have to. There'd been that German pilot who deliberately crashed his plane. What could you do to stop him?

So why trust them? You didn't know them. There were safeguards in place, but they could be easily circumvented. So was it wise to put your life in their hands, just to get somewhere quickly?

Right now, it seemed a foolish thing to do.

'This isn't funny,' Jill Stearns said. 'If it's meant to be a joke, I'm not laughing.'

'No,' Varun said. 'It isn't. There's nothing funny about being on a runaway plane with a rogue pilot.'

'I wouldn't go that far,' Marcia said. Jeff thought there was a slur in her voice, and wondered again where she had got the booze. 'And there's two of them in there. We always have two pilots. If one dies or falls ill, the other can step in.'

'The other one's not doing much,' Kevin Anderson said. 'In fact, did anyone see another pilot?'

Ramos had not; no one else said they had.

'The door was closed,' Marcia said. 'Normally it's open. So maybe—' she paused. 'Maybe there's only one.'

'Look,' Jeff said. 'This is ridiculous. They can't just start flying whatever route they want. I'll go and talk to them.'

Jill shook her head.

'That's fine. I'll go.'

She stood up and walked through the galley to the cockpit door. She knocked three times.

The door did not open.

'Hello?' she called.

She knocked again. 'Hello?'

'Try the door,' Chip Markham said.

She grasped the handle and tried to turn it. It did not move.

'Hello!' She shouted this time and rattled the door, trying to shake it open.

There was no reply. Not even a message *to please step back from the cockpit door.*

'What the *fuck* is going on?' Jeff said.

Jill turned to face the cabin. She shook her head. 'I don't know.'

She took a deep breath.

'Can you hear me?' she said. 'Is anyone there?'

The Pilot

Is anyone there?

Of course someone is there.

They are working it out, bits of it, slowly.

Something is wrong.

The pilot is misbehaving. She is – what was it they called her? A rogue pilot? It was rather a flattering description, in some ways.

But there are two, they remember. That is the safeguard.

But there are not two. Not this time.

There is just her.

The two that are supposed to be here are probably just waking now, in the pilots' room at the rear of the hangar, to discover the door is locked, the barrel taken from the handle. They will be angry, their tongues furry and their heads aching.

Jill Stearns has tried the door, to see if she can talk to her. That shows they have not yet realized quite how serious this is. If they had, they would know there is no reasoning with her. She will not change her mind because they have persuasive arguments.

She has her own arguments. Her own reasons.

The door, of course, is locked. Perhaps they could force it, if they really tried. Perhaps they will. But it won't change anything. They need her, whatever happens. What exactly would they do without her? Attempt a landing?

They might as well jump from the plane and take their chances that way.

Can you hear me?

Yes, I can hear you.

But you don't need to know that. Not yet.

Chip Markham

This was pathetic. Stearns was supposedly a calm-headed CEO, but there she was, banging on the door like a toddler trying to get its mother's attention. What was next? Begging?

Yes, it was clear something was happening that shouldn't have been, but this kind of behavior was not going to help. They needed to be calm and think this through, and Chip had an idea where to start. In Chip's experience, people always wanted something, and once you knew what it was you could start negotiating.

So the question was what did the pilot want, and how could they give it to her so they could get out of here? Stearns whimpering at their feet was hardly going to do it.

And then there was what Miller had said, about an email. He needed to know what that was about.

'Jill.' Stearns looked back at him. 'The email he' – he pointed a thumb at Miller – 'mentioned. What is it?'

'It's nothing,' she said. 'A hoax of some kind.'

Chip's chest tightened. It was a sharp, uncomfortable feeling. He'd have to visit his doctor when they got back.

'What kind of a hoax?' he said.

'I can share it,' Varun said. He opened his laptop and

touched the screen. 'It was sent as we boarded, just before the Wi-Fi went out.'

'What does it say?' Kevin Anderson said. 'Read it out.'

Miller caught his eye and held it for a moment. Those two didn't like each other, Chip saw. He didn't know why, but it was interesting to note.

Varun began to read. 'Dear Mr. Miller. Your company is in dire legal trouble. I hope you read this email promptly, as the reasons will become clear shortly. Certainly before you land.' He looked around the cabin. 'That's it. There's no signature.'

Chip paused. There was something odd about it, something he could not put his finger on. 'Read it again,' he said.

Miller nodded and, repeated what he had said.

It came to him, and Chip nodded. 'They knew about the flight?' he said.

'Maybe,' Anderson said. 'But so what? Anyone can track a flight, even a private jet.'

'But how would they know Miller is on it?' Jeff Ramos said. He stood up, almost aggressive, and folded his arms. His shirtsleeves were rolled up – that was new, Chip noticed – and the muscles in his forearms rippled. He was in good shape for a man in his fifties.

'They might be able to figure it out,' Miller said. 'If they knew the date of the board meeting, they could assume I'd attend and then travel back on the jet.'

'But what if you'd stayed on for another meeting?' Chip said. 'Or gone to New York for the holidays? If you'd decided not to take the jet, they'd have no credibility. They had to be sure you were on the plane, which means that one hour ago, they knew *for certain* that you were on this plane and would read their email.'

'So they were watching me?' Miller said.

Chip shrugged. 'Possibly. Or they're close to you, in a position to know your movements.'

78

'Who fits that profile?' Miller said. 'Someone who works for us?'

'That's one option,' Ramos said. 'There could be others.'

'Maybe,' Kevin Anderson said, 'it's someone who wants to play a game?'

Chip looked at him sharply. 'The pilot?' he said. 'Is that what you're suggesting?'

'Yeah. Makes sense, no? Send a sinister email to add to the tension. And that's what she said: she wants to play a game. Whatever the fuck that means.'

The prickle in Markham's spine came back. It was accompanied by a tightness in his chest. There was something going on here, something that was not good.

And they were trapped on a plane.

Which was, he was now sure, no accident.

Mary Jo Fernandez

This could not be happening. She should never have come on this flight. She should have used her return ticket and gone home the way she had originally planned. Then she would have been fine. She would have made it home to take care of her husband.

But they had brought her on this plane, and now she was trapped. Why and by whom she had no idea. There was an email saying something about legal trouble; the pilot was flying them in the wrong direction; there was no Wi-Fi: it was a mess.

She didn't know what was going on, but she did know it was nothing to do with her. If the company had a legal problem it was not her problem. She just wanted to get home. Ray needed her.

It had been hard enough to leave him for one night. His cancer – first diagnosed way back when he was forty-four – had come back early in 2020. He had felt some pain early in the lockdown, but had not been able to go to the doctor. By the time he did, it was too late. The cancer was in his spine, and it was not treatable. The oncologist had told them it would have been the same had he come in March, instead of May, but Mary Jo couldn't shake the feeling that if they

80

had got the diagnosis earlier there might have been a treatment. She couldn't stop thinking that they had missed their chance, and it tortured her.

The prognosis was two to three years, and they were nearly two years in. Since the end of summer, his health had deteriorated sharply, and he was in constant pain. He found it hard to walk unassisted, which left him largely bed-bound, but even then he was not comfortable. He said the only time he was pain-free was when Mary Jo lay beside him.

Never mind all these pills, he said. *You're the best medicine.*

Corny, yes, but no less true for that. She knew exactly what he meant. She had felt the same way since the early days of their relationship. They had met in junior high: she was in sixth grade, and he was in eighth. He had his problems: his dad had died in a car crash when he was ten, and his mum struggled to make ends meet for him and his two sisters, but they were a loving, warm family. Her situation was a mirror image. Her mom had died of lung cancer, leaving her and her brothers in the tender care of her father, Bernie.

Big Bernie – as he was known – did not struggle to make ends meet. He would have, if he'd tried, but he didn't bother. As long as there was enough for him to pay his bar tab – and sometimes he didn't even do that, because how could the owner of the bar throw him out – he was fine.

Big Bernie. A character. Feared, a little, but loved. Tolerated, at least, because he didn't have that name for no reason. He had it because he had earned it, because from time to time he lost his temper, and no one wanted to see him do that again. So if he was late on his bar tab it was better to give him a few days to pay, or maybe even to wipe the slate clean.

That didn't work with his children. The rages and bellowing and slaps and insults stayed with Mary Jo. Sometimes he'd hug her, sober and remorseful, and tell her he loved her, but the slate stayed marked. It could be not erased that easily.

And as for her brothers: well, it wasn't slaps and insults. It was fists and boots and bruised and broken ribs.

And no hugs and apologies, either. He saved those for his daughter, although she wished he wouldn't. The guilt – that she was not being beaten like her brothers so maybe what they got was worse than it would have been if she took her share – was worse than the pain he would have inflicted.

She escaped to Ray's family. Vinnie, her older brother, escaped to the army. Tommy, her younger brother, escaped into the same bars that Big Bernie drank in. He became his dad's shadow. Little Bern, they called him. Or sometimes Baby Bern. He'd confessed to her once that he hated the name – he wasn't like their dad, not at all – but what could he do? Who could stop them, if Big Bernie allowed it?

So when Ray said she was the best medicine, she understood what he meant. He had been her best – her only – medicine all her life. As long as there was Ray, she was fine.

And as long as there was her, he was, too.

But soon he would be gone. And she had no idea what she would do without him. There was their daughter, Katherine, but she lived in Seattle. Perhaps she'd go there to be near her. But she didn't want to be a pain. Kath needed to live her own life.

Maybe Kath would make her a grandmother and need someone to help with the baby. Mary Jo would do that. She'd do whatever Kath needed.

But it would be without Ray. That was the worst thing about losing him. It wasn't just the man who would be gone, it was their dreams. The travel they would have done in retirement. The sunsets they would have watched together. The museums they would have visited. She loved modern art – it spoke to her in a way that more traditional art didn't – but Ray laughed at it. She'd been hoping to take him to MOMA and convert him.

None of that would happen now.

At least she could care for him in whatever time he had remaining. At least she could lie with him and take away his pain. That was a great comfort to her.

So she had not wanted to go away even for one night. Her neighbor – a retired nurse – had agreed to check on him, make sure he ate, make sure nothing happened to him – but Mary Jo had hated the idea of being away.

And now it wasn't clear she'd ever get home.

Marcia Fournier

She was glad, now, of the numbness from the vodka. Without it, she would have been freaking the fuck out. They were on a plane that had left the route it was supposed to be following, the Wi-Fi was down – switched off, no doubt – there was a threatening email, and the pilot had not come on the intercom and said, *Nothing to worry about, ladies and gentlemen, simply a brief diversion.*

No, she had come on and announced they were going to play a fucking *game.*

So thank God she was half-drunk. The only problem was that there wasn't any more to drink. She would happily have slugged as much as she could and then passed out until this was all over.

If all went well, she'd wake up in a plane that had safely landed. If the worst happened, she wouldn't wake up at all. Either was OK with her. All she needed was another drink, or two.

But there was no more vodka, so she'd have to go through this conscious.

She shifted in her seat. That wasn't the only problem. She also really needed the bathroom. She had to go, badly. It reminded her of her daughter, Kerry, as a toddler. *Mom, I need to pee. I need to pee badly.* Marcia would always give the same reply: *Don't pee badly! You'll make a mess. Pee well!*

Well, now she was Kerry. She needed to pee, badly. She didn't want to: she hated how public the small cubicle was, but she had no choice.

She undid her seat belt and turned to the aisle. The nurse, Mary Jo Fernandez, was sitting bolt upright, her hands flat on her knees, her eyes closed. She was pale, her skin sallow.

Marcia put a hand on her shoulder. The woman's eyes flew open and she snapped around to face Marcia.

'What?' she said. 'What is it?'

Marcia felt suddenly ridiculous. What was it? Why *had* she got the nurse's attention? It was the drink; without it she would have kept herself to herself, slipped to the bathroom unnoticed.

Although without the drink, she would not have needed the bathroom at all.

'Nothing,' she muttered. 'Just—'

'What?' Fernandez said.

'Just that – it's going to be OK.'

The nurse stared at her. The words felt incredibly weak.

'I'm going to the bathroom,' Marcia said. 'Should have gone before we took off.'

Jill Stearns

Jill had resisted it, but she no longer had any option other than to accept that the obvious conclusion was the only conclusion: there was something amiss here. The Wi-Fi, the route change, the email: individually, she could easily have explained them away. Wi-Fi could break, air traffic control could re-route them, some activist could have sent an email to try and waste their time – or even to alert them to a real lawsuit that was coming their way. It would have been quite a coincidence to have them all take place simultaneously, but coincidences happened.

It was the pilot's words that had tipped the balance. That line about playing a game. If it had been some kind of prank, the pilot would have said what it was by now – some Christmas frivolity or goofy pilot joke. But it wasn't that. The silence had gone on too long.

She turned and looked down the cabin at her colleagues.

'OK,' she said. 'It seems we have a problem.'

'No shit,' Kevin Anderson said. 'And I thought everything was hunky-dory.'

She didn't rise to the insult; she could hear in his voice how frightened he was.

'I agree,' Chip said. He too rose to his feet. 'We got any solutions, Jill?'

'I tried the door. I don't know what else we can do.' She looked from face to face. 'The problem is, we're powerless. It doesn't look like we have any options, other than to wait.'

There was a click, and the door to the bathroom opened. For a moment, Jill thought there was a stowaway, but it was Marcia who emerged. She looked flushed, her neck red, and there was a film of sweat on her forehead.

'Sorry,' she said. 'Carry on. I heard what you were saying. I needed the bathroom. I'll sit down. Please. Keep going.'

She hurried down the aisle to her seat. As she went to sit down, she stumbled and had to grab the armrest to save herself. Jill wondered whether there was something wrong with her. That was the last thing they needed: someone falling ill.

'As I said, we don't have many options.' That was the worst thing: the sense of powerlessness. It wasn't something she had any experience of, outside of her dealings with Mila. They were at the mercy of whoever was behind this. 'So for now, we wait.'

She studied her colleagues. Kevin Anderson was pouting, arms folded, looking tough; Chip was thoughtful; Varun, anxious; Marcia looked ill. Ramos was still and calm, as though nothing out of the ordinary was going on.

Almost as though he was not surprised.

She caught the eye of the nurse, Mary Jo.

'No,' Mary Jo said softly. 'No. We cannot just wait. We cannot do nothing.'

'I understand,' Jill said. 'But I don't see—'

'I have to go home,' the woman said. Her voice rose. 'I have to go home!' She banged the back of the seat in front of her. Kevin Anderson's head bounced forward. 'My husband needs me!' She was shouting, her face red and twisted. 'He's dying, and he needs me with him!'

'He's dying?' Jill said. 'Is he sick?'

'Cancer. It came back.' She shook her head. 'We've been together since high school. He's in pain, but he says' – her words were swallowed by her sobs – 'he says I'm the best medicine. As long as I'm there, he's OK. I didn't *want* to leave him! I should have stayed home, but I came and now this is happening. Please! I HAVE TO GO HOME!'

'I'm sorry,' Jill said. She fought to stop her own panic from overwhelming her. 'I'm so sorry. But I – I just don't know what I – we – can do.'

'Hello!' Mary Jo shouted, her voice raw. 'Pilot! Are you there? What do you want?'

Her words met with silence.

'Please!' she screamed. 'I have to go home! Please!'

There was no reply.

'Can you hear us?' she said, her voice falling away. 'Can you hear me?'

The Pilot

The woman – Mary Jo Fernandez – complicated things. She had not been expecting her; she did not recognize the name when it was added to the passenger manifest. She studied her as she crossed the tarmac to the plane. She had an air of self-consciousness that suggested she was not altogether comfortable. The others were in twos, talking about their shared interests. She walked alone, not part of any clique.

And then there were her clothes. She was wearing dark chinos and a blue shirt under a red, quilted gilet. Her shoes were blocky and comfortable. Functional, inexpensive clothes.

She did not fit. She was not one of them.

But the pilot did not know who she was, and she didn't like it, nor did she like what she had said.

My husband needs me. He is dying, and he needs me with him! I have to go home!

There had been real emotion in her voice, and the pilot had wondered what was wrong with her husband. She had felt a wave of sympathy swell before she pushed it away.

Whoever she was, and whatever her problems were, it was nothing to do with her. The woman was here now, and she would suffer the fate of the others.

89

And it was time to let them know what that was. They understood the situation now. They understood that they were powerless. That the pilot had them where she wanted, and they would do what she wanted.

That was important for what came next. They had to know she was in control.

Mary Jo had asked the question.

Can you hear us? Can you hear me?

So she would answer it.

She reached for the intercom and switched it on.

'Yes,' she said. 'I can hear you.'

Chip Markham

Everyone froze.

Chip felt a sense of relief. He had been tense – he could feel his face flushing. It happened a lot these days. It was a blood pressure problem, probably from the Scotch. But now she had spoken and the heat in his cheeks dissipated.

She had opened negotiations. He focused, hard. He had not been in this situation before – how could he have been? – but had been in situations like it. High-pressure negotiations which seemed impossible to resolve, with both sides seemingly millions of miles apart and with no common ground, until, at the last minute a solution was found.

In his experience it didn't matter how far apart you were. What mattered was that you were at the table, that you were prepared to talk. Once you got that far there was bound to be a solution. It was simply a case of finding it.

And she had spoken.

'Good,' he said. 'I'm glad you can hear us. I take it that our change of route was not at the request of air traffic control?'

It was a few seconds before the reply came.

'Correct.'

'So it's a decision you made?'

'Evidently.'

It felt strange to talk to a disembodied voice. But then everything about this was strange; what was important was that he established a dialogue.

'And the Wi-Fi? You switched it off?'

'I did.'

Now they were talking, it was time to get to the real question.

'Are you going to take us to our destination? Are we going to Portland?'

There was a faint buzz coming from the intercom. It stopped for a few seconds, then came back.

'No,' the pilot said. 'I am not.'

Behind him, Mary Jo, the nurse they had given the money to, let out a low groan. 'No,' she said. 'Not this.'

'Where are we going?' Chip said.

'That depends on you.'

'How does it depend on us?' he said. 'What can we do?'

'Play the game,' she replied. 'And if you give me what I want, then I'll take you to Portland. If not' – she paused – 'we keep heading east.'

'There is nothing east,' Jeff Ramos said, his tone almost amused. Chip wished he would shut up and leave this to him. The tightness in his chest got worse. 'Just the ocean. We'll run out of fuel well before we hit land.'

She didn't reply.

'This is ridiculous,' Kevin Anderson said. 'What's the damn game?'

Chip caught his eye and shook his head. They both needed to butt out.

'Like I said.' His voice was steady and reasonable. 'What can we do?'

'Like I said,' she replied, her voice equally steady. 'Give me what I want.'

92

'What do you want? Can you spell it out, exactly?'

'For you to play the game.'

'OK,' Chip said. 'We can do that. Tell us how.'

The buzz on the intercom returned. 'It's a murder-mystery game,' the pilot said. 'We're going to solve a crime.'

'Look,' Kevin said. 'Let's cut all the bullshit, shall we? If you want something from us, just say what it is. We can work this out. There's no need for—'

There was a squeal of feedback.

'Enough.' The pilot's voice was hard now. 'You're going to do what I say.'

'Kevin,' Chip said, 'shut the fuck up, will you? So, the game. What crime are we going to solve?'

'I'm glad you asked,' the pilot replied. 'It's a murder. One of you is a murderer, and we're going to find out who.'

Stacy

If it wasn't for the machines she was hooked up to, Cherry could have just been asleep. She was lying on her back, her jaw slack and her mouth half-open. A tube came out of each nostril and ran up to a machine that presumably provided oxygen. She had a pulse oximeter on her left forefinger – Stacy had used them during her military training – and a drip in her right arm. To the left of her bed a heart monitor gave a steady beep.

Stacy sat on a chair by the bed and held her hand. She squeezed Cherry's fingers; there was no response. She studied her daughter's face. Her skin was sallow, with a yellowish tinge, her lips redder than usual. There were dark circles around her eyes, much darker than they should have been. Her chest was rising and falling slowly.

Her first emotion was relief: for the past hour she'd been fearing she would hear that her daughter had died, or suffered some serious, long-term damage. It appeared that the worst had passed, and for that she was deeply grateful. But the relief started to fade, replaced with a sense of shock at the sight of her sweet, beautiful five-year-old in a hospital bed. Yes, she was alive, but this morning she'd been her normal self. There had been no sign at all of what was to come.

And then there was Ella.

If it was Nicole, her mom – and Stacy was pretty sure it was, although she had seen her from a distance, and had hardly been at her best – then that meant two five-year-olds were in hospital on the same day, which could hardly be a coincidence.

She took her phone and typed a message to Nicole.

All good? We're at the hospital. Cherry was taken ill – not sure what it was – but seems to be on the mend now.

Dan put a hand on her shoulder. 'Look at her,' he said. 'Look at our little girl.' He leaned over and kissed her forehead. 'She better be OK. I couldn't stand it if—'

'Don't say it,' Stacy said. 'She'll be OK.' Her phone buzzed and she opened the message. It was Nicole:

Oh my God, us too. Ella felt ill at school and by the time I got there she was in an ambulance. She's unconscious. I'm frantic. What was the issue with C?

Don't know exactly. She's out of the ICU though. I'm sending good thoughts for Ella.

Thanks. Glad she's stable. It makes me feel better.

'Who's that?' Dan said.

'Nicole.' She put the phone down. 'I saw her.'

'What do you mean?'

'Here, at the hospital.'

'Nicole's here? I didn't see her.'

'She was just arriving as we came in to see Cherry. I saw her from the window.'

'Why's she here? Is she OK?'

'It's Ella. She's sick too.'

Dan frowned. 'Really?'

'Yes. Same situation. She got a call from the school. Ella was in an ambulance on the way here. Same as Cherry.'

Dan sat down and looked at her.

'What the hell's going on?'

Dr. Williams

Dr. Neal Williams was finding it hard to get off the phone. It was Mindy, his party planner, and she had some urgent questions about the guest list.

His wife was turning forty. He hated parties, but they had young children and he worried she didn't get enough time away from them, so he had decided to throw a surprise party for her.

The problem was that he had no idea what he should plan. He had started with a save the date to all of the friends he could think of: her college roommates, the few names he could find from high school, the moms from the preschool, her colleagues at the historical society where she had worked before their first son, Riley, had come along.

Then he had worried that wasn't enough, so he had asked one of the preschool moms for help.

Is there anyone else I should invite?

You have her yoga friends, right?

He did not.

And there's the group of women who she sometimes goes out with.

He had never heard of this group. If pushed, he would

97

have said he assumed that the preschool moms, the yoga class and her colleagues covered it. He asked who it was.

It's quite a loose group. Just a bunch of friends who occasionally get together. Whoever can make it.

How would I invite them?

Would you like me to take care of it?

He indicated that he would.

It turned out there were forty-two women who said they would come, most with partners, almost all with kids.

A total of nearly one hundred and fifty.

What would they eat? He couldn't cook that much. And what would they do? He had a cornhole set, but they'd need more than that to pass the time. And drinks: he'd need a bartender.

That gave him the idea: he could get it catered. And maybe a band. And babysitters, so the adults could have a good time.

It was a fine theory, but he had woefully underestimated the amount of effort it would take to plan a party of this size. After a week of phone calls he realized he was in deep shit. The invites were sent. No party was planned. And this party was like a wedding, just minus the ceremony and the vows.

Which gave him an idea. His sister had a friend who was a wedding planner. Maybe she could help.

It turned out she could, for a small fee, if by small you meant small fortune. Fortunately he had the venue – they had a large backyard – but his sister's friend felt they needed a tent. A marquee tent, she called it, like they have at Royal Ascot, whatever that was.

A tent, a party planner, catering for one hundred and fifty guests, a band, babysitters and drinks: it added up to a grand total of – no, he stopped himself before he did the math. If he knew officially what it cost – even though he kind of did really – he would not be able to enjoy it.

'Mindy,' he said. 'I'm at work. There's a patient I need—'

'One more thing. Do you want oysters?'

Oysters? That was hardly going to help with the bill.

'I – I haven't—'

'Dr. Williams?'

It was Roland, a nurse who had just started working at the hospital.

'One second,' he said. He gestured to his phone. 'Be right with you.'

'Oysters are available,' Mindy said, 'but we have to order today. It's eighteen dollars a dozen, but if you get ten dozen it's sixteen per dozen. I'd say maybe half the guests will want them, and they'll want two or three each, so maybe eighteen dozen?'

What the fuck was she talking about? Eighteen, sixteen, dozen this, dozen that? He was lost, and his attention was needed elsewhere.

'Dr. Williams,' Roland said, his voice more urgent now. 'There's another one.'

'Hold on, Mindy,' Williams said, and addressed himself to Roland. 'Another what?'

'Child with liver failure. Just arrived in the ER.'

'Neal,' Mindy said. 'We really need to—'

'Sorry, Mindy,' he said. 'I have to go. Just do what you think is best regarding the oysters. OK?'

He put down the phone. Roland looked at him, eyes narrowed.

'Oysters?'

'Party. I'll explain later. You can come. You said there's another one? With the same symptoms?'

Roland nodded.

'Unconscious?'

'Yes. Exactly the same.'

'Boy or girl?'

'Girl. From the same school.'

'OK. Talk to the hospital admin – Diane is the best bet – and get them to talk to the principal and have that school closed for the day.'

'Will do.'

'Where's the patient?'

Roland beckoned to him. 'Follow me.'

Stacy Evanston

Stacy put her hand on her stomach. She was momentarily taken aback; it was a protective gesture she remembered from her first pregnancy.

It's real, she thought. *I'm actually pregnant. My body knows. Now, of all times, I'm pregnant.*

She watched Dan. He was smiling at Cherry, stroking her forehead. She had had boyfriends before him – some better looking, some more athletic, some with better grades – but she loved him in a way she had never thought was possible. What surprised her most was that she *admired* him. She wanted to be like him. She wanted the calm self-assurance, the confidence that he was doing the right thing, living his best life.

He wasn't jealous of others. He didn't want a faster car or a newer truck – OK, maybe a newer truck – or a bigger house. He didn't crave more money. He didn't want what others had. He had the gift of enjoying what he had, right there in that moment.

Once, early in their relationship, he had gone out to get breakfast and come back with bagels, cream cheese and some fruit.

Look at that orange, he said. *It grew on some tree in Florida and now here it is. And we get to eat it. Sweet, juicy, delicious. Is there anything better than that? Really? You could go to the ends of the earth looking for something better, but this orange is as good as it gets.*

And he'd meant it. That was how he lived his life. And even when – like before, in the waiting room – his calmness deserted him, she loved him even more, because it was proof it wasn't an act.

And when they got through this, she'd give him the news he wanted.

Another child.

'She's beautiful,' she said. 'And she's lucky to have a dad like you.'

'Nah,' he said. 'It's me who's lucky. She's the best. *You're* the best.' He stroked her cheek. 'When she's better we'll do something special. Disney. Something like that.'

'Disney in California, or Disney in Florida?'

'Florida, of course. We can go to—' he stopped and stared at their daughter '—Cherry?'

Stacy jumped to her feet. 'What is it? Is she OK?'

He didn't reply, his attention focused on Cherry.

'Dan? What is it?'

'She's waking up,' he said, and grinned at her. 'She's back! She heard Disney, and now she's back!'

Dr. Williams

Dr. Williams read the chart. The girl's liver was failing; the bloodwork was unequivocal, but he didn't need it to know what was happening. The problem was visible in the yellow tint in her skin and around her pupils, and he had a recent similar experience.

They had stabilized the first girl – Cherry – and she seemed to be getting better, so they were following the same course of treatment. Without knowing what was causing this, it was all they could do.

And he had no idea what was causing it. Sudden onset of liver failure was rare and normally associated with prolonged lifestyle choices that damaged the organ. He doubted very much that these two five-year-olds were hard-core drinkers and drug-takers. It could be the result of fetal alcohol syndrome – just about – but the chances of that in two kids in the same school on the same day were minimal. More than minimal. Virtually impossible.

And it was the fact there were two of them that bothered him most. If it was one, he might have accepted they would never know what was behind it. A girl got sick; a girl recovered. Sometimes things just happened and there was no explanation.

But two of them suggested a common cause, possibly linked to the school. Maybe they had been somewhere else together, in which case it could be that. Either way, whatever had caused one to fall sick had more than likely triggered the other.

He could only think of two causes: a hepatitis virus which was not vaccinated against – and those were pretty rare in the US – or a toxin of some type. For them to get hepatitis they would have needed to come into contact with the blood or fecal matter of an infected person, which did not seem likely in Barrow, Maine. As for a toxin: well, he had no idea what could cause something like this.

He'd called a doctor friend, Peter Hall, who worked as a liver specialist in Portland. Pete had no immediate suggestions; he requested the charts and said he'd take a look, but to really determine what was going on they'd need to do more tests.

He put down the chart and walked around the bed to look at the girl. Ella Farmer. Long, thick brown hair, a pink T-shirt with sequins in the shape of a whale that reversed if you brushed them to reveal a new picture.

Her breathing was shallow. He felt her pulse. It was weak, weaker than he remembered. He checked the screen.

Her oxygen level was low. Not critical, but low; lower than when she came in.

That was not a good sign.

He pressed a button to call a nurse. It was Roland who arrived.

'What do you think?' he said. In his experience, nurses were often able to assess whether there was a problem equally as reliably as the doctors. They saw this stuff every day.

Roland pressed his index and forefinger to the girl's neck. He looked at the screen.

'Hmm,' he said. 'I think we need to do something.'

'Intubate? Get her on oxygen?'

Roland nodded. He looked worried, and there was a sense of foreboding in his voice. 'Exactly. I'll get on it.'

2

Ella's parents were in the waiting room. Her dad was sitting upright in a chair, staring at his phone. He was wearing smart gray pants and a jacket; he looked like a professor from the local college. Her mom was looking out of the window.

He held the door open. They walked quickly across the waiting room.

'Come through,' he said. He led them to a consulting room.

'How is she?' her father said, before he sat down.

He hated this part of his job. No parent wanted to hear what he was about to say.

'She's still in intensive care,' he said. 'I'm afraid we had to put her on a ventilator. She was having difficulty breathing.'

Ella's mom sat down heavily. The blood drained from her face.

'What's happening?' she said in a whisper. 'What's doing this to her?'

'We can't be sure,' Dr. Williams said. 'It's . . .' he paused '. . . it's highly unusual.'

'You said it was a liver problem, when we arrived?' Ella's

dad said. He was fighting to keep his composure, to project an air of professionalism.

'That's right. Her liver is inflamed, and it's not working well.'

'How can that be?' he said. 'She's *five*.'

'I know,' Dr. Williams said. 'I have the same question. It's possible it's something environmental.'

'Like what?'

'Again, I don't have an answer. I wish I did, but I don't.'

'So what can you do?'

'We'll keep monitoring her. If she continues to need assistance breathing, we'll provide that. I've consulted with a liver specialist, who is looking at her case as well. He'll be coming up from Portland later today.'

What he didn't say was that it didn't add up to much. Their options were limited. Ella was, to all intents and purposes, on her own.

Her dad nodded. 'Thank you. And if there's anything we can do, please, just ask. If you need authorization for a treatment – covered by insurance or not – you have it. Don't hesitate, Doctor Williams. She's our little girl.'

He could feel their anguish; it was palpable. As parents they would do whatever they could to help their daughter; he had no doubt that if he had said the only treatment was for one of them to give up their liver, they would have offered it up in a heartbeat.

'We will,' he said. 'We'll do everything we can.'

He opened the door and stepped into the corridor. Nurse Miranda Chan looked up from the nurse's station.

'I'm glad you're out,' she said. 'I didn't want to disturb you, but I was going to have to come in if you didn't get done in the next few minutes.'

He had a horrible feeling that he knew what was coming.

'What is it?' he said.

'There's another. A boy this time. Six years old.'

'No,' he said. 'No. It's not possible.'

'Yes it is,' Miranda replied, her expression grim. 'It's more than possible. It's happening.'

December 23rd, 2022

Jill Stearns

Jill looked around the plane.

One of you is a murderer, and we're going to find out who.

Static came through the intercom and the pilot spoke again. 'Here's my question: Who is it?'

'This is Jill Stearns,' she said. 'I'm the CEO of—'

'I know who you are,' the pilot said.

'Then you'll know that this is preposterous,' she said. 'No one on this plane has killed anyone. There's been a mistake.'

'No,' the pilot said. 'There's been no mistake.'

'I think there has. It's inconceivable that anyone here has committed murder.'

'One of you has,' the pilot said. 'And I want to know who.'

'Why do you think this?' Jill said. 'Who has been killed?'

'One of you knows,' the pilot said. 'And I'm going to give you a chance to come clean. You have twenty minutes to confess. If you do, this is over. We land, you go to the police and tell them what you've done, and your colleagues go home.' She paused. 'If you don't, then I'll take steps to make you.'

'Listen,' Jill said. 'We can work this out. But you need to tell us what's going on here. You need to tell us what it is that you think has happened. Then we can explain, and move on.'

'There is no explanation,' the pilot said. 'You have twenty minutes.'

The buzz faded as the intercom switched off.

Jill shook her head. 'Please,' she said. 'Give us a chance. At least give us the opportunity to try and explain. Then if there has been a mistake we can move on. I'm not saying there has, but it's at least possible. Give us a chance. That's all I'm asking.'

There was a long silence, broken by Marcia coughing. 'I think she's gone,' she said. 'Now what?'

Chip Markham

This had rapidly spiraled out of control. He didn't know what was going on – the most likely explanation at this point was that the pilot was deranged, but that didn't help the situation. It made it worse, as there would be no way to reason with her.

So he was stuck on a plane with a crazy pilot, headed east over the Atlantic Ocean.

He wouldn't have minded, this time last year. Or the year before. Anytime, really, in the five years since Sandra, his wife of nearly thirty years, had died. He'd had a good life, and the prospect of it ending didn't bother him at all. He'd come close on two occasions to killing himself – his preferred method was to drink a bottle of Scotch, close the garage door, climb into his Land Rover and turn the engine on – and there were times he still considered it.

The truth was, with Sandra gone, he'd had nothing to live for. They had a son, Matthew, but he didn't speak to Chip: their relationship had fallen apart when he was a teenager, and Chip had not known how to repair it. Matthew lived in San Diego; he'd spoken to Sandra most weeks, but refused to talk to his father, and Chip had convinced himself he didn't care. Matthew was the past, a lost cause.

And he did not chase lost causes, even if part of him would have liked to.

He'd considered rekindling things with Marcia – she would have resisted out of pride, though that wouldn't have lasted – but he had decided not to. The companionship – and sex – would have been welcome, but he didn't want to invite her neediness back into his life.

So, most days he got by, but there were times – Christmas and Thanksgiving were two of the worst – when, without Sandra, he saw all too clearly how empty his life was, and he couldn't face the question that rattled around his brain: *Why bother? Why bother with this for ten, twenty, thirty more years? Why bother for ten, twenty, thirty more* days?

He was lonely, and sad, and bored, and he'd had enough.

And then the pandemic had arrived, and the office had closed. His world had collapsed into nothing: just the four walls of his house and endless video calls. The most serious suicide attempt had come a month into the first lockdown; he had drunk the Scotch, climbed into his car, and turned the key.

A carbon monoxide detector had gone off, the alarm penetrating – as it was designed to – his drunken stupor. He had woken slumped over in the front seat, his head throbbing and his pants stained with urine. His first feeling was gratitude, followed swiftly by a burning shame that he had lacked the courage to put an end to this farce that was his life.

The second attempt had come three days later. This time he had disabled the alarm and drunk more whiskey.

It had made him vomit, and he had woken again, ending up crouched over on his garage floor, sputum dripping from his mouth. As the exhaust fumes gathered around him, he had realized, however faintly, that he didn't want to die, and that he was done committing suicide.

But he reserved the right for the future.

So the prospect of being trapped in a plane with a crazy pilot would not have concerned him at all. He would have met his fate with equanimity.

Until a month ago, that was.

It was a Friday night and he was in the office – he put the weekend off as long as he could these days – reading an email from Jill about a potential acquisition that she had decided was not a fit for the company. It was irritating; he'd been working on it for some time and now it seemed the effort had been wasted.

He closed his computer and felt the bite of anxiety in his chest at the thought of the two days ahead of him. What would he do with the weekend? Wake up, go for a walk? Watch some sport, read the papers?

He'd eat alone, that much he knew. Open an expensive bottle of red wine – perhaps one of the ones he and Sandra had bought on one of their trips to the West Coast – and drink it, pretending to himself that it was delicious, when, without her it could as well have been from a fifteen-dollar box.

Everything was like that. That was the problem: the world was colorless. His life had been work and Sandra: that was enough for him. He hated golf and tennis, and he had let his friendships slide years ago. It was just his job and his wife.

But she was gone, and his life was cut in half. Getting through Saturday would be hard enough.

And then there was Sunday. Another day to endure before the work week started.

It was pathetic. He was pathetic. If his colleagues had known he was like this they would have lost all respect for him. At work he was a composed, urbane, wise presence; they would never have guessed he was a nervous wreck at the thought of a weekend alone.

But then, that Friday, it had all changed. He was about to pour a Macallan – his third of the evening – when the doorbell rang.

He paused, the bottle in his hand. He wasn't expecting anyone, and he never had visitors. The house was at the end of a long private drive, invisible from the main road, and if any political canvassers seeking signatures or salesmen did consider venturing down it there was a sign on the main gates telling them not to bother.

So his doorbell never rang, and whoever it was he didn't want to talk to them.

He waited to see if they tried again. Maybe they'd leave if he didn't answer the door.

It rang again, then, after a brief pause, again.

He put down the bottle and headed for the front door. He unlocked it and pulled it open.

There was a man in a puffy black jacket, a mask covering his face. It took Chip a moment to recognize who it was.

'*Matthew?*' he said.

'Hi, Dad,' his son replied.

It was the last person he would have expected. His relationship with Matthew was broken, irrevocably broken. He could see it was his fault; he had failed as a father. Could he have done better? He had no father figure to model himself on – his own dad had walked out when he was a toddler and his mom had never remarried – which was an excuse of sorts, so he'd have said maybe. But he was stubborn. Sandra had tried to tell him to reconcile with Matthew, but he had refused, convinced he was right.

The problem was that Matthew didn't live up to his expectations. He was a quiet child, slow in movement and thought and prone to daydreaming, a combination which didn't endear him to his teachers, or to his father.

114

He was late for school, forgot his bag, didn't do his homework: Chip could never understand why he didn't just try harder. Yes, he was interested in other things, but so what? This was school, and an expensive, exclusive, elite school at that: it was important, and Matthew was wasting the opportunity he'd been given.

Worse, he didn't seem to care that he was failing. Later, Chip had come to suspect that he did care but didn't know how to fix it, and pretending he didn't was a defense against his father's expectations. At the time, he had seen it as wilful and deliberate and aimed at his dad.

So the more he saw of it, the harder he pushed Matthew to conform, and the more Matthew refused. When he was fourteen, they got into a screaming match, and Chip told him it was time to shape up and start working properly.

If I'm such a disappointment to you, why do you bother?

Chip struggled for an answer.

I don't know.

So I am?

Are what?

A disappointment to you?

His reply had haunted Chip ever since.

I suppose you are.

He should have apologized immediately. When he failed to do so, he should have apologized the next day, or the next week, or sometime afterward.

He knew that now, but he didn't then. He was too proud and too stubborn, and he thought he could make Matthew more like him. As a result, he and his son fell into a stand-off. Sandra warned him that he was damaging his relationship with their only child, but he told her it was a lesson for the boy, a lesson in the real world.

And then, at eighteen, after years of a distant, cold, relationship, Matthew went to art college.

115

Art college.

It was as though he was trying to antagonize Chip. Of all the paths to choose, his son had chosen *art* college.

Home of the dropouts and washouts and losers.

At the end of his first year there was a show, and Chip showed up, under pressure from Sandra.

The art – if it could be called that – was a mishmash of shapeless blobs of color and sculptures that looked like a two-year-old had done them. He had walked around in disbelief. After a while, Matthew had come over to him, a tentative smile on his face, his arm around an Asian girl in paint-spattered dungarees.

This is my dad, he said. *What do you think of the show?*

Chip shook his head. *You did this?*

Matthew nodded.

It's – it's good.

His son's smile faded. *Is that it? Is that all you have to say?*

It is good, Chip said. *Really. But I don't understand it, I guess—*

Matthew looked outraged. *You don't* understand? *That's Chip Markham for I think this is trash.*

People were looking at them. Even though this was an art college, Chip didn't want a scene.

Isn't that it, Dad? You think it's trash?

Chip bristled. His son was acting out still, aged nineteen. He felt the eyeballs on him. This was becoming embarrassing, and he was getting annoyed.

That's not what I said.

It's what you meant.

No. I meant the words I said. If I'd meant something else, I'd have said it.

Matthew sneered. *You're a douche. I don't care what you think of my art.*

116

I like your – he paused – *work.*

My art.

Your art.

No you don't. You're a fraud, Dad. A bullshitter.

He knew he shouldn't bite – he was the adult in the conversation – but there was a lot of water under this particular bridge.

Yeah, Chip said. *Then maybe it's time I didn't bullshit you. You want to know what I think? I don't think this is trash. It's not that good. This is crap. Is that what I'm paying for? Because I'd just as soon—*

Forget it, Dad. You'll never understand.

And that was it. After that he had seen Matthew when he was home in the summers, he had attended his graduation, but their relationship was frosty. When he had moved to San Diego, Chip had offered to help with the deposit on a house, but Matthew had refused.

They had not spoken since. He had seen Matthew at Sandra's funeral, but, other than a stiff hello, they had not said much to each other. Matthew made it clear he wasn't interested.

And Chip understood. He hadn't earned the right to anything else. He had treated Matthew like a failure, because he thought he *was* a failure. He *was* disappointed in him. He hadn't lived up to his expectations.

It was only since Sandra was gone that he saw it was his expectations that were the problem, but it was too late to fix them.

And now Matthew was at his door.

'This is unexpected,' he said.

'I've been thinking,' Matthew said. 'Maybe we can do better.'

Chip nodded. Suddenly all he wanted was to do better. He gestured behind him, to the house.

'Come in,' he said.

117

'I will. But first, there's someone I'd like you to meet.'

Matthew turned to the car behind him and nodded. The rear door opened, and a woman got out. Chip had seen photos; it was Matthew's girlfriend, Esme.

She was holding a baby.

'This is Otis,' Matthew said. 'Your grandson.'

Matthew had decided, after becoming a father, to give his own father a second chance. He had stayed for the weekend, and on the following morning, Chip had made the apology he should have made years before.

It wasn't all perfect between them, but it was a start.

Otis, though, was perfect, and Chip loved him from the moment he first held him. His only sadness was that Sandra wasn't there to meet him.

They left on the Sunday evening, with a promise to return. A promise that had turned into a plan to have a family Christmas.

Chip looked out of the window. The sun was setting to the west, low over the ocean.

They were arriving that night for Christmas. So now he did mind whether he made it home.

He minded a lot.

'Jill,' he said. 'This can't go on. We have to do something.'

Kevin Anderson

Chip was saying *this can't go on*, which was all very fucking well, but what was he going to do about it?

This wasn't the office, where some subordinate would quail at the sound of his voice. Not that they called them subordinates, of course, but that's what they were, it was a fucking joke to think otherwise. They were underlings, peons, staff: if the big boss said, *Don't let this get in the way of all the important work you have but when you get a chance, I'd love to know more about that market research report that came out*, what that meant, and they all knew it, was that everything else would be dropped until the market research report was fucking well analyzed and digested and turned into a PowerPoint presentation, every page of which had been scrutinized and pored over so that every word and number was ready for the CFO.

It was gross, it really was. An utterly obscene spectacle. Jill liked to walk the floors, shaking hands and projecting an air of informality: *We're all equal! All just members of the team! Really we are!*

They were nothing of the sort.

The employees were there to serve. Chip and Jill and their C-Suite buddies – Kevin included – were the modern equivalent

119

of the princes and kings and queens of medieval city states. They sat atop their little piece of the world until someone came along and overthrew them. They had no loyalties other than to themselves; they ruled by fear. The deal was explicit: upset me and you won't receive my favor – a property or military command or lucrative tax collecting post – or maybe, if really pushed, I'll throw you into a hellish prison. In modern corporate America it was no different, but in place of favors and prisons were the promises of promotions and bonuses and the threat of unemployment.

It was – as it always had been – about power, and the struggle to get and retain it. All the *we have a flat hierarchy* and *we're a collaborative, team-based company* was bullshit and self-serving hot air.

If you made it to the top, it was great. If not – well, more's the pity.

Kevin was a boss, and the people that worked for him knew it. He could ruin their day with a critical comment, make them physically ill with worry if he decided to. He didn't pretend to deny it. He didn't act like their friend. He wasn't their friend. Either they did what he wanted and made him look good or he got rid of them.

There was a lot of money at stake if they didn't. More than people thought. He, as chief operating officer, got paid one point five million dollars, plus the same as a bonus, plus three million in stock options.

Every fucking year.

He loved it. Loved the money. Every fortnight when he got paid, he loved seeing the money roll in. It made him feel like a god, it was a numerical representation of why he was better than everyone else. And when he got his bonus: it was almost erotic.

But he always knew that Chip – not to mention Jill – got *much* more.

120

Which was why when he heard her talk about *mission* and *values* and how she *loved what this company does* he knew it was a crock of shit.

She wanted the money. As did he. As did *everyone*.

And they were the people who held the key, who could make or break your career. So yeah, people did what he and Chip and Jill said.

But this was not the office. This was the real, actual world, so what was Chip going to *do* when the pilot, as she would, ignored him?

Reprimand her? Go to HR and have her put on a performance management plan? Give her a shitty bonus?

No, he was going to do nothing. He was going to act big and talk tough, but none of that made a blind bit of difference. They were at the mercy of this madwoman, and nothing Chip said was going to change that.

And she was clearly insane. There was no murderer on this plane. Sure, they were selfish and greedy and would have – most of them probably had – betrayed their friends and family members to get the next job. Yes, they had sacrificed their relationships with wives and husbands and boyfriends and girlfriends and children in order to attend one more meeting, send one more email, get one more promotion. Work was everything to them, and while it may not have made them good humans, it made them successful, which was a price they were more than willing to pay.

But they weren't murderers. The idea was ludicrous, but it was clear the pilot – whoever the stupid bitch was – had made up her mind there was, which was why she had gone to such extraordinary lengths to do this.

And whatever Chip or anyone else said was not going to change her mind. She was not rational, so no rational argument was going to matter.

And if words were useless, then that left action.

121

And he had a plan.

He pictured himself landing and texting Katie – she was the perfect example of why he wanted his job, wanted the salary and the bonuses, a hot little twenty-eight-year-old like her wasn't interested in him for his good looks and charm, and they both knew it – telling her *Hey, let's meet up, the craziest thing just happened* and her replying *what? What happened* and him saying *I was on the jet* – that was a good start in itself – *and some mad bitch took us hostage* and her replying again *OMG, that's unbelievable, are you OK?* and then the closer, the line that would seal the deal and get her out to dinner and into his bed where he could finally fuck the shit out of her, *Yeah, it's fine, I sorted it out. It was a bit of a risk but I got it done.*

So, yeah, he had a plan. And it was going to work.

Varun Miller

Was there a murderer on the plane? It seemed barely credible, but how could he be sure? And if there was, then he – they all – were caught up in something that could end in disaster.

No: it must be some fantasy of the pilot. She was mistaken about this, and they would convince her of that and it would be over. Unless she was making it up. Unless this was an excuse to kidnap them and crash them into the ocean in an attempt to make herself famous. Dead, yes, but famous all the same.

He wished he had read the email as soon as it had arrived. He would surely have realized it was foolish to stay on the flight, and now he would be on the ground, making his way to another airport, or driving the fifteen hundred miles home.

He could see it, an alternative path, tantalizingly, *agonizingly* close, a path which would have kept him safe.

Kept him *alive*.

Because he was sure he was going to die. They were all going to die.

He felt his mind start to race, his thoughts – his ability to think at all – scrambled by panic. He took a deep breath, then another, then another.

There had to be a way out of this. There was *always* a way out. He just had to find it.

He couldn't leave Ari fatherless. If he died it would be OK for him. It would be fucking awful for his wife and son. He didn't want to die; in fact, now he was facing it he realized he was *terrified* of dying. There was so much he wanted to do, most of it with Ari, and he couldn't bear the idea of having it taken away from him.

But ultimately, he knew that if he did die, then it would be over. He'd be gone. He'd been brought up a Catholic, but he'd given up on all that many years ago. There was no afterlife; just oblivion. It wasn't like you started experiencing nothingness. There was no you to experience it – you went back to the same state of non-existence that had prevailed before you were born. So, and he had no doubt about this, once he was dead it was not him that would suffer. It was his son and his wife.

Just like all the others that would be left behind.

Behind him, the nurse stood up. 'Listen,' she said. 'Pilot, I'm talking to you. I know you can hear me. I *know* you can hear me, so even if you don't answer I'm going to say my piece.'

There was no reply.

'Fine,' she said. 'I'm a nurse. I don't work for this company. I'm not part of this. My husband is dying, and I need to go home. So please, let me.'

'Would you mind?' Kevin Anderson said. 'I don't think this is helpful. We need—'

'I'm not *trying* to be helpful,' Mary Jo snapped. 'I just want her to know who's on the plane. I've got nothing to do with this. With you. With any of you. I haven't killed anyone.'

'How do we know that?' Anderson said.

'Kevin,' Stearns said, raising her hand. 'Please. Not now.'

124

'Well, how do we?' Kevin said. 'We don't know her. We've all been on this plane many, many times, and the first time she's on it this happens. Is that a coincidence?'

'Yes,' Mary Jo said. 'It is.'

'Well, I don't trust coincidences. You're a nurse, right?' He didn't wait for a reply. 'Who has easier access to people they want to kill? Me? Or you? Surrounded by sick people, maybe you feel you're on a mercy mission. Some patient you give too much morphine to?'

'I help people!' Mary Jo said. 'I've never harmed a patient.'

'So you say.'

'Kevin.' The CEO shook her head. 'Stop.'

The nurse slammed her hand into the headrest. 'Is anyone going to own up?' she shouted. 'Well? *Is* anyone? Because one of you needs to!' She turned to the man, Kevin. 'It's not me! It's one of you. That's how we get out of here. That's how we go home! So come on!'

No one spoke. Varun checked his phone, even though he knew it was pointless, hoping there was a signal.

Nothing. It was crazy. You could *always* get a signal these days.

But not here. Not on this awful plane. He was on the local network – the router was working, distributing its signal around the plane, but it wasn't connected to anything. The pilot had disconnected it from the satellite network. He had no idea how – presumably there was an antenna of some kind that she could have unplugged, or a function on the router that she had switched off.

The router which his phone was connected – uselessly – to.

Maybe he could talk his way into the cabin, offer to negotiate with her, then, when she wasn't looking he could turn the Wi-Fi back on. He could retreat, negotiations over, but when he returned to his seat there would be a connection to the outside world.

125

Who was he kidding? Even if he could distract her, which was unlikely given how suspicious she'd be, he didn't know which switch of the many hundreds there were in the cockpit.

His only connection to the router was through the local network, which was the problem in the first place.

Although he was connected. He paused.

It was possible there was a setting on the router that could be changed to connect it back up to the outside world. If someone could get access – could hack into it – then maybe they could change the setting.

He had coded in high school, had built his own computer, and had, to impress his first girlfriend, Madison, hacked into the school's online records and changed the name of their teacher to Maleficent.

It had been a while, but it was worth a try.

And it was the only plan he had.

Kevin Anderson

All this was a waste of time. Chip, the nurse they'd shipped in for the photo opportunity, Stearns begging: nothing they said to the pilot was going to change things. It was time for some direct action.

He unclipped his seat belt and stood up, his hands on the tops of the seats on either side of him.

'Kevin,' Jill said. 'What are you doing?'

'Sorting this out.'

Saying it like that – like something Clint Eastwood would have said – made him see that the only mistake he'd made was not to do this immediately. He was buoyed by the words, by the low, tough growl he'd said them in.

'It's probably best to sit down,' Jill said. 'We don't want to do anything that will make this worse.'

'It won't make it worse.'

He made his way down the aisle, walking his hands from seat back to seat back. As he reached Jill she stepped partly into the aisle.

'I'm serious, Kevin,' she said. 'We need to be cautious.'

'Fuck cautious,' he said.

She held his gaze for a long time. For a moment he thought

she was going to stay in his way – and then he would have had to somehow push past her, because he wasn't going back to his seat – but she stepped aside.

He walked past her. On his left was the main cabin door. In front of him was the cockpit door.

He rapped on it, hard.

'Open up,' he said.

There was no reply.

He rapped again. 'Open. Now.'

He grabbed the handle and tried to turn it; it was locked and wouldn't move. He turned to the cabin. Six faces looked at him, half-skeptical, half-expectant.

Maybe he's the hero, they were thinking. *Maybe he's going to save us.*

'There's a metal bottle in my bag,' he said. 'Pass it up.'

Miller leaned over and opened his bag. He took out a bottle. It was matte silver, and heavy looking. 'This one?'

Kevin nodded and held out his hands. Miller threw it and he snatched it from the air. It was full of water; he unscrewed the cap and took a sip. It was a very cool move.

He tapped the base of it on the door handle. It rang out with a metallic tang. He tapped it again, readying himself. This was the moment. This was when he would smash this thing open.

He tapped it again to find his range, then slammed it down as hard as he could.

The clang was deafening in the small space and someone let out a yelp. The impact shuddered through his arm and shoulder, leaving him dizzy for a second.

The handle lowered about a quarter of an inch, which was something.

'It's coming,' he said. 'It's working.'

He hit it again, the impact jarring, then again, then a third time. It did not move any further. He lifted the bottle above his head then brought it down with all the force he could muster.

'Shit,' he said. 'It's stuck.'

He grabbed the handle and pulled, trying to rattle the door, then kicked it in frustration. He shoved his shoulder against it, seeing if it would move.

He was starting to look a bit foolish. More than a bit, but it wasn't over yet. Maybe if he hit it hard enough he could open it. He was a big man, a former football player, who still weighed two hundred and twenty pounds, most of it muscle. He kept fit – it was mainly money that kept Katie interested, but that wasn't all.

He took a step back, then launched himself toward the door.

He braced himself for a painful impact on his shoulder, for the door to spring open, or at the least to buckle so he could force something in between the door and the frame and lever it open.

But he hit nothing.

Instead, the plane lurched savagely down and to the left and he went flying to the right, his feet off the ground, his body momentarily weightless. And then he slammed into the galley cupboard, knocking the door open and sending packets of nuts and pretzels in every direction.

As he found his bearings, the plane lurched up and in the opposite direction and he flew across the cabin. He put a hand out to steady himself. It snapped into the wall, his full weight on it. He heard a loud crack and saw his wrist bend at an unnatural angle and had time to think *that's not right* before the pain bloomed and he realized it was broken, badly broken.

The plane leveled out and he sank to his knees, clutching his wrist. He looked down and saw the flash of bone protruding through his skin. It was shockingly white, like pristine freshly fallen snow.

And then the pain came. Oh, God, the *pain*.

He screamed. He felt faint, his vision swimming, and he slumped to the floor, his back to the wall.

He was breathing heavily. He fought to control it. He looked up at his colleagues; they were pale, frozen in their seats. Jill was gripping the armrests, her knuckles white.

She relaxed her grip and stared at him, a half-smile on her lips.

'That went well,' she said.

He bit back the pain. 'Fuck you,' he muttered. For a second the pleasure of saying it muted the pain, but then it came roaring back, and he let out a high-pitched squeal.

There was a hand on his shoulder. It was the nurse. Her expression was a mixture of pity and disgust.

'Let me take a look.'

He looked up at her, his vision blurred by tears. He wondered if he would vomit; that was all they needed in this enclosed space.

Mary Jo turned to Marcia. 'Are there towels in the bathroom?'

'I think so.'

'If there are any, would you grab some?'

Marcia nodded and jumped up. She came back with a handful of paper towels and one neatly folded cloth towel, a gold emblem on it. Mary Jo took them and went over to Kevin. She crouched next to him.

'Put your legs flat on the floor.'

He did as he was told, and she took his wrist in her hands, then placed it on top of the towel. Blood seeped across the white cloth.

His wrist was badly damaged. It was bent sharply to the left, a sliver of bone visible just above the top of his thumb.

'It's going to need surgery,' she said. 'But I'll see if there's anything I can do.'

The plane bumped as it went through some mild turbulence. He winced in pain.

'Fuck,' he said. 'This really hurts.'

'I'll bet.'

She touched his fingers in turn. 'Can you feel that?'

'Yes. I think so.'

'You *think* so?'

'I can. It's just the pain swamps everything else.'

'That's good.'

She studied his wrist. 'It's broken. But how badly and where, I can't say. You'll need an X-ray, and then an orthopedic surgeon will have to decide how to reset the bones.'

'Can you do anything?' he said. 'Can you fix it?'

She shook her head. 'Not here. You'll have to wait to see a surgeon. It'll hurt but you'll be OK.'

'You can't straighten it out?'

'No. I can't do anything. It could easily make it worse.'

'Jesus,' he said. 'The pain's one thing, but what's worse is the feeling that it's wrong, somehow. It's in the wrong place.'

'I have some ibuprofen,' she said. 'That could help with the swelling, and the pain, at least a little. Is there ice onboard?'

'In the fridge,' he said. 'Opposite me.'

She turned and opened the fridge. It was full of water and soda and fruit juice. At the top was a small freezer compartment. She took out the ice tray and shook the ice cubes into the towel, then wrapped it around them and placed it gently around his wrist.

'Feels better already,' he said. 'It'll be even better when it goes numb.'

'That's the plan.' She took a bottle of water from the fridge and refilled the tray. 'Hopefully we land before they freeze, but just in case.'

131

The Pilot

There was little more than an hour of fuel left. In another twenty – maybe thirty – minutes they'd be too far from land to make it to Portland.

And not long after that, anywhere else.

So things had to start moving.

She did not doubt they understood she was serious now. One of them had tried to break in, hitting the door with some metal object. She was certain that it would hold – these doors were made to withstand assault – but she didn't like it.

She could have asked him to stop. She could have *demanded* he stop. But she did not want to give the impression that this was – in any way – a negotiation. That this was a conversation between equals. That she asked for things and they decided whether or not to do them.

No. That was not what this was, and it was important to establish that right away.

It was important because of what would come next.

So she had gone into a steep dive, at the same time veering sharply left. It was a useful physics lesson for him: when you were on a plane traveling at five hundred miles per hour, you too were traveling at five hundred miles per hour.

And when the plane suddenly changed course, you carried on in the same direction until something stopped you. Something like the ceiling or wall of the plane you were in.

It sounded like he had hurt himself, at least if the screams were anything to go by.

Good. It would raise the temperature back there. Sharpen their minds.

And they would need that, very soon.

Jeff Ramos

Kevin Anderson. What a fool. Typical of him: full of bluster and empty threats. He had to do something, had to be the big man. He'd been like that since the day he showed up at the company. Cocky, arrogant, full of an inflated sense of his own ability. Well, he was paying the price now.

Good. He deserved it. Ramos hated people like Anderson. He'd met plenty in the military. No interest in personal sacrifice or teamwork; plenty in the grand gesture and playing the hero. It never worked, never met any purpose other than massaging their ego. Fucking asshole. When they got out of this, he'd make it his mission to turn Anderson's professional life into a daily hell.

'OK,' he said. 'It's time to make some progress. Remember, she can hear everything. Has anyone got anything to say? Any confessions?'

He looked from face to face. They all shook their heads.

'What a surprise. Jill, do you mind if I say something to our pilot?'

'Be my guest.'

'Ok,' he said. 'You made your point. But no one here is going to confess, because no one here has killed anyone.

134

The idea's ludicrous. So let's move on. You tell us what you want, and we'll see if we can get it for you. Cash. Influence. A profile for your cause. Whatever you want. But this has to stop.'

After a long silence, there was a click and then the buzz of the intercom.

'Is that it?' the pilot said.

The buzz faded away. Ramos frowned.

'What do you mean?' he said.

'Is that your final answer?'

'To what?'

'To my question. Who is it?'

He looked around. Jill shrugged.

'Yes,' he said. 'Final answer.'

There was a long pause. 'I see.'

The intercom went dead.

'You have nothing else to say?' Ramos asked.

The click came again.

'I do have something to say.' The pilot's voice was lower than before, more serious. 'I know one of you is guilty of what I say. I gave you a chance to confess. So now I have no choice but to force the issue.'

'In what way?' Jill Stearns said.

'You confess,' she said. 'You tell me which one of you did it, and we fly to the nearest airport. Or you don't.'

'Or we can't.' Stearns said. 'Don't forget that. Maybe we can't.'

The pilot laughed. 'Maybe. But that makes no difference.'
She paused.

'One of you confesses, or I bring this plane down, and we all die.'

135

Elizabeth Carter

He was their only child.

That was the first thing she thought. He was their only child.

Their son, Nathan. Nate. 'The boy'. Natey. Nate-dog.

They'd wanted more, two minimum, maybe three or four. That had been the plan. She sometimes looked at photos of her and Scott in their twenties – physical photos, taken before everyone had a camera in their pocket – and they looked like different people. Not just younger: different. Full of hope. Unaware of how cruel life could be.

Unaware of how cruel it *would* be.

For a while she had thought of Nathan as their third child. She had miscarried the first two. She hated the word: *miscarried*. It suggested she had done something wrong, failed to carry the baby correctly.

She had done nothing wrong; she had done everything right. She had followed all the advice, eaten none of the proscribed foods, taken folic acid, gone to all the check-ups. But she had lost the babies.

She joined a large group of women who had been through the same thing. *A quarter of all women have miscarriages.*

That was what Stella, her best friend had told her. Someone else said it was a third. Either way it was a lot. It happened: it was hard and painful, but it happened.

After the first miscarriage she consoled herself with that, and with the other thing everyone said. *Don't worry. You'll get pregnant again. It'll be OK next time.*

And she did get pregnant.

It wasn't OK.

Another miscarriage, this time at eighteen weeks, when she'd started to believe it was going to be OK, she was going to be a mom and Scott was going to be a dad. She held on to some doubts, unwilling to fully commit, but Scott couldn't help himself. In his mind he was already taking his baby for walks in the park, changing its diaper – they never found out the gender, it was too risky – sitting up at night with it.

He was devastated. The first time he'd been her rock; this time he retreated into himself. She could smell what he feared: it'll never happen.

She could smell what he thought: there's something wrong with her.

There wasn't. She got pregnant again. It was a grim, joyless pregnancy. Neither of them dared to believe. They hardly mentioned it. No nursery was decorated. No baby clothes were bought.

So when Nathan was born it was a bit of a scramble. She had cried, after the birth, on and off, for days. Tears of joy and relief and happiness. Scott was the same: they would look at each other and then at Nathan and the next thing they'd be crying and hugging and thanking the universe for the blessing it had given them.

And then – a year later – she was pregnant again. This time they allowed themselves to enjoy her pregnancy. They found out it was a girl, bought her clothes, picked out her name – a name Elizabeth could never hear without a catch in her chest, a name she would never let pass her lips – and then she had gone into labor.

It was all fine.

Until it wasn't. Until a doctor rushed in and she was wheeled out into the operating theater positioned usefully by the delivery room. A whirl of activity; no one telling her what was happening, everyone too focused on saving her and the baby to have time to talk to her.

They saved her. For months she wished they hadn't.

Her daughter was stillborn.

Stillborn. Another word she hated, and not only because of what it meant. The baby wasn't born still. It was dead.

The baby – her baby – was dead.

The grief was so deep, the pain so intense, she thought she would die from it. It was only Nathan that pulled her through.

It was the last time they tried. She couldn't go through it again.

The experience changed them. How could it not? They became wary and insular, unwilling to take a risk with their son. They kept him close, made sure he was always watched, never allowed him to be in danger. Every time he got a cold she panicked; every time he got a fever she was sure he would die.

Meningitis. That was her particular fear. But he never got it.

He'd got something else.

After all that, something serious was wrong. The school had called to tell her Nathan had collapsed in class and was on the way to the hospital in an ambulance.

He was her only child. Her only surviving child. He couldn't be taken from her. What would be left for them? He was their lives, their hope. Everything she had dreamed for him – for them – was fading away: Nathan scoring for the junior

138

high basketball team, playing sax in the band concert, graduating high school, waving goodbye as they left him at a college, hopefully not too far away.

If they lost him, it would be the end of everything.

And she would never forgive who was responsible. She would make it her life's work to bring them to justice.

And if she couldn't, she would pursue them to the ends of the earth to get her revenge.

Dr. Williams

The boy – Nathan Carter – presented in exactly the same way as the two girls. A coma, and an inflamed liver. Dr. Williams had no doubt now that it was something environmental – what, he had no idea – but to have three young children arrive on the same day with the same rare set of symptoms was almost impossible to explain any other way.

Which raised a big question: what the hell was it, and how many more victims would there be?

He sat at the desk, studying the notes. There was nothing to indicate what had caused these symptoms. They would need to do some tests to determine that, but he didn't want to interfere with any of the patients before they were more fully recovered.

The first girl – Cherry – was inching forward, and he hoped she would be able to go home soon enough – maybe the next day. Her parents would need to monitor her, and the hospital would want to see her to check her liver function was returning, but he was confident she would recover.

The other two were in a much more precarious situation. Neither had regained consciousness, and both were still in the ICU. If they followed Cherry's progress then maybe they'd be OK, but there were no guarantees of that. They could have had a more serious exposure to whatever was causing this, or simply have reacted differently.

These were the worst moments of a medical career. The thought of those children in such a critical state was sickening. He couldn't imagine what it was like for the parents; he didn't like to try. It only made it worse, made the pressure to find a way to solve it even greater.

Perhaps Dr. Hall could help. He was due any minute from Portland. He was a liver specialist, so hopefully would be able to shed some light on the situation. If he couldn't, then all they could do was wait.

There was a cough and he looked up from the notes. Roland was standing by the desk.

'There's a call for you,' he said. 'From the school. Where the kids were. I spoke to the principal earlier and asked for it to be closed until further notice.'

Dr. Williams reached for the phone on the desk. Roland shook his head, and held out an iPhone. 'I gave my number. So they could definitely get through.'

'I'm not sure you're supposed to do that.'

'Maybe. But I wanted to make sure they could reach us.' He pressed the screen and handed the phone over. 'It's off mute.'

Williams put it to his ear. 'Dr. Williams.'

'This is Carol Smalling. I'm the principal at Paul Tyler Elementary.'

'You've had an interesting day.'

'You could say that.'

'I understand you closed?'

'Yes. Do you think it's something at the school?'

'I don't know. I can't think of what it would be, but it's possible.'

'How are they? The nurse who called mentioned liver damage? I just don't understand how that could have happened.'

141

'It could be a virus, or bacterial, but the most likely culprit – at this stage – is a toxin.'

'Like what?'

'I don't know. A fungus? Something they found in a store cupboard? Hard to say.'

'This is crazy,' the principal said. 'I've been teaching for over thirty years and I've never known anything like this.'

'Me neither,' Williams said. 'But we'll get to the bottom of it.'

'Are the children OK? Are you allowed to say?'

'I can't give details,' he said. 'But it's still a serious situation.'

She started to say something but the words caught in her throat. 'I'm sorry,' she said. 'It's very difficult. I just think of their parents and siblings – it's upsetting.'

'I can imagine.'

On the line he heard the sound of a door opening and a voice in the background.

'Excuse me one moment,' she said. 'I have a visitor.'

He waited for a moment, listening to the sounds of her conversation, until she returned.

'Dr. Williams,' she said, her voice breathless. 'There's another. That's four, now.'

Stacy Evanston

The nurse pressed a button and the head of the bed raised up with a mechanical whirr, lifting Cherry into a sitting position.

'We need one of those at home,' Dan said. 'Very comfy.'

'You can get them,' the nurse said. 'But I think they're quite expensive.' She took a glass of water from the table. It had a lid and a paper straw, and she held it up to Cherry's lips.

'Thirsty?' she said.

Cherry nodded and began to drink. 'Do you have any juice?' she said.

'Just this for now,' the nurse replied. 'This water has some things in it to help you get better.'

'Like medicine?'

'Exactly.' She waited for Cherry to stop drinking. 'How do you feel?'

'Sleepy.'

'Good sleepy, like bedtime? But if someone read you a story you could stay awake? Or sleepy like you *have* to go to sleep?'

'Good sleepy. Are you going to read me a story?'

'Maybe later. But for now I have work to do.'

'Will you read me a story, Mom?'

'I didn't bring a book,' Stacy said.

'Maybe I can find something,' the nurse said. 'I'm sure I can. I'll be right back.'

'Thank you,' Stacy said. 'But there's no hurry.'

'Not a problem.' The nurse smiled. 'See you in a bit.'

'I wonder what book they have,' Cherry said. 'I hope I like it.'

'If Mom reads it you will,' Dan said. 'She can do her funny voices.'

'It's not me who does funny voices,' Stacy said. 'That's a dad thing.'

'Sorry,' Dan said. 'I thought you did. You mean to say that's just your voice?'

She rolled her eyes. 'Very funny. I can tell you're feeling much more like your normal self.' She looked at her phone. 'I haven't heard from Nicole. I'll try and call.'

'I hope everything's OK.'

'Nicole?' Cherry said. 'Ella's mom?'

It was amazing how much she picked up, even at five. They were going to have to be careful what they said in front of her.

'Yes. I need to talk to her.' She glanced up at Dan. 'Nothing serious.'

Dan sat on the bed. 'Let me tell you about Bangor,' he said. 'I was just there. There's a big airport.'

Stacy went over to the window and called Nicole. The phone rang three times, and then went to voicemail.

It had not rung out, then gone to voicemail.

It had rung three times, which meant Nicole – or someone else, maybe her husband, Jonah – had cut the call instead of answering it.

Which meant they didn't want to talk.

Stacy's scalp prickled. That wasn't good. It could be nothing. It could be that they were talking to the doctor and didn't want to be interrupted.

But it could be that she didn't want to talk to anyone at all. Well, if it was the former, she'd call back when she was done with whatever it was. If not – Stacy pushed the thought away. She didn't even want to imagine it.

Steve Murdoch

Steve Murdoch knew who was responsible for this. It was his bitch of an ex-girlfriend. She had left her gear lying around and the kid had got hold of it somehow.

He should never have let her pick him up from school. He didn't normally; she wasn't really supposed to see him on her own, for this very fucking reason, but the school had shut and Bren had needed someone to go and get him, and Kris – she was called Christina but when she shortened her name she spelled it with a K – had said she would. He was at work and he couldn't get away and Kris had texted to say she'd heard the school was closing and she could get Bren and keep him for a few hours if that helped.

Stupidly – and he had the idea he would regret this for the rest of his life – he had agreed. It got him out of a short-term problem and how much damage could she do in one afternoon?

Well, there was a reason why for the first year after they split she had to have a court-appointed social worker monitor her visits with Bren, and he had just been reminded of it. She was incapable of looking after herself, never mind a child.

He should have seen the signs when they met. They were there, for sure: once she started she was incapable

146

of stopping herself drinking. On one of their first dates they had gone to dinner and he had watched her drink two cocktails, most of a bottle of wine, and then a large vodka and soda at a bar. Afterwards she had invited him back to her house, a small cape in Barrow, and he had been amazed to see her open the freezer when they got in and pour a large glass of vodka on ice; he had consumed half of what she had and couldn't face another drop, but her appetite was undimmed.

She was the same with everything: food, exercise, socializing, sex. She always wanted more. She was forever being invited to parties and gatherings and he went with her. It was intoxicating, especially for someone like him, who was naturally quite reticent. He had always found it hard to meet people, but with Kris he was pitched into a whirl of fun and good times.

And then there was the sex. It was constant. First thing in the morning before work, *Quick*, she would say, *we have time*. First thing when they got back from work. One memorable occasion *at* work. His office was in a 1970s office block in Portland where everyone had their own cubicle and there was a warren of meeting rooms. Kris had dragged him into one, pushed a chair against the door, and, that had been that.

And then they would go out in the evening and who knew what would happen? Sex in a bathroom, a park, the car.

He wondered, often, what she saw in him. He assumed others did too, but he just figured that, while it lasted, why not enjoy it?

And that was the problem. He assumed it would end at some point, so he didn't pay attention to the things he should have paid attention to. Sure, she drank too much, but at least she worked out every day and she functioned well enough, so why should he care? Yes, in the long term it would have to be sorted out, but he'd be history by then.

Except they didn't break up. And she didn't sort out her drinking. It got worse, and then the accident happened.

Driving home – drunk, of course – she ran off the road and into the side of a bridge. Thankfully no one else was involved, but she shattered her right femur. The surgery was a success, in that it would leave her able to walk again, but she would have a limp, and her days of serious exercise were over. Before she could even worry about that, though, she first had to spend a month immobile, some more months on crutches, then many more doing PT.

The pain was awful; the remedy was a prescription for narcotic painkillers.

She *loved* them, and by the time she didn't need them for the pain it was far too late. She needed them for everything else, but the doctor, when she was good and properly hooked, decided it was time to cancel the prescription.

Opiates are expensive, so she did what all the other addicts did: went for the cheap option. Heroin. There was a flood of it in Maine, and she took full advantage of the torrent.

Steve, incredibly, didn't realize. She was back at work, on her feet, and he assumed her state in the evenings was down to the amount she was drinking. He was seriously concerned by this stage, and he told her so, but she laughed it off with the addict's mantra: *I can stop anytime I want. I'm just having fun.*

He didn't believe that for a second, and he was getting ready to give her an ultimatum: me or the booze, when the next accident happened.

She told him she was pregnant.

She was supposed to be on the pill. He suspected she had been so drunk she had missed one or more days, but she swore blind she hadn't: the pills just hadn't worked.

It was OK, though. She could get an abortion. He told her it was sad, but they weren't ready for a child, so they should schedule it as soon as possible to minimize the emotional impact.

Her response was categorical.

No fucking way.

Those were her exact words. *No fucking way.*

Then: *I can't believe you think I would do that. This is my* child. *There's no chance whatsoever I'll kill it. No way. I love it already.*

He tried to change her mind but nothing he said made any difference. She was having the baby.

For most of her pregnancy, and for the first few months of Bren's life, she stayed clean. *See,* she said. *Told you I could stop.*

Except she couldn't. By the time he was three she was worse than she had ever been. The booze was gone: she had lost her job and it was too expensive. Steve refused to buy it for her, so she turned to meth and heroin, which – he learned in horror, from an ashen-faced friend – she paid for by selling sex. It was when she admitted to this that he ended it once and for all.

He got custody of Bren; there was no question of that, and her visits with him were supervised.

After that she spiraled into an even deeper hole. Every time his phone rang he wondered whether it was the police calling to tell him she had died, maybe of an overdose, or by freezing to death on a winter night, or at the hands of some deranged punter.

Recently she had claimed to be clean and on the last occasion he had seen her – when he was dropping Bren for his visit – she had seemed better. Her skin was less waxy, and there was a light in her eyes. Some human warmth: not just the vacant stare of the last few years.

Which was maybe why he had agreed to let her pick Bren up from school.

149

What a fool he was. Once a junkie, always a junkie. He should have known better. And now he was paying the price.

She had called to say his son was in an ambulance; she was following in her car. She had gone to make him some macaroni and cheese and heard what sounded like cries of pain; when she went into the living room he was passed out on the couch. Unable to revive him, she had called an ambulance.

What did you leave out for him to find? he shouted. *Meth? Vodka? Heroin?*

Nothing. I'm clean. There's none in the house, I promise.

Yeah, right. You fucking did this, Kris. You're not fit to be a mom. And this is the proof. You prefer that shit to your kid's welfare. It's fucking disgusting.

Steve, I promise. I'm clean. And I love him. I'd never hurt him. You know that.

What I know is you'll never see him again.

Now, though – even after all this – he felt guilty. He shouldn't have said all that. He'd seen a therapist after they had broken up and she had made him understand that addiction was an illness, and Kris needed treatment, not criticism or harsh judgment.

He believed that to be true, and he wanted to help her, but believing the theory was one thing. Watching someone destroy their life was another, especially when they were a parent. Bren loved his mom, and, knowing that, how could she do what she was doing?

But he kept reminding himself it was an illness. She needed help and support.

Now, though, as he drove to a hospital to see his son, he found it was hard to muster anything other than hatred and regret.

Dr. Williams

Another one. Another boy, same age, same school. He was at home when it happened; the ambulance drivers reported there could be drug or alcohol-related causes, but Dr. Williams didn't think so.

This was identical.

He closed the door to the office and sat opposite Dr. Hall.

'One more, a boy,' he said. 'There could be others.'

Dr. Hall nodded. 'Very possible. Likely, even.'

'What do you think?'

'Near impossible to say.' He read the notes. 'The bloodwork from the first girl is back. There's no suggestion of a virus. I suppose it's possible there was a bacterial cause that doesn't show up – something in the water supply, fecal contamination, maybe – but that seems unlikely. And if it was in the water, we'd be seeing more cases. It could be contained to the school's water supply, but even then presumably many more people would be exposed.'

'Which leaves?'

'A toxin.'

'Like alcohol? Or another drug?'

'Yes, but there's no indication of that in the bloodwork.'

'Then what?'

Hall shrugged. 'Don't know. Something they found and ingested? A fungus, possibly. We should find a mycologist and see if there are any fungi that cause this kind of thing. It would make sense. Some of them have psychotropic effects, which would explain the unconsciousness.'

'If it is that, what do we do?'

'What we're doing now.'

'We have to get to the bottom of this. To stop it happening again.'

'Neal,' Dr. Hall said, 'I agree. But it's possible we might never know.'

Dr. Williams opened the door to Cherry's room. He smiled; she was sitting up, the remote control for the television mounted in the corner grasped in her hand.

It boded well for the others.

'Hello, Cherry,' he said. 'How are you?'

'Good. I'm watching *Peppa Pig*.'

'One of my favorites.'

'Is it?'

'It certainly is.'

A look of surprise – and faint disbelief – passed over her face before she turned back to the television.

He sat on the edge of the bed. Her mom was sitting to her left; her dad was by the door. 'She seems a lot better,' he said.

'Can she go home?' her dad asked.

'Not yet. We'll want to monitor her, and also do some more bloodwork to see if we can determine the cause, and also how she is. We'll also ultrasound her liver to check on the inflammation.'

'Do you think it's still there?'

'Yes, but I imagine from how she's doing that it's less

severe than before. We gave her some pretty powerful anti-inflammatories, which work quickly on someone her age. It could leave scarring, but the liver has an amazing capacity to regenerate. We'll keep an eye on her, though.'

Her dad folded his arms. 'Is it over? At least the worst of it?'

'She's not out of the woods yet, but she's moving in the right direction. I just want to know what happened, so we can prevent it in the future.'

Cherry's mom looked at him.

'I know,' she said. 'We all do.'

Steve Murdoch

Steve Murdoch paced the waiting room. He'd been there an hour and the light was fading outside. A nurse had told him Bren was with the medical team and he would get news as soon as it was available.

He couldn't believe he was here, and he could forget blaming Kris for it. This was his fault. She was an addict; she should never have been left with a child. Yes, technically she was the one who was there, but it was the person who put a kid in that position who was at fault, and that person was him.

There was no way around it. This was all his fault.

He let out a sharp, involuntary cry. An elderly woman turned to look at him, then looked away when she saw him notice.

He sank to his haunches, his face in his hands. He felt like a different person, hollowed out and empty.

'Mr. Murdoch?'

A doctor was standing there. He looked tired, his eyes red.

'Yes.'

'I'm Dr. Neal Williams.'

'Are you taking care of Bren?'

'We are. We're doing our very best.'

He did not like the sound of that. The doctor had not said, *Yes, and he's fine now.*

'How is he?'

'He's still in the ICU. He's in a critical condition.'

'What is it?' Steve said. 'Meth? Heroin? Alcohol?'

'I'm sorry?'

'What caused it? It sounds like an overdose.'

'Mr. Murdoch, why would your son be overdosing?'

'His mother. She's a junkie. He was at her house. He wasn't supposed to be, but the school closed and I let her pick him up. He must have got into her drugs.'

'We'll certainly check for that, but I don't think it's the cause.'

Steve stared at him. 'Then what is? This is exactly what an overdose looks like. Believe me, living with his mom I got some experience of that kind of thing.'

'I would agree, Mr. Murdoch. But he's not the only one. There are three other kids – all from his school – with the same symptoms.'

Steve paused. He felt a mixture of relief – it wasn't an overdose – and fear. It was something else.

'Then what is it?'

'That's not clear.'

He asked the question no parent ever wanted to have to ask. 'Will he be OK?'

'I can't offer any guarantees at this point.'

Steve couldn't support his weight. He slumped into a chair.

'Please,' he said. He caught the doctor's eye. 'Please don't let him die.'

Dr. Williams held his gaze for a moment, then looked away.

'We're doing everything we can. I promise you that.'

Stacy Evanston

Stacy woke up on the cot in Cherry's room. Her back was stiff; the cot was narrow and sagged in the middle, and she had struggled to get comfortable. She sat up and stretched, then got to her feet. She swung her arms left to right, glad to feel the tension lessen.

Cherry was still asleep. For a second Stacy thought she was not breathing and her back tensed again in panic, but then she saw her daughter's chest rise and fall.

She picked up her bag and walked out of the room. A nurse – Gloria, her name tag said – was in the corridor, arranging medical supplies on a cart.

'Morning,' she said. 'Sleep well?'

'Great. Perfect.'

'You don't have to lie. I've slept on those cots. My son was in here for a few days.'

'Is he OK?'

'Fine, now. He had an infection. It took a while to clear. So I know how uncomfortable they are.'

'They're not that bad. And I don't mind.'

'I know. We'll do anything for our kids, right?'

Stacy nodded. It was true; like most parents, she really would

156

do almost anything for her child. She wondered exactly where the line was. What would she not do for Cherry? Lie? Steal? Kill?

'Bathroom this way?'

Gloria nodded. 'Coffee?'

'I'd love one.'

'I'll bring one to the room.'

In the bathroom she opened her bag and reached in for her toiletries case. Dan had gone home the night before and brought her toothbrush and toothpaste, as well as a change of clothes, but there was something else in there, next to the case.

A cardboard box.

The pregnancy test she had bought the day before after dropping Cherry at school.

She smiled. It was the morning – which was when you were supposed to take the tests – so why not? She could tell Dan when they got Cherry back home. It would be a double celebration.

She sat on the toilet and held the test in the stream of urine, then sat there, holding it in her lap, waiting for the second red line to appear.

Slowly, it swam into view.

She inhaled sharply, then sucked in her bottom lip.

She was *right*. She was pregnant!

She let out a squeal of excitement, then stood up. She wanted to run out into the corridor and announce her news, but she stopped herself. Dan should be the first to know.

When she got back the coffee was on the table by the cot. She sat on the end and sipped it. Dan was at home: after bringing her stuff he'd stayed a while, then left. She typed a message.

Woke early. Not the best night's sleep! But C's OK. Still sleeping,

157

I'll be there soon. Hopefully we can bring her home today.

Fingers and toes crossed.

She didn't add the other reason she wanted to get Cherry home: so she could tell him she was pregnant. She could have told him here, but it wasn't the right place. Home was the right place.

Did you hear from Nicole yet?

She had not. No returned call, no message. It gave her a knot in her stomach, but she reassured herself that it was just that people handled stress in different ways, and some wanted to be left alone. Nothing more sinister than that.

Nothing yet. I'll try later, but I don't want to bother her.

Makes sense. See you soon. Love you.

Love you too.

She realized now how much she *did* love him. It wasn't just a phrase you said at the end of a text message. It meant something, and you saw exactly what at times like these. He and Cherry – and now Baby Two – were everything to her. Her life was built around them in the most pervasive, all-encompassing ways. They were there in everything she did.

And the thought of losing one of them was unbearable.

She bent over Cherry and kissed her forehead. Her

daughter's eyes fluttered open. They were bright and clear, a trace of yellow still there, but she could see it clearly.

Cherry was going to be fine.

Dr. Williams

'How's Cherry doing?' Dr. Williams asked.

Gloria tapped on her keyboard and turned the screen to face him. 'Stable, this morning. A lot better.'

He studied the screen. 'The bloodwork from yesterday?'

'Not back yet.'

'OK. I'll take a look at her.'

He walked down to Cherry's room and knocked on the door.

'Good morning,' he said. 'Everyone OK?'

Cherry's mom nodded. 'Seem to be.'

'And our patient? How's Cherry?'

She was eating some applesauce. He sat on the bed.

'Feeling OK this morning?' he said.

'Yes.'

'Not sick?' He put a hand on her forehead. 'No fever?'

She finished the applesauce and held the carton out to her mom. 'Can I have some more?'

'No loss of appetite,' he said. 'I think, young lady, you might be ready to go home today.'

'I like it here,' Cherry said. 'I'm in charge of the remote.'

Dr. Williams laughed. 'Yes, I'm sure that makes all the difference. But hospitals are for sick people, so if you're better

160

we can't keep you here.' He turned to her mom. 'We'll wait a little longer, but you can start to get ready.'

The expression on her face moved from relief to joy. Tears welled in her eyes.

'Thank you,' she said. 'I can't tell you how grateful I am.'

'We're all just glad she's OK. When the time comes a nurse will take you through the discharge instructions. Things to look out for, medications. If you have any questions, reach out at any time.'

'What kind of things to look out for?'

'Just to monitor her temperature, those kind of things. The nurse will explain. And we'll want to do some follow-up care. Maybe see her tomorrow, and the day afterwards. Just to be safe.'

'OK. And thank you, again.'

'My pleasure.'

The door opened and Gloria put her head around it.

'Dr. Williams,' she said. 'Are you free?'

She was smiling, but the smile did not reach the rest of her face. She held his gaze, an urgent look in her eyes. She was being polite in asking if he was free, but her expression told a different story. It said, *You need to come, now.*

'Of course. Cherry will be going home today.' He gave a wave to her, and to her mom. 'Have a safe trip.'

He closed the door behind him. Gloria's smile was gone.

'What is it?'

'It's one of the others. Ella. She's getting worse.'

Nicole Farmer

Nicole Farmer sat in an uncomfortable chair, her head resting on the wall of the ICU room Ella was in. Her sciatic nerve was firing and causing her intense discomfort; she had tried moving into another position, or standing and walking around the room, but none of it made it better. It was the stress: the muscles in her lower back were tense, and that was causing the nerve pain.

She didn't care. All she could think about was her daughter.

Jonah was standing by the door, staring at Ella. She was unconscious, a tube coming from her nostrils, a drip in one arm and some kind of monitoring equipment on the other. Cherry, her best friend, was somewhere in the hospital. She wondered whether she was in the same state, hooked up to machines to keep her going.

What the hell was going on? Liver damage? A coma? It didn't feel real. She had answered the call from the school and the next thing she knew she and Jonah were following an ambulance to the hospital to hear their daughter was in the ICU.

And then this nightmare had started. It was like being in a long, dark tunnel with no sense of progress towards the end.

Everything had shut down: she was in stasis, waiting for what came next, wishing for it to be good news.

Terrified it would not be.

Her phone lit up in her bag. It was on silent mode. She did not want to be disturbed. As she glanced, though, she saw it was from Stacy.

Cherry had the same thing. So if Stacy had bad news, she could expect the same. But if it was good news, then maybe, just maybe, that would give her some hope.

She reached for her phone and opened the message.

Hi. We're heading home later. Cherry's doing much better. Hope it's the same for you.

For the first time since their arrival she felt a surge of optimism. She was pleased, of course, for Stacy and Dan. If they were going through the same as her and Jonah, then how could she not be glad it was over? But the real surge of excitement was what it meant for her. Did that make her selfish? Maybe, but mainly it made her human.

She read it again.

Cherry was *doing much better.*

Whatever had caused this for Cherry, had caused it for Ella.

So maybe Ella would soon be doing much better.

She didn't want to tempt fate, but she had to tell Jonah. Or should she? Would saying *I think she might be* OK cause her not to be? Was that simply foolish superstition? More than likely, but why risk it?

No: it would help him. He deserved to know.

'Jonah,' she said, her voice loud among the hum of the machines. 'I got a message from Stacy.'

He looked away from Ella. 'Oh?'

'She said—'

163

There was a loud alarm from one of the machines, then an insistent beeping.

'What's that?' Jonah said. 'Did you touch something?'

'No.' She looked wildly around the room. 'I don't know what it is.'

Ella was still lying there, her chest rising and falling, but her face was flushed.

'Oh God,' Jonah said. 'Something's happening.'

The door flew open and three nurses rushed in. One bent over Ella and checked the tubes; the other read the screens. She called out some instructions and did something to the drip.

'Get the doctor,' she said. 'Now.'

One of the nurses nodded, and ran out of the room. The other began to undo the brakes on the bed.

'What's happening?' Nicole said. 'What are you doing?'

'We have to move her to theater,' one of them said. They began to wheel the bed and the machines to the door. Jonah followed them. 'It's better if you wait here,' she said. 'I'm sorry.'

Nicole watched them leave. The door swung shut behind them and she stood, her hand in Jonah's, in the silence of the room.

Stacy Evanston

They were home by early evening.

It was odd to be back; she almost didn't recognize the house. It felt like they'd been gone for months. So much had happened that she found she was surprised the house was unchanged, that they hadn't left in summer and come back in the depth of winter.

She opened the front door. The smell was familiar and comforting and she felt that she, they, were home.

It could have been so different. If they had come back without Cherry – the thought sent a shiver down her spine – it would have smelled the same, but it would no longer have been home. It would have been just a house, a house she would never have wanted to see again.

Cherry pushed past her and ran into the living room. She grabbed the remote control.

'Can I be in charge?'

Stacy nodded. 'For now, yes.'

Dan came up behind her and put his arms around her waist. He kissed her neck.

'She's busy,' he said. 'Want to come upstairs and check out a few things with me?'

'I do.' She turned and kissed him. She would tell him about Baby Two when they got upstairs. 'Let's go.'

Her phone started to ring in her back pocket.

'Ignore it,' he said. He took it out and slid it onto the table by the door. 'They can wait.'

She kissed him again, and glanced at the phone over his shoulder. It was Nicole. She pictured Ella in the hospital bed, eyes opening as she came to. She was a few hours behind Cherry, so it'd be around now she was recovering; no doubt Nicole was calling to tell her. She felt a weight lift. This whole thing was going to be OK, in the end. They could figure out what the hell had happened later.

'I have to take it,' she said. 'I'll be quick.'

He turned and headed upstairs. 'I'll be waiting.'

'Hi,' she said. 'How are you?'

Nicole answered the call. There was no response for a few seconds, then there was a guttural sob, followed swiftly by another, and another.

Stacy's chest tightened, a hard ball forming in her sternum. *Oh God*, she thought. *Please, no.*

'Nicole?' she said. 'Nicole?'

Nicole tried to speak, but each time her words dissolved into sobs.

'Nicole,' she said. 'What is it?'

'It's Ella,' she said, each syllable punctuated by a racking sob. 'She's – she's dead.'

The Pilot

She looked out of the cockpit window. Nothing but bright blue sky and dark blue ocean as far as the eye could see. A feeling of absolute peace settled on her.

She had done what she had promised herself she would do, and now she would go through with it, whichever way it went.

A safe landing, or a fatal crash. Live or die; it made no difference to her. That was what made her dangerous. She didn't care. A steep descent into a frigid ocean had its merits for her. Not that the temperature would matter. They would all disintegrate on impact.

She was ready for anything. She was ready to die. She had been for a long time. Even if their flight ended with them touching down safely, she might not carry on. But she would decide that when – if – it happened. Perhaps she would feel better about life, more optimistic.

Perhaps not. She didn't mind. She would cross that bridge when it was in front of her.

She was at peace, although in the calm, one small thing disturbed her.

The nurse.

If she really was a nurse, then she was not part of this. It was the 'if' that she focused on. She had a suspicion that it was a trick of some kind. Why would a nurse be on the plane? It was possible – likely, even, the more she thought about it – that the nurse was not a nurse at all, but someone pretending to be a nurse.

Everybody loved nurses; if you were trying to appeal to someone's conscience you would do it with a nurse.

A nurse whose husband was dying.

Yes, the more she thought about it, the more obvious it was. It was too convenient. She pictured them passing a note around: *Say you're a nurse, that you're innocent and need to be let go.* The 'nurse' writing on it: *Even better if I have a dying husband, right?*

So forget the nurse. In any case, she had no choice. She could not back down now. And innocence made no difference. Some of the others were innocent too, but she had no problems with killing them. Why was the nurse any different, really?

She looked down at the distant ocean. Would she do it, in the end? Would she kill them all, and herself?

She'd asked herself that question many times. She'd known that the only way to find out was to put herself in this position.

And now she was here, she knew she would.

She would do it without hesitation. Either they gave her what she wanted or they died.

Their families would mourn them. Children would be left parentless, parents childless.

She knew all this, but she didn't care.

Marcia Fournier

You tell me which one of you did it, and we fly to the nearest airport. Or you don't. In which case, I bring this plane down, and we all die.

The words hung there for a moment, incomprehensible. She thought: *We're going to die* then *I need a drink*.

Her skin prickled with sweat and her breath shortened. She forced herself to think, forced the tightening coil of panic to unwind, as much as she could.

The pilot was saying she would crash the plane and kill them all – herself included – unless one of them confessed to a *murder*?

It was ridiculous, but it was real. It reminded her of the sensation she had before the craving for a drink came. As the day wound down, she became certain that something was wrong, that she had messed up somehow, that something bad was going to happen and she was the cause.

She no longer knew whether it was the alcohol that caused it or the alcohol that cured it. It certainly stopped the anxiety while she was drinking, but did it make it worse in the morning? Did it fuel the beast that lived inside her, the beast that seemed to hate her, seemed to think she was

169

responsible for everything bad in the world, told her that no one liked her, she was awful at her job, she'd be found out eventually and everyone would laugh at her humiliation, saying to each other *I knew it would happen sooner or later, she's been on borrowed time for years*. Did the alcohol make that voice louder?

She had no idea. It was so long since she had tried to live without it that she couldn't remember what it was like.

All she knew was that, for a blissful few hours, the voice in her head and the coil in her stomach were gone.

But now they were there, despite the vodka. Because this time it was real.

You're going to die. This plane is going down and you're going to die. And you'll die a drunk. So much for your plans to get clean. You should have done it sooner, but you're too weak.

Her mouth was dry. The coil in her stomach became a sharp pain, her heart racing. She wanted now, more than ever, another drink.

But there was no more.

She felt dizzy with panic. For a moment she found herself wishing for the plane to crash, so this could all be over. If she couldn't have a drink, she'd rather be dead.

She caught herself, held that thought in her mind.

If she couldn't have a drink, she'd rather be dead.

Was that who she had become? Had she sunk so far?

For a moment she thought that this was it, the catalyst for change, the point at which the curtain lifted and she saw the path forward, and she was sure she'd never drink again. And then the thirst came back.

She opened her bag. Perhaps there was something in there. She knew there wasn't, but perhaps there was. Perhaps a miracle had occurred.

Was this really what God used His miracles for? Conjuring

170

alcohol out of thin air for aging drunks? She let out a stran-
gled laugh.

Jeff Ramos stared at her.

'What the fuck did the pilot just say?'

He was half-standing, his elbows on the seat in front of
him.

'Did she say what I *think* she said?' He looked around
the plane. 'Did she?'

'She did,' Jill Stearns said. 'Unless I misheard.'

'She said she's going to crash this thing unless one of us
confesses to a *murder*?'

'I know.' Jill's voice was soft. 'I know.'

'Then whoever did it better fucking confess,' Jeff said.

There was a long silence.

'Nobody did it,' Jill said. 'No one here is a murderer.'

'She can hear you,' Kevin Anderson said. He was wincing,
his shattered wrist resting on his thigh. 'Remember that.'

'She needs to know,' Jill said. 'This has gone far enough.'

'So we tell her that and we all die?' Ramos said. 'Is that
the plan? Because if it is, count me out. I don't like that plan
at all.'

'What's the alternative, Jeff?' Jill said.

He looked around the plane, his eyes narrowed.

'Let's deal with the elephant in the room, shall we?' He
sniffed. 'She's not done this on a whim. If she just wanted to
kill some evil big food executives, there's an easier way. She's
done this for a reason. And one of you knows what it is.'

'I don't think so,' Jill said. 'I think she's mistaken, and we
need to let her know.'

'What if she isn't?' Jeff said. 'What if she's right, and one
of you *is* a murderer? That one of you needs to own up right
now.' He stared at Jill. 'What if it's you?'

'What if it's you?' Jill said. 'You seem very certain she's right.
I think she believes it to be the case, but she's mistaken. People

171

ascribe all kinds of things to companies like ours. That doesn't mean they're right.'

There was a cough. Mary Jo was holding up a piece of paper. She put a finger to her lips and passed it to Jeff Ramos. He read it and passed it on to Chip. Chip added something, then handed it to Marcia.

Someone say they did it. Someone say they did it, and then we land and get off the plane.

Underneath, in red ink, were the words Chip had added:

Who? And how do you answer when she says what did you do?

Marcia took her pen from her bag. She unclipped the top and hovered it over the paper, then began to write.

I'll do it. And I'll think of something. Marcia

Kevin Anderson

It was agonizing. He had never felt pain like it. At first it had been a sharp, knife-like pain that was, in retrospect, quite bearable. It was the kind of pain he recognized: a kick or stamp on the football field, the flaring pain from a punch. This was of a different order, yes, but it was that kind of pain.

Now, though, it was as though it had occupied his entire body. With every beat of his heart his wrist pulsed in pain. It was as though his blood was having to force its way through damaged and broken pathways, tearing them apart anew each time it did so. His own body was in rebellion against him.

Even if they did make it back, there'd be no bedroom reunion with Katie tonight. He needed this thing fucking fixed before he tried anything that energetic, although he was looking forward to telling her how he did it.

Tried to smash the door down. Someone had to do something. The rest of them just sat there like sheep. At least I tried.

So they knew what this was about now, at least. He felt strangely calm. He wasn't scared of dying. He wondered whether it was his wrist taking his mind off it. At least he'd be done with the pain.

He didn't think so, though. He just wasn't scared of death. So what if he died? A brief moment of pain – not as bad as what he was experiencing anyway – and then nothing. He never got scared, really. He got angry when he didn't get what he wanted, but he was never scared. Whatever happened to him he could deal with, and he didn't really care what happened to other people. If Katie was unavailable to him because she was doing something else, that would be annoying; if she died, he'd simply move on. Likewise if she got fat, or ugly. She'd no longer be of use to him, so why would he waste his time on her?

He'd understood early in his life that other people were just objects to him. He couldn't imagine them thinking things or feeling things or having any kind of interior life. They were simply there, and as long as they were of interest or use to him he'd keep them around. When they weren't, he'd get rid of them.

Why other people didn't do the same, he couldn't fathom. He had college friends who hated their wives, who complained they never got laid, pulled out of weekends away with the boys because they'd get too much grief from their better half. Why not just do it anyway? Or divorce them and find someone else? It was easy enough; if you were a half-decent man in your forties, you could have your pick of the lonely divorcees and desperate women who had never married and were faced with ever-dwindling options.

So why not? Was it fear of upsetting the wife? But you hated her, so why did that matter? Or damaging the kids? So what? Loads of kids had parents who divorced. They'd get over it.

The main question, though, was simple. If you wanted a divorce, why would you care what anyone else thought?

The note the nurse had written was making its way around again. Jill handed it to him.

I'll do it. And I'll think of something. Marcia

Marcia. She'd been hot, once. When he'd joined the company twenty-two years back, he'd tried flirting with her. They didn't have the word back then, but she was a MILF. And there was something slightly desperate about her, a vulnerability that he found irresistible.

It hadn't worked though. The one that got away. He'd still do it. For someone in her early sixties she was doing OK. So if the opportunity arose, why not? It didn't hurt anyone.

So she was going to confess. It was worth a try. She should be careful, though. It was possible that the pilot would land this thing, then let the rest of them off and keep Marcia onboard. Maybe take off again just to throw her out, or maybe she had a gun and bang! Bye bye, Marcia.

He could picture the scene.

No! I was just saying it to get you to land! It wasn't me!

Not a position he'd want to be in. He could have written his warning down, but then she might not have gone through with it, and at the moment it was their best chance. So fuck that. Let her try. If it went wrong for her and the rest of them were fine, that was a price worth paying.

He looked around the cabin and nodded, then gave Marcia a thumbs up. *Thanks,* he mouthed. She gave a bashful smile.

He pushed the note toward Chip. He was sitting silently, his palms on his thighs, his gaze fixed on them.

'Here,' he whispered. 'Take it.'

Chip waved it away. He started to shake his head, his mouth opening and closing silently. His eyes were scrunched up and his hands were clenching into fists, then relaxing, then clenching again.

The shaking of his head sped up, and Kevin saw that he had tears running down his face.

He reached around the seat and took the note. Chip didn't seem to notice.

Well, well, Chip had lost it. It was never the ones you think. He'd have had Chip down as cool under fire, not this gibberish wreck.

Except maybe that wasn't what it was. Chip had turned gray.

'Chip?' he said. 'You OK?'

Varun Miller

It was working. He was amazed to find that it was working.

There was an antenna somewhere that connected the plane to a satellite network, and then to a router, which broadcast a network. The network was still there, but the router wasn't connected to anything.

His supposition that the router was not physically disconnected from the satellite, that it was just a configuration within the router itself, in which case it could be switched back on, if he could gain access to it, was right.

And he had hacked into it. Not to any of the plane's systems – they were presumably on a separate network so that passengers couldn't get into them – but into the router itself.

Which meant he could switch on the network.

If he could work out how. The problem was he couldn't. He could hardly announce what he was doing and ask for help, not that he thought any of them would know any more than him. Jeff Ramos might have an idea – he was Chief Technology Officer, so he knew some of this stuff, although he was in the position more for leadership, and long service, than any real tech savvy – but that was it.

So he had come a long way, but not far enough.

And then he saw it. He saw how it could be done.

He typed a few commands and there it was. It was on.

At least partially. The issue was that there were two bands, a broadband and a narrowband, and all he could reactivate was the narrowband. Whether that was by design or as a result of his lack of skills was another question.

He was, however slowly, connected to the internet.

Which meant many things, but most importantly that he could call for help.

He closed all the applications so that they didn't use up any bandwidth, then opened Google Maps to find out where they were. By zooming out he could estimate how many miles – about one hundred and fifty – they were off the coast, and which town they were east of.

He closed the window, opened his email and typed a message to his assistant, Sharon.

Plane hijacked. Send help. Acknowledge receipt.

He added the location, and pressed send.

A minute passed, then another. He couldn't understand why she hadn't responded. Sharon would still be working, and she would definitely have seen the email; the message was in the subject field. *Plane hijacked.*

If it had gone through, that was. Perhaps there'd been some failure of the system, or the connection had been lost.

Shit.

He was so close. Ari and Susheela were there, within his reach, tantalizingly close. Yet so far. And the pilot had made herself clear. She was going to kill them all. Varun didn't doubt for a second that she was serious. She wouldn't have gone to these lengths if she wasn't.

Which made it all the more imperative that Sharon get the email.

He waited another minute, then another.

And then it flashed up in the corner of his screen. An incoming email.

What? Are you serious? No – I know you are. I'll call the authorities. Hang in there, Varun!

He had done it.

He had got a message out. Help was on the way.

He typed another message.

Thank God. Tell them to hurry. And tell Susheela and Ari I love them.

Chip Markham

He was going to throw up all over himself. The nausea was overwhelming and he had a cold sweat all over his body. He had written on Marcia' s note and, as he handed it over, had started to feel very ill.

He had never felt anything like this before. It had pervaded every cell of his body. All he could think was *I'm going to die. This is it. This is the end.*

And then he thought of Matthew and Otis and Esme – how they were going to have Christmas together. He had ordered a turkey. He had no idea how to cook one, but from the recipes he'd read it seemed easy enough, a matter simply of putting it in the oven for a few hours, but in case it was a disaster he had some backup steaks. Even he could cook a steak.

He'd been planning to tell Matthew and Esme to take it easy, have a break, while he played with Otis and assembled all the presents. Pass them a glass of champagne – he had a case of vintage Laurent-Perrier – and let them relax. He'd been planning to make it perfect, low-key and classy, a warm, happy family Christmas.

He had been waiting for one for years. Decades.

And it was going to be the first of many. He had messed this up the first time around and he wasn't going to mess it up again. He didn't care if Matthew wasn't the son he had imagined; he shouldn't have bothered imagining anything and just enjoyed what he had, but he had been too stupid and arrogant to let himself.

Well, he was going to make up for his mistakes.

Except now he was going to die – either of whatever was causing this excruciating pain or when the plane crashed – and none of that would happen. He would die without having fixed the biggest mistake he had ever made. He would die a failure. Rich, successful, yes: but no less a failure for that.

It was that which paralyzed him. The realization his life had been a waste. He had been given the chance to redeem it but that had been snatched away from him.

And all they had to stop it was Marcia Fournier pretending she'd done whatever this crazy bitch thought had happened. It wouldn't work. All it would do was waste time and fuel and bring the end nearer.

He knew now there was no chance of it working, because there was something bigger than some nutjob hijacking a plane going on. Jeff had said it: she was doing this for a reason.

Chip agreed, but he was surprised how quickly Jeff had reached the conclusion. He had seen it clearly and early, and he was unusually unperturbed.

Did he know something? Or was it that he stood to gain something from this? Maybe cause a crisis and ride to the rescue?

It all made sudden sense. That was it. He had to tell the others. He started to speak, but all that came out was a gurgle.

He clenched his fists, fighting to control his breathing. His heart was beating too fast; it felt like it was jumping, banging into the walls of his chest.

181

It felt wrong. His hand was tingling, then it felt cold and numb.

He started to sweat, beads forming on his forehead. It was hard to inhale, iron bands encircling his chest.

He leaned forward, his vision dimming, darkening.

And fading, slowly, to black.

Jill Stearns

There was a strange, troubling sound coming from Chip. She looked at him, saw the pale froth on his lips.

'Shit,' she said. 'Chip? Are you OK?'

He looked anything but OK. He was pale, his temples wet with sweat.

And he was leaning forward, his eyes closing, his right hand raised to his chest.

It was obvious what was going on. He was having a heart attack.

'Mary Jo,' she said. 'Chip's in trouble.'

Mary Jo gave her a long, piercing look, then unclipped her seat belt and stood up.

'I'm not going to do anything,' she said. 'I'm talking to you. The pilot. So keep the plane level. There's a medical emergency.'

'Heart attack?' Jill said.

'Maybe,' Mary Jo replied. 'I'll take a look.'

She knelt by the man and took his wrist in her hand. It was the second wrist she'd held in the last ten minutes.

'His pulse is faint and irregular, but he has one,' she said. She beckoned to Jill. 'We need to lift him so his knees are

183

close to his chest. Put his back to the window and we can put his feet on the seat, facing the aisle.'

They maneuvered him into the position Mary Jo wanted. His eyes were closed, his breathing shallow.

'Stay with him,' Mary Jo said. She went to her seat and opened her backpack. She took out a small medical kit and dug around. She pulled out a pill packet, then grabbed some of the paper towels Marcia had brought for Kevin.

She opened a bottle of water and poured some on the paper towels. She handed one to Jill. 'See if you can bring him round. Put this on his forehead.' She passed the water bottle to her. 'And if you can, get him to take a sip.'

Jill pressed the paper towel to his brow. His eyes fluttered open. She lifted the water bottle to his lips.

'Have a sip.'

She tilted it up and he drank a little. Mary Jo unwrapped the pill packet and took out two small, round, white tablets.

'Aspirin,' she said. 'It'll thin the blood. Make things a bit easier.' She pressed them to his mouth and he parted his lips. Jill lifted the bottle and he swallowed them with some more water.

'Thank you,' he said, his voice a troubled wheeze.

'You're welcome.'

She wiped the sweat from his forehead with the paper towel.

'How do you feel? OK?'

He shook his head and tapped his chest.

'Take it easy,' Mary Jo said. 'Try to relax. You need to avoid stress. Not easy on this plane.'

Chip gave a weak nod. He seemed to strain to say something, but all he managed was a feeble groan.

'Want to say something, Chip?' Jill asked.

He tried again, but a look of pain crossed his face. His eyes slowly closed.

Jill caught Mary Jo's eye. 'How is he?'

Mary Jo raised an eyebrow. 'Not good.' She looked at the cockpit door, and spoke again, her voice raised. 'He had a heart attack, God damn you. He had a heart attack and he needs to be in a hospital! Have you no mercy?'

She waited before asking the same question again. The words disappeared into the silence.

'Have you no mercy?'

Marcia Fournier

This was the perfect opportunity. She had signed up for this in a moment of – what? Drunkenness? Anxiety? It was hard to tell – and now she was committed. If she was honest, she hadn't fully considered it. *I'll think of something*. But what? What would she think of?

And when? Would she just come out with it at some point?

Now, though, it was obvious what she should do. Chip had had a heart attack. The tension in the cabin was high.

What better moment for a confession?

She took a deep breath. 'I have something to say,' she said. 'I want to confess.'

Everyone – except Chip – turned to look at her.

'It was me,' she said, her voice growing louder. 'It was me.'

The intercom buzzed as the channel opened. 'What's your name?' The pilot's voice was suspicious.

'Marcia Fournier. I did it. You have what you want now.'

'Do I?' the pilot said.

'Yes. You have your confession. You said one of us has to confess and then we land. Well, it was me.'

'It was you who did what?'

This was the moment. This was the moment when her *I'll*

think of something became real. She hesitated, and then it came to her.

'I don't want to say.'

'You're going to have to.'

'I don't want to. I'm not going to.'

The buzz of the open line went dead. The panic started to mount in Marcia's chest.

'You said you would land the plane,' she shouted. 'You lied!'

The line opened again. 'I did not lie. Tell me what you confess to, and I'll land the plane.'

There were many things Marcia could confess to – the affairs – Chip was one of many, all of them short-term, all of them harmless enough, all of them as corrosive of her self-esteem as they were necessary to make her feel good about herself – the secret drinking, the abortion she'd had in college when she'd got pregnant by Anton, her best friend Rayna's husband, who Marcia had slept with a month after their first child was born. They had been at the wedding of a mutual friend in Atlanta. Rayna stayed at home with the baby; they drank too much and one thing led to another and then, at 3 a.m. she was staggering to her own hotel room where she knelt in front of the toilet and threw up, as much from shame and self-hatred as alcohol.

It was a theme in her life, the inability to resist temptation. It had aways been that way. She didn't want to have affairs, but if she sensed the opportunity she couldn't turn away. It was the thrill, the rush, the *escape*. It was the same with alcohol. She could confess to all that now, tell them about the vodka she'd smuggled aboard and drunk from water bottles. She wanted to. She wanted to put it all out there and beg for absolution.

But there would be no absolution. Her sins would not be washed away. They would still be there, reminding her of who she was, who she *really* was.

And it wouldn't help. That wasn't what the pilot was asking for.

'I'm not saying,' she said. 'Not in front of everyone. These are my colleagues and friends and I'm too ashamed.'

'Tell me what it is you did.'

'No! I won't humiliate myself in front of them. We can talk about it when we land – presumably you want to do something like that – and I'll tell you everything. But not now.'

It was a good answer. Convincing. She waited for a response. The line went dead.

The Pilot

Was it her? Was it Fournier? It certainly could be. It could have been anyone on the plane – except maybe the nurse, if she was a nurse – that was why they were there.

But *was* it her?

She couldn't be sure. And she had to be sure. None of this would work if she wasn't.

And this was something she had anticipated. A false confession, rescinded when they landed, which was why she'd asked for confirmation.

She had assumed that if it was a false confession it would be revealed, but Fournier had a reason. Plausible.

Not certain, but plausible.

But it would be certain if she gave details of what she was confessing too. And certainty was required, so that left her with no choice.

She pressed the button and spoke into the microphone.

'Not good enough.'

The reply was immediate. 'It'll have to be. I'm not saying what I did.'

'Then nothing has changed. Time is running out. Either you tell me what you did, or we all die.'

She cut the connection. There was nothing more to say.

189

Barrow, Maine 2018

Stacy Evanston

Ella was dead.

Ella: that beautiful, shining, spark of life, hope for the future, was gone. Stacy could barely believe it was possible, much less that it had happened.

The phone call had more dissolved than ended; after Nicole had told her Ella was dead, Stacy had said *I'm sorry, I'm so sorry* over and over, but Nicole had not been able to reply.

Stacy had listened to the sound of her friend crying and then the line had gone dead.

She had placed her phone face down and put her head in her hands and let the tears come. She had not realized she was wailing until Dan came downstairs, his expression a little disappointed, and sat next to her, his arm around her shoulders.

'Stace,' he said. 'What is it?'

'Ella,' she said. 'She's—' She couldn't face the word. 'She's gone.'

It took a moment for him to understand, then the blood drained from his face.

'What?' he said. 'That can't be right. There must be a mistake.'

She shook her head. 'That was Nicole. Ella's dead, Dan.'

He started to shake. 'No,' he said. 'No.'

'I know,' she said. 'It makes me think about Cherry and how it could have been her.'

'Don't,' he said. 'I don't want to go there.'

She had been about to say something else, but she stopped herself. Cherry was alive, but what if she wasn't out of the woods yet? What if the illness – or whatever had caused it – was still in her, still lurking somewhere in her system, ready to flare up again?

She needed to call the doctor. She needed to ask him if Cherry was truly OK.

But first she needed to see her daughter. She got to her feet, her legs unsteady beneath her, and walked to the living room. Cherry was on the couch, the remote control in her hand, her eyes fixed on the television.

Stacy sat next to her and pulled her close to her chest. Cherry wriggled away.

'I can't see,' she said. 'You're squishing me.'

'I love you,' she said. 'I love you so much.'

'I love you too, Mommy,' Cherry said. 'But can you let me watch my show?'

Dr. Williams

Dr. Williams sat at the desk, the case notes for all four of the children in front of him.

He was exhausted, mentally and physically. It had been a long shift – technically it was over, though he couldn't leave yet – but it was what had happened that had drained him.

The girl had died.

This was the worst part of the job. He could take any amount of sleep lost to night shifts or angry patients or incompetent administrators but losing a patient was awful.

And when that patient was a child, it was unthinkable.

Could he have done something else? Had he missed something? Was he at fault, in any way, however small?

He would ask himself those questions for a long time. Maybe forever.

They had discussed this in medical school, talked to experienced doctors about the demands of the job, about not becoming attached to patients, about remaining dispassionate and calm, about the inevitability of death.

About how you had to do that because lives were at stake.

About how even if you did everything right, sometimes it still wasn't enough.

He'd understood all of that in the abstract, but it wasn't until you got here – to a hospital, with real, sick patients – that you realized you didn't understand it at all.

And when it was a child—

He stopped himself and studied the notes.

Ella, unconscious, liver failure, deceased.

Bren, unconscious, liver failure, in intensive care.

Nathan, unconscious, liver failure, also in intensive care.

Cherry, unconscious, liver failure, seemingly recovering.

Why the difference? Why was one of them recovering?

He read the notes again, from the start. Cherry had vomited in class, then gone to the nurse's office where she lost consciousness. It was the same for Ella and Nathan, a little later than Cherry, but the same basic progression. Bren had made it as far as his mother's house.

But other than the timing, they were all the same.

Something flitted around at the back of his mind. There was something there, something his subconscious had noticed but he was not seeing. Gloria walked past his door. He called to her.

'Got a minute?'

'For you, Dr. Williams? Always.'

He handed her the notes.

'What am I missing?' he said. 'There's something, I can feel it. But I can't put my finger on it.'

'What are you looking for?' she said.

'They all had the same symptoms, but one has recovered. The others are either dead, or in critical condition.' He caught her eye. 'Why did one recover?'

She smiled. 'You're the doctor.'

'That's not helping me much right now. Take a look.'

She read through the notes.

'See?' he said. 'Same symptoms, different outcome.'

'Not *quite* the same,' she said. 'There is one difference.'

193

He leaned forward. 'Which is?'

'In what way?'

'Cherry vomited.'

'The others didn't?'

'They may have, but it doesn't *say* they did.'

He paused. 'It would make sense,' he said slowly. 'If they ate or drank something and one of them vomited, early, then that person would maybe – almost certainly – recover more quickly.'

'We pumped their stomachs when they arrived,' Gloria said. 'But that extra hour? Could it make a difference?'

'Oh yes. It could make *all* the difference. You're a genius, Gloria. But we need to find out if they vomited or not. I'll call the principal. The boy, Bren, was found by his mother. Is she here?'

'The father is. She may be too.'

'If she is, could you ask her? If not, find out some other way.'

Gloria nodded. 'On my way.'

Steve Murdoch

'Mr. Murdoch?'

Steve looked up from the chair he was slumped in. A nurse was walking toward him.

'Yes?'

'I'm Gloria. The doctor has a question he'd like me to ask you.'

'Anything. If it'll help.'

She consulted the notes in her hand. 'It was your wife who found Bren?'

'Yeah. She's not my wife. We—' he waved it away. 'Never mind. It was Kris, yes.'

'Do you happen to know what state he was in when she realized he was in trouble?'

'He was unconscious.'

'Had he vomited?'

He couldn't remember what Kris had said. 'I don't know. Why don't you ask Kris? She's here.'

'We haven't been able to find her. She was waiting in the east wing, but she's not there.'

Steve let the words sink in. Bren – her son – was in intensive care and she wasn't where she was supposed to be. He'd been through this before with Kris, every time she'd not come home or not showed up at a birthday party or taken money from his wallet, money he was planning to use to pay rent or buy food or enroll Bren in a summer camp. It was a familiar feeling: disappointment, anger, at her for doing it and himself for being so foolish as to think she'd change, sadness at what she was doing to herself, because he loved her, he really did, in a pitiable, tragic way.

And here it was again.

'I'll call her,' he said. 'Give me a minute.' He paused. 'How's Bren?'

'The same, I'm afraid.'

He lost his breath for a moment, then picked up his phone. She didn't answer, so he called again. Once more, she didn't pick up. He typed a message.

Where are you? Medics need some info.

'Sorry,' he said, reminded painfully that he was used to apologizing for Kris. 'She's not answering, for some reason.'

Then his phone buzzed.

I'm outside. There's a garden. What do they need?

Fucking typical. Outside, smoking meth or drinking vodka. She couldn't stop. She really couldn't stop.

They need to know if Bren had vomited.

Dots scrolled on the bottom of the screen.

No, he hadn't. I would have seen it.

He looked at the nurse and shook his head.

Dr. Williams

Dr. Williams dialed the school principal. She answered on the second ring, her voice taut and anxious.

'Carol Smalling.'

'This is Dr. Williams.'

'Oh God,' she said. 'Has there – has another student—'

'No,' he said. 'Bren and Nathan are still in a serious condition, but they're alive.'

'Thank God. I don't know how I would cope if another – If we lost another child.'

'That's why I'm calling,' he said. 'I have a question you might be able to help with.'

'Anything at all.'

'I'm wondering whether Nathan or Ella vomited before they lost consciousness. I know that Cherry did.'

'I – I don't know,' she said. 'They were taken to the nurse's office.'

'Could you check?'

'Of course. I'll call you back immediately.'

He put his phone down. The door opened, and Gloria walked into the office. She shook her head.

197

'No vomit, at least according to the mom. I'm not sure how reliable she is, though.'

'She'd probably know. So if he didn't say he had vomited, the balance of probabilities suggests not.'

'I'd say so. The others?'

'I'm waiting to hear from the school.'

As he spoke, his phone rang. 'This'll be them,' he said, and picked it up.

'Hi!' It took him a moment to recognize the voice. 'It's Mindy.'

'Oh,' he said. 'Right. Yes. How can I help?'

'I sorted out the oysters. I wanted to check in on one thing. They need to know if you need a shucker?'

'A what?' he said.

'A shucker. Someone to open them.'

His phone buzzed. Someone else – maybe the principal – was calling.

'I'm sorry,' he said. 'I have to go.'

'But I need to tell them—'

He cut the call and switched to the incoming one.

'Dr. Williams.'

'This is Carol Smalling. I talked to the school nurse.'

'And?'

'She said as far as she could remember – and she asked me to emphasize that it was a very stressful situation so she couldn't be totally sure – but she thinks they did not vomit. She's pretty sure she would have remembered it, because she remembers that Cherry *did* throw up.'

'Thank you,' Dr. Williams said. 'That's very helpful.'

'Is there anything else I can help with?'

'Not for now. I'll call if there is.'

He hung up and looked at Gloria.

'Three didn't, one did,' he said. 'And those three are either very sick or dead. It's something they ate or drank. We just have to find out what.'

Stacy Evanston

It felt strange to be telling him good news at a moment like this, but she had to do it. He deserved to know.

Cherry was asleep on the couch, her head in Stacy's lap. Stacy eased it onto a cushion and walked into the kitchen. On the way she grabbed her bag from the stairs.

Dan was chopping an onion. He was a good, if basic, cook; if they were both home then it was he who made dinner. His repertoire was limited to what he called 'hearty and wholesome' – stews, soups, roast chicken or beef or pork, baked fish, maybe a curry or pot pie. If pushed, she would have admitted that she found it a little repetitive; she would have preferred some more salads, some delicate pasta sauces, vegetarian recipes, but she didn't complain. She could make those herself if she wanted.

'Starting off with an onion,' she said. 'That's not like you.'

'Adds flavor,' he said. 'The finer you chop it, the more flavor you get.' He winked conspiratorially. 'Pro tip.'

'What are you making?'

'A soufflé.'

'Really?' This was a radical departure, although she didn't see where the onion fit in.

'Nah. Spicy parsnip soup and chicken thighs.' He wagged his head from side to side. 'Might splash some teriyaki on, if you're feeling exotic.'

'Try this.'

She reached into her bag, leaving her hand inside.

'What is it? Some kind of sauce?'

'Not exactly.'

She took out the pregnancy test and showed it to him.

'Is that what I think it is?'

She nodded. He took it and looked at the little window.

'Two lines means yes?' he said, in a low, quiet voice.

'Two lines means yes,' she replied.

'When did you take it?'

'This morning. I wanted to wait until we got home to tell you.'

He laughed, then smiled, then hugged her, squeezing her hard against his chest. 'Stacy,' he said. 'Stacy, Stacy, Stacy. I can't believe it. This is the best news ever. Well, other than Cherry.'

'I know. I'd almost given up thinking it would happen. My period was late and I had a feeling I was pregnant. It feels like it did with Cherry.'

'When is it due?'

She laughed. 'A long time! I'm like, three weeks pregnant.'

'I know. I just – that's what people ask, right?' He put his hand on her stomach. 'There's a baby in there. *Our* baby. It's amazing.'

'Isn't it.' Tears welled in her eyes. 'It's been so long.'

'How do you feel?'

'Fine.'

'No morning sickness?'

'Not yet. And I didn't have much last time, so fingers crossed that doesn't change.'

'I will get in some avocados, though.' He raised an eyebrow.

'You know how you get about your avocados when you're pregnant.'

'And cottage cheese.'

'I'd forgotten the cottage cheese.'

During her first pregnancy, Stacy had developed cravings for avocados and cottage cheese. She liked avocados but she had always hated cottage cheese: the claggy texture, the soft, suspicious lumps, the hint of rottenness in the taste, but it didn't make any difference. For about three weeks all she wanted to eat were avocados full of cottage cheese.

Although 'wanted' didn't cover it. It was an all-encompassing *need*. They were the only things she wanted to eat. One day she had come home and Dan had been sitting at the table, an avocado and cottage cheese in front of him, and she had blown up.

You're eating my food!

He held up his hands. *It's OK. There are loads more, as well as at least three tubs of cottage cheese in the fridge.*

I don't care! Whether there was more wasn't the point; she simply couldn't stand the idea he was eating her food. She jumped forward and grabbed his plate. *Give that to me.*

Stacy, he said. *One of the problems is that there's nothing else to eat, and I'm hungry. If you let me eat this one, I'll go right out and buy some more.*

No! Eat your own food.

He stood up. *OK. See you later.*

She settled down with three avocados and a bowl of cottage cheese, flicking through the channels on the TV. She had just finished when the door opened, and he came in.

He was holding a large box and wearing a wide smile.

This should do it. He put the box on the table. *This was all they had.*

It was full of avocados.

There's another box with cottage cheese in the car. Now can I have one?

Incredibly, her instinct was to say no, but she inhaled deeply and held her breath for a few seconds.

Fine. But only one, OK?

She leaned forward and kissed him. 'There's some time before all that,' she said. 'And there's some before Cherry wakes up. Any thoughts on how to spend it?'

'One or two.'

'Me as well. I wonder if we're thinking the same thing?'

He put his hands on her hips.

'I think we may be,' he said.

Dr. Williams

Dr. Williams sat opposite Sandy Price, the hospital's COO. He was a dark-haired man with round glasses; in the prior year he had lost a lot of weight. There had been speculation he was ill – he wasn't very popular so some of it was more like wishful thinking – but it turned out it was no more than an effective diet.

The door opened and Dr. Hall came in. He sat down and checked his phone.

'Peter,' Dr. Williams said. 'Thanks for coming up.'

'Not a problem. It's an intriguing case. I'm eager to hear what you have to say. I have nothing to offer yet myself, I'm afraid.'

'I have an idea,' Dr. Williams said. 'There was something in the notes.'

Sandy Price leaned forward. 'You have an explanation for the sick kids?'

'I have a theory.'

Price unfolded his hands in a gesture that said *speak*. 'And?'

'And I think they ate or drank something that was highly toxic.'

'Could be,' Price said. 'It's possible.'

'Could be?' Williams said. 'And it's more than possible. It's likely.'

'You don't know that,' Price replied.

'No. But I have reason to believe it.'

Price started to shake his head, but Peter Hall raised a hand. 'Let him finish, Sandy,' he said.

'Thanks, Peter.' Williams tapped the desk. 'The girl who recovered vomited, and the others didn't.'

Dr. Hall nodded. 'Which makes you think—'

'That Cherry Evanston cleared the poison – the toxin – from her stomach before it was all absorbed. The others didn't.'

'It's an interesting theory,' Hall said. 'But we shouldn't jump to that conclusion. There could be other explanations.'

'Maybe,' Williams said. 'I wondered about that. But I couldn't think of one.'

'Viral in origin?' Dr. Hall said. 'Perhaps the other three got a larger viral load at exposure? Similar for something bacterial.'

'Anything I can think of that's either viral or bacterial would have shown up on the tests,' Williams said.

'Tests can be unreliable,' Dr. Hall said. 'Perhaps the pathogen evaded the tests. Or they were faulty. Or it's something rare that we don't test for normally.' He held up his hands. 'I know. These are unlikely suggestions. But I'm just pointing out that we can't say for certain it's a toxin they ate or drank.'

'It's the most likely explanation,' Williams said.

'What would it be?' Price asked. 'Bleach? Something they found in the janitor's room?'

'No,' Williams said. 'I don't think so. It would have to be something that overloaded the liver and its ability to process it.'

Hall pursed his lips. 'Nothing comes to mind,' he said. 'Alcohol, maybe, but it's not that.'

'There's an easy way to find out,' Williams said. 'We can ask them.'

'Assuming they regain consciousness,' Price said.

'Yes,' Williams replied. 'And even if not, we can ask Cherry Evanston. She'll remember if she ate something unusual.'

'I really don't think this is the right avenue to pursue,' Price said. 'I don't want to waste anyone's time, or upset the child.'

Williams stared at Price. Why the hell was he getting involved in this? He was an administrator. 'It's not a waste of time,' he said. 'It's the obvious next step.'

'I don't want to upset her,' Price said.

'I'll tread carefully.'

'You might make her feel culpable,' Price said. He looked at Dr. Hall for support. 'Don't you think, Peter?'

'Partially,' Dr. Hall said. 'I think it risks upsetting the family. Maybe we can give it a day or two.'

'Peter,' Williams said. 'This is ridiculous! I'm not surprised by him' – he made a dismissive gesture toward Sandy Price – 'but you should know better. You know I have to ask them.'

Dr. Hall nodded slowly. 'You're right,' he said. 'We have to ask.'

Price looked at his watch. 'OK. It's getting late. Maybe tomorrow is better?'

'Maybe,' Williams said. He stood up. 'That's that, then. I'm exhausted, and I'm off shift, so I'll see you in the morning.'

'Yes,' Price said. 'And thank you for all your effort. It's very much appreciated. By all of us.'

'My pleasure,' Williams said.

Price turned to Dr. Hall. 'Peter, could you stay for a few moments? There are a couple of items I need to discuss with you. Mainly administrative. Tedious, but since you're here . . . ?'

Dr. Hall shrugged. 'Not at all. Happy to help.'

Steve Murdoch

Steve Murdoch sipped his coffee. It was weak and tasteless and he didn't really want it, but it passed a few minutes: walking to the café, filling a cup, adding milk, paying, walking back. It wasn't much, but it took no effort. It was the kind of mindless activity that was pretty much all he was capable of.

At the other end of the waiting room were a man and a woman. The man sat motionless; the woman paced. They were a few years older than him – maybe mid-forties, and he wondered what they were here for. Probably a parent, given their age.

Which was the way it should be. Sad, yes, but not this perversion of the normal order of life. His parents were in their sixties, and in good health, but he knew at some point they would die. He would grieve them, he would miss them, they would leave a huge gap in his life, but he would not have to deal with the unfairness, the wrongness of it.

Bren had been reading his first chapter book last night. It was something simple but he was beaming with pride at his achievement. Steve had hugged him and said, *This is the beginning of a lifelong journey for you. You'll be reading for the rest of your life.*

Don't be silly, Daddy, Bren replied. *I'll finish this book before I'm six!*

Not this book! All the other books.

That couldn't be taken from him. Bren's life was ahead of him, not behind him.

He took another sip and watched the woman pace. She walked along the windows, back and forth, ceaselessly. There was something familiar about her that he couldn't place. Perhaps she'd been in a meeting he'd attended, or maybe he'd just seen her around town.

He definitely recognized her, though.

The door to the medical rooms opened and a doctor came out. It wasn't the same one he'd seen earlier. He looked at Steve, and then headed toward the couple.

He reached them and started to talk. Steve could hear the low murmur of his voice, but couldn't make out the words.

Whatever he had said was not good news. The woman let out a wail unlike anything Steve had ever heard. It was inhuman, a noise ripped from her soul, the sound of pure grief. She fell to her knees and clutched her head in her hands. The man slumped in his chair and started to shake his head.

The doctor crouched in front of them, his hand on the woman's shoulder. He said something, then got to his feet, and walked back to the medical rooms, his face grim.

It did not seem like the death of an elderly relative.

The woman slowly stood up. She was facing him directly.

Steve's back tightened.

He recognized her now.

He knew where he'd seen her.

She was a parent of a kid at Bren's school, Nick maybe, or Nathan. Yes, that was it: Nathan.

He took another sip of his coffee. It tasted like ashes, and he spat it back into the cup.

Dr. Williams

Williams was just opening his second beer – he wasn't sure he'd finish it before he fell asleep – when his phone rang. It was the hospital.

'Williams.'

'Dr. Williams. This is Gloria.'

He knew why she was calling, but some part of him held out hope that it was for another reason.

'What is it?'

'We lost another one. Nathan.'

It felt as though his heart had dropped into his stomach. He closed his eyes.

'When?'

'Half an hour ago.'

'Do the parents know?'

'Dr. Hall talked to them.'

He didn't ask how they were. There was no need.

'And Bren? How is he?'

'No improvement.'

He pushed his beer away. He didn't want to drink any more.

'If he gets worse, call me. OK?'

* * *

She called back twenty minutes later. He was reading about liver failure and possible unusual causes. When he saw the number, he wanted to throw the phone across the room.

It was Gloria, again.

'It's bad news. The other boy – Bren – is getting worse. It doesn't look good.'

His vision began to swim.

'Thanks for calling. I'm on my way.'

When he reached the ward, Gloria was waiting for him.

She shook her head.

'I'm sorry,' she said.

'When?'

'A few minutes ago. There was nothing they could do.'

'I'll talk to the parents. Where are they?'

'The father's in room seven. The mother's on her way.'

'Hang on.' The voice came from the end of the corridor. It was Dr. Hall. 'I'll talk to them.'

'I'd like to,' Williams said.

'It's fine. I was there.'

'I've been there from the start.'

'Neal,' Hall said. 'This is not the time for an argument. You're off duty. It's OK. We got this.'

'I'd like to talk to them.'

The door opened and Sandy Price walked in. He was in an expensive-looking down jacket.

'I was just leaving when I heard,' he said. 'So sad.' He looked at Williams. 'I thought you had gone.'

'I came back. I wanted to be here.'

'I understand,' Price said.

'I'm going to inform the parents,' Dr. Hall said. 'They need to know.'

'I'll do it,' Williams said. 'Honestly, I'm happy to.'

209

Price gestured to Williams. He nodded toward an empty office. 'Join me for a moment,' he said.

Williams followed him in. He closed the door behind them.

'Is everything OK?' Price said. 'I know this has been a strain.'

'Everything's fine. I feel I should be there for the parents. I know the most about the case.'

'Dr. Hall is a fine doctor.'

'That's not the point!'

'Please don't raise your voice,' Price said. He paused, as though he'd noticed something. 'Have you been drinking?'

'No!'

'Really?'

'Not really. One beer.'

'Neal,' Price said. 'I have every sympathy with you. This has been a tough situation. But you need to go home, and go now, before any more damage is done.'

Price held his gaze. His expression was serious, and Williams knew he had no option but to leave. Even one drink was too many.

'OK,' he said. 'I'll go. But tomorrow we need to find out what happened. I'll talk to the family of the girl who survived. Find out what the hell they ate.'

Price stared at him.

'That's for tomorrow,' he said. 'Good night.'

Stacy Evanston

Stacy's phone rang. She didn't recognize the number. Normally she wouldn't have answered, but after the last few days she didn't want to miss anything important.

'Stacy Evanston,' she said.

'Mrs. Evanston? This is Dr. Williams.'

She did not want this call. She did not want to know what he had found out and why it was bad news for Cherry, why there was some complication that meant she would have to take her daughter back to the hospital for further tests, or worse, that there was serious, long-term damage to her health.

'Yes,' she said. 'What is it?'

'Do you have a moment?'

'Is there a problem,' she said, 'with Cherry?'

'No,' he said. 'It's not that.'

'Then what is it?'

'There were other children,' he said. 'Who were sick at the same time.'

'Ella was Cherry's friend,' she said. 'It's so sad.'

'There were others too.'

'Did they – are they alive?'

'I can't say too much. No specifics, but two others died.'

She heard herself gasp. That was three now, which made Cherry all the luckier.

'The others had a slightly different situation to your daughter,' he continued. 'None of them vomited in the immediate aftermath of – well, of encountering whatever it was that caused this.'

'You think that's important?'

'I think it could be critical. I'd like to talk to your daughter, if I could, and ask her if she ate or drank anything unusual. A plant, a fungus, anything.'

'She's asleep,' Stacy said.

'Maybe tomorrow? First thing.'

'We'll be here,' Stacy said. 'You can call on this number.'

'It's probably better if I come in person. Is that OK?'

'I think so. I don't see why not. But let us know before you arrive, in case she's sleeping, or there's something else going on.'

'Why don't you call me and let me know what's convenient? I'm at the hospital from six in the morning until two in the afternoon, so sometime after that?'

'OK,' she said. 'We can talk tomorrow.'

2

Stacy woke just after nine. It was – how long? – months, more likely years, since she'd woken up that late. Perhaps on a weekend in her twenties after a late night, but certainly not since Cherry was born. Dan was an early riser, so when she was a baby he would often get up at five or six and take her for a walk, but even on those days, Stacy would be awake by seven thirty, eight at the latest, ready for whatever the day brought.

One morning she had woken to total silence. Not a quiet house, but a quiet *world*. She recognized it immediately: it was the kind of silence you got during a snowstorm. Not a major, windy nor'easter, but one of the long, soft storms that went through the night, dropping inch after inch of snow, until, when you woke, the world was buried in white and nothing was moving. No cars, no people: the world was at a standstill.

And no Dan or Cherry.

She looked out of the kitchen window and saw the footprints – nearly wiped out by fresh snow already – headed for the back gate. There were two sets, both the large oval of snowshoes, but one set thirty-six-year-old-man-sized, the other four-year-old-girl-sized.

213

The snow was still falling in thick waves.

Her phone buzzed.

Severe weather warning: Blizzard

Excellent. Well done, Dan. A morning walk in a blizzard with your four-year-old, in – she checked her phone – temperatures that were well below those in the freezer.

She imagined them in the forest, huddling together for warmth. Dan would have some romantic notion of Cherry, her upturned face watching the snowflakes falling, melting as they landed on her rosy cheeks.

But it wouldn't be like that. She'd be wailing with the discomfort of it all, begging to go home.

She didn't like it, he'd say. *I thought it'd be fun.*

It's a blizzard, Stacy would answer. *She's four.*

But at least he tried. She loved him for that.

An hour later, she was starting to get worried. Dan's phone was on the kitchen counter, so there was no way of contacting him. The storm had thickened, the air white and impenetrable. She was wondering whether to put on her snowshoes and go and look for them, when the front door thudded open.

Jeepers! It was Dan's voice. *It's cold out there.*

Stacy got up and walked into the hall. *You guys were gone for a long time.*

Cherry's face was red, white rings around her lips. Her eyes were dark pinpricks, her coat slick with water.

Are you OK? Stacy said

Mom. Cherry's tone was intense, and Stacy readied herself for Cherry's denunciation of her father, of a screed about how he had made her do this awful thing. *It is so cool out there. We saw deer tracks! Dad said I can hunt one, one day!*

She glanced at Dan, who shrugged.

That's amazing! I'm so glad.

214

And we weren't cold. Well, a bit.

This morning was different. She heard the sound of the TV, of Dan bashing around some dishes in the kitchen.

The sounds of a family home.

A home that could so easily have been devastated, like three others had been.

She would talk to Dr. Williams with Cherry and see if there was anything they could do to help. She reached for her phone. He had said he would be done by two, so she'd call and leave a message for him to come straight after work. The sooner they did this, the better.

The receptionist answered the phone.

'Hello, this is Stacy Evanston. My daughter left yesterday, and Dr. Williams wanted to see her this afternoon. I was hoping to leave a message for him?'

There was a pause.

'What did you say your name was, again?'

'Stacy Evanston.'

'Thank you, Mrs. Evanston. Could you hold for a moment?'

Stacy listened to the tinny music. After a few minutes, a man's voice came on the line.

'Mrs. Evanston? My name is Sandy Price. I'm the COO of the hospital. I understand you are looking for Dr. Williams?'

'Yes. He wanted to see my daughter, Cherry, today. She was—'

'I'm aware of your daughter,' he said. 'I'm very glad – we all are – that's she's OK.'

'Well, Dr. Williams was hoping to see her today. He wanted to ask her some questions about whether she'd eaten anything out of the ordinary. I was calling to arrange a time with him.'

'Yes.' The man – Sandy Price – gave a sort of sigh. 'I'm sorry to be the bearer of bad news – but Dr. Williams will be unable to see you today.'

'Is he OK?'

215

'I'm afraid not. Dr. Williams passed away last night.'

The words did not sink in.

'Did you say—?'

'Yes, I did.'

'That's crazy! What happened?'

'It isn't public knowledge yet, but he committed suicide.' Price paused. 'It's not clear what happened exactly, or why, but from what I've been told he'd been under a lot of stress – well before your daughter's case – and it became too much for him. I'm so sorry to have to tell you this.'

Of all the things he could have said, suicide was perhaps the last she would have expected.

'I'm sorry for you, too,' Stacy said.

'Thank you. And if there's anything we at the hospital can do for you, please don't hesitate to reach out.'

December 23rd, 2022

Marcia Fournier

That had not gone very well.

No – that was an understatement. It had been a complete and utter bust. A failure, doomed from the start. When she had written the words – *I'll figure it out* – she'd had a rush of adrenaline, the feeling that her moment had arrived. She'd felt confident – yes, she would figure it out! She was strong and capable, and nothing was beyond her.

Yeah, right. She was half-drunk and deluded. This was the perfect microcosm of what her life had become, although become was now quite the word. It was too passive: it was what she had made her life into.

Well, she'd had enough.

'I'm sorry,' she said.

'It's fine,' Jill Stearns replied. 'It was worth a try.'

'Jill,' Marcia said. 'It's not that I'm sorry for. I'm sorry for lying. Just now – to the pilot – but for all the other lies.'

She looked from passenger to passenger.

'That's what I'm sorry for,' she said. 'It won't matter to you – why do you care if I lie? – but I'm sorry for all the lies I've told. To you, to my friends, to Mick, to my daughter, to my beautiful granddaughter, even to myself. Because I have lied to myself now for years. Every day I wake up and tell myself this is the last time I wake up hungover. The first lie of the day. Others follow. "How many drinks have you had, Marce? Just two, Mick."' She snorted, a sardonic laugh. 'Try six. Or eight. "Brought your own water on the plane, Marcia?" You asked me that last week, Kevin. I had two of these' – she pulled out one of the empty bottles – 'just like I did today. But they're not water.' She leaned forward. '*Vodka*. That's right. Half water, half vodka. It doesn't even taste good. It's just enough to get me through the flight, but not enough so I can't drive home. Functionally, that is. Legally, I should be nowhere near the wheel of a car.'

'Marcia,' Jill said. 'You don't have to tell us this.'

'I want to. I want you all to know. I want Mick to know. Because if you don't, then I'll never stop telling myself the biggest lie of all.' She took a deep breath. 'The lie that I can stop any time I want to. That's my take on the alcoholic's delusion. That I have control – any kind of control. At least, that's true for me. I have no control of this at all.'

Jill put her hand on Marcia's shoulder. 'It's so brave to do what you just did,' she said. 'We'll be here for you. I promise.'

She felt light, almost ethereal, like a heavy burden had fallen from her shoulders. It was a physical sensation of letting go of a great weight. And her mind was clearer than it had been for years.

She felt, despite the situation, optimistic. It was a feeling she had forgotten.

'Thank you,' she said. 'It's a long way to go, but this is the first step.'

'This is great.' Kevin Anderson tapped the back of his seat. 'Lovely to see all these happy-clappy good times, and I'm glad you chose now to hit rock bottom. I wish you all the best in your recovery journey. But there are more pressing matters at hand.' His voice rose. 'Is anyone going to fucking *do* anything?'

218

Varun Miller

Help is on the way.

He read the email from Sharon again.

Help is on the way.

Varun looked over at Kevin Anderson. He was staring at Jill Stearns, tapping his fingers on the plastic table in front of him.

Is anyone going to fucking do anything?

Who did he think he was, talking like that? Varun was more than happy to ask tough questions, have difficult conversations, tell people hard truths – he was a top lawyer, after all – but in his view there was no excuse for bad manners. His father was a local politician in the Pennsylvania town where he grew up, and, at the end of his thirty-year career the town had held a ceremony to honor him. At the end, his bitterest political opponent had risen to her feet and gazed across the packed chamber.

The guests had held their breath. Up until that point, everything that had been said was little short of gushing praise.

Diana Christensen was less likely to be so glowing.

I'll keep this short, she said. *Ram and I have disagreed on almost everything for the last three decades. In my view, he was wrong on pretty much every question and issue we faced. But, despite that, he never once treated me with anything other than respect and good manners, which is not true of many of the people I have encountered in this chamber. I have been insulted, had my integrity questioned, been called foul, unrepeatable names, been threatened: but never, once, by Ram. Yes, we disagreed on almost everything, but I use that word – almost – deliberately. Because the one thing we agreed upon is our respect for other people and a belief in the importance of our shared humanity.*

His dad said, in the days before he died, that this was the highlight of his career. Varun hoped to match it, someday.

Kevin Anderson would never match it. He was everything Varun's dad was not. Crass, selfish, arrogant, pleasure-seeking and utterly self-centered.

Because the truth – and Varun would tell him, one day, in a polite and respectful way – was that he was not a victim of reverse discrimination. If anything, he was over-promoted. His judgment was clouded by his prejudices, and he was lazy. The two went hand in hand: it was easier to arrive at an opinion by consulting your prejudices than by considering all the facts.

And Varun thought it would be good to let him know that, even if his father would not have approved.

Look at this situation: Kevin was swearing, nursing his broken wrist, having failed to do anything to solve the problem. Varun, on the other hand, had summoned help.

That was the difference between the two of them. Kevin thrust himself forward, acting the Big Man. Varun got the job done.

And he was looking forward to letting Kevin know.

Jill Stearns

So what next?

Mary Jo was sitting with Chip, her hand around his wrist, taking his pulse. Whatever happened, he was going to need immediate medical care, although right now it seemed that was a luxury he would not be afforded.

They were going to crash into the ocean, she was sure of it, so never mind his heart. He was going to die like the rest of them.

This was supposed to be a simple flight home, just like all the others she'd taken, and it had turned into *this*.

Chip Markham, in serious jeopardy. Kevin Anderson whimpering in pain. The others, terrified of what might happen.

Her, equally scared. It was funny what form that fear took. She wasn't thinking about the moment the plane hit the water, or whether there was a heaven or hell – instead, she was wondering what Mila's news was.

A baby? A marriage? Now she didn't care which. She just wanted to know, and to tell her daughter she loved her and supported whatever decision she took. Because this had shown her how fragile life was, how – despite the care you took to build a solid foundation, to work hard and have savings and good health and a home – you were never far from it all crashing down. Security was an illusion that allowed you to carry on. Without it, you would be paralyzed by the knowledge that you were suspended over a bottomless void.

She tapped Mary Jo on the shoulder.

'How is he?'

'No better.'

'Tell me about your husband.'

'You really want to know?'

Jill nodded. 'If you're happy to tell me.'

Mary Jo's expression was faraway for a moment, then she smiled. 'We've had it good,' she said. 'We met young and realized we were the one for each other, I suppose. And we managed to pull it off all these years.'

'Kids?'

'One. Nancy. She lives out west now. You?'

'A daughter, Mila. I love her, but it wasn't easy.'

'Teen years?'

'The very same.'

'You know,' Mary Jo said, 'we had some struggles in those years. She was depressed, stayed in her room all the time. I used to wonder what we'd done wrong, where our relaxed, confident daughter had gone.'

'She was OK?'

'She came out of it, eventually. She had a therapist and the right medication and she came out of it. A year later one of her classmates – not a close friend, but someone she knew – killed herself. She, too, had suffered with depression, but had not made it.'

'I'm sorry to hear it.'

'That's when I realized we were lucky. Nancy was the canary in the coal mine. Nowadays my younger colleagues deal with anxiety and depression in their teenage children

222

all the time.' She held Jill's gaze. 'What are we doing to our kids? What kind of pressures are they under?'

'I know what you mean. I see it at work. We have these amazing graduates show up and all they've done is get grades and build their résumés. It seems fun is not on the agenda anymore.'

'You know what I said to Ray – my husband – once? I said, "I'm glad she survived her teen years."' She shook her head. '*Survived*. Is that what we hope for now for our kids: survival?'

'And now Ray is sick?'

'Very. A year, maximum. We've been fortunate,' she said. 'But I can't help feeling cheated. I was looking forward to the golden years, you know? Retirement, travel, grandkids. But I guess that's not going to happen.'

'That's very sad,' Jill said. 'I'm sorry.'

'And now it looks like he won't even have me around for his last few months.'

'We can't be sure of that.'

'Really? No one's confessing. No one knows what they're supposed to confess *to*. Which means the pilot is deranged, and that's hardly reassuring. We don't even know what this is about.'

She let go of Chip's wrist, and held Jill's gaze.

'That's what's so crazy. We don't even know that.' Her voice rose. 'Could I ask you a question?' she called out to the cockpit. 'What are you hoping someone will confess to? Who exactly, has been murdered? Can you at least tell us what this is about?'

223

The Pilot

What *was* this about?

It was about justice.

It was about fairness.

It was about finding out the truth.

She had listened to all that heart-wrenching stuff from the nurse – if she was a nurse – and she had reached her conclusion.

It was bullshit, designed to make her doubt herself. Well, it wouldn't work. It just made her heart harder.

That was the only way that this meant anything. Without that it was just her personal crusade. So maybe it was time to let them know exactly what had happened.

She reached for the microphone. She pressed the button to switch it on.

'Ella Farmer,' she said. 'Do you recognize that name?'

She waited for a reply from the cabin. There was none.

'Well,' she said. 'Do you?'

The silence that followed enraged her. She knew that back there, the name Ella Farmer meant something, to one of them.

One of them had been thinking *if I just keep quiet then maybe this will go away.*

But now they knew.

Ella Farmer. When they heard that name they would understand that this was for real, that the time had come to pay the price.

The question was whether they would, or whether they would have to be forced to.

She looked at the fuel gauge. Fifteen minutes, maximum, before it was too late.

She had given the name. It was time to move to the endgame.

'Did you hear the name?' she said. 'Ella Farmer. Does that mean anything to you?'

Kevin Anderson

Ella Farmer. Does that mean anything to you?

So this was it, then. The reason for all this. Someone called
Ella Farmer.

'Ella Farmer,' he said. 'Who knows that name?'

There was silence in the cabin.

'Anyone?' Kevin said. 'Does anyone recognize it?'

'Not me,' Ramos said. 'Never heard it in my life.'

Jill: 'Me neither.'

He looked at Marcia. Maybe this was the reason she drank.
'Do you know the name?'

'No. I'm sorry. I've never heard it.'

'So no one here knows Ella Farmer?'

In the seat at the front, Chip groaned. Mary Jo stood up
and walked over to him.

'Chip?'

His skin was gray. A line of spittle unspooled down his
chin. She felt for his pulse. It was, if anything, weaker.

'Were you trying to say something?'

He groaned again, his eyes fluttering open.

'Water,' he said.

Mary Jo opened the fridge and took out a bottle of water.

She opened it and held it to his lips. He took a weak sip. The water spilled out of his mouth and ran over his lips.

'The name,' she said. 'Do you recognize it? Or did you just need a drink?'

He nodded, his face creasing in pain with the effort.

'I do.' His breathing was ragged, the words hard to make out. 'I know it.'

'How?' Mary Jo said. 'How do you know it?'

'The girl,' he muttered. 'She was a girl. She died.'

The words hung in the air, the implication shocking.

'Fuck,' Jeff Ramos said. 'This is *real*.'

Chip Markham

He was slipping in and out of consciousness. There were moments when he was awake, aware of what was around him, hearing what the others were saying, feeling thirsty or panicked or in pain, understanding that his breathlessness was a problem, a big problem, and wishing for the tightness in his chest to loosen, and then the world would start to fade and the pain would dissolve and he would allow himself to settle into the blissful feeling of nothingness.

But then he would fight to come back to himself. Some survival instinct would kick in, some desire to struggle, because he knew that if he let himself slip too far he would never come back. It would be the end, and he didn't want it to be.

He wanted to see his son and grandson, wanted to celebrate Christmas with them, wanted to right all the wrongs of the past. He saw it now, saw how to be a father – late, yes, but better late than not at all – and he couldn't stand the idea of it being taken from him.

It was unfair, and the unfairness made him angry and the anger made him fight, so he clawed his way back to consciousness, but then the pain came, the shooting pains in his arm and the feeling that his heart wasn't working right, that it was jumping around in his chest, that it was fluttering on the edge of madness, and it was hard to breathe and he felt weak and tired and he wanted to sleep, to fall back into the darkness.

He had to stay awake. He had to stay awake or he would die, and he would never see his son and grandson again.

And he had to tell the others that he had suspicions about Ramos.

Mainly he needed to stay awake for his family.

But he couldn't.

He sat, his knees to his chest, his back to the fuselage, the plane's engines thrumming against his spine, and he breathed in and out, shallow, hard-to-win breaths.

Through the pain he heard the pilot talking. *Did you hear the name? Ella Farmer. Does that mean anything to you?*

And then the nurse was talking, the one who had helped him. She was asking if anyone knew the name, and he wanted to help her. He *did* know the name – at least, he thought he did.

He remembered it from a long time ago. Who was it? How did he know it?

Ella Farmer.

It was a girl, wasn't it? A young girl. But why did he remember the name? His mind was hazy. It was an effort even to think.

He tried to speak, but his mouth was too dry. The nurse gave him water. The words came.

The girl. She was a girl. She died.

The nurse held both his hands.

How? she said. *How did she die?*

He closed his eyes and tried to remember. It was there but he could not grasp it. The name swam in front of his face.

A girl. Who was she?

229

He didn't know. All he remembered was the name.

But he knew that the name meant trouble.

Big trouble. It came back to him now, all of it.

He felt the tiredness close in and he understood that his time was over.

And given what was coming, he was glad.

And then – thankfully – all was darkness.

Varun Miller

He listened to Chip's words. The girl had died. That changed things; as Ramos said – this was real.

The nurse asked him how, but there was no answer. A look of alarm spread across her face and she bent over Chip.

'Is he OK?' Jill Stearns said.

The nurse glanced over her shoulder. 'No. He's far from OK.'

'But he's alive?' Stearns said.

'For now.'

'If it was him,' Kevin Anderson said, 'and he dies before he confesses, we're all fucked. Can you wake him up?'

The nurse shook her head, her mouth half-open in indignation. 'No, I cannot. And I wouldn't, if I could.'

'Why not?' Anderson said. 'He knew the name. It was probably him who did it. He was about to say so. It's in all our interests if he does.'

'You don't know that,' she said.

'It seems likely.' Anderson stood up and leaned over her shoulder. He started to reach out to shake Markham awake with his good hand, but winced in pain. He sat back down, his broken wrist cradled in his lap.

'Chip, he called. 'Wake up. We need to hear what you have to say.'

Chip did not respond.

'Kevin,' Stearns said. 'This isn't helping.'

He looked at her and laughed. 'Like you've done anything? Let's be honest. Hardly the fearless leader, are you?'

'I'm sorry to be a disappointment,' she said. 'But this is hardly the time for that.'

He laughed again. 'We can talk about it later. Discuss how you did once we're all safe and sound. How about that?'

She stared at him and Varun saw in her eyes how she had got to where she had. Her face was fixed in a slight, almost pleasant smile, but her eyes were hard and empty. She blinked.

'I'll look forward to it.'

Varun opened his laptop and loaded the web browser. It was like the early days of the internet, the page slowly assembling itself. He typed the girl's name into Google and hit search.

He watched as the results came in. There were Facebook posts, news stories, an online tribute site. He selected the tribute.

'What are you doing?' Anderson said. He nodded at the laptop. 'That thing working?'

'Trying to see if I can get it to,' Varun said. 'Maybe pick up a signal somehow.'

'Yeah?' Anderson looked suspicious. 'Anything?'

Varun didn't want to tell him he had a connection. He could have – maybe he should have – but he had a sudden hatred of Kevin Anderson and did not want anything to do with him.

'Not yet. I'll keep trying, though.'

He tilted the laptop toward himself to hide the screen. The tribute site had loaded.

232

A Tribute to Our Beautiful Daughter, Ella

As many of you know, Ella went to be with the angels. We were blessed with her presence, but for too short a time. She was the light of our lives, and

He skimmed over the text, looking for details of what had happened.

It is a comfort that she did not suffer for long. The illness that took her arrived swiftly and carried her away before she experienced too much pain. We would have loved a chance to say

He read it again. *The illness that took her.*

She had died of an illness. There was no murder here. This was all a mistake.

He read to the end, just in case.

Her service was held at the Church of Our Lady, in her home town of Barrow, Maine.

He froze.

Barrow, Maine.

He knew Barrow, Maine. He'd lived there.

The company had a research and manufacturing center there, one of the largest facilities in the country. It had been one of the first, and although there had been moves to close it over the years, it had survived. It was part of the company's history. There wasn't much else in the town besides it.

He had worked there for a few years, around the time the girl had died.

He looked around the plane.

They *all* had.

233

Barrow, Maine 2018

Stacy Evanston

Dr. Williams was dead.

Ella, Dr. Williams.

And two other children. It was all over town. Four sick kids, three of them dead. Ella, Nathan and Bren.

All dead.

Cherry could have been one of them. She had vomited; the others had not. That one small detail had saved her life and condemned the others to an early – way too early – death. She swung between relief and guilt that she alone got to keep her baby.

The others would want answers, would pursue the doctors and the hospital until they found out who was responsible. Stacy would have done the same.

And there was the doctor, too. Another victim. Had he felt too much pressure, too much guilt at the loss of the kids? Was he negligent in some way? He had seemed to be doing all he could, but maybe he had made a mistake. It would all come out in the end.

Her phone buzzed. It was Molly, a friend from her spin class.

'Hi,' Stacy said. 'How are you?'

'Good. But that's not the question,' Molly said. 'How are *you*?'

'All things considered?' Stacy said. 'We're as well as could be expected. Alive, at least.'

'I heard about Ella. I also heard about the others.'

'I know. I can't imagine what they're going through. And four deaths in a small town? It'll be devastating.'

'Four?' Molly said. 'There's another?'

'The doctor. Dr. Williams.'

'The doctor *died*?'

'I know. Crazy, right?'

'How?'

'Suicide. I tried to call him yesterday and the hospital – the COO or someone – told me. Apparently he'd been having a hard time and this put him over the edge.'

'That's terrible,' Molly said. 'You said Dr. Williams?'

'Yes. I think his first name was Neal?'

'Oh God. I know his wife. It's her birthday soon. He was planning this huge party' – she started to cry – 'she must be devastated.'

'I'm sorry, Mols.'

'And then there's Ella's mom and dad, and the other parents.'

'Did you know them?'

'I didn't,' Molly said. 'It was two boys. Bren Murdoch and Nathan Carter.'

Stacy closed her eyes.

'I know Nathan,' she said. 'Bren, too. Cherry was in class with him in preschool. He lives with his dad. He's a really great guy.' She felt her lips start to quiver. 'This is so hard, Molly.'

'I know. But I'm glad you're OK. And Cherry.'

'The doctor thinks it's because she vomited and the others didn't. Maybe they ate something toxic, and she managed to get it out of her system.'

235

'Thank God. Can we get together? I need to see you. Give you a hug.'

'Tomorrow morning?' Stacy said. 'Come anytime. I need that hug.'

'Tomorrow it is. Love you.'

'Love you too.'

She put the phone down. What *was* it that they'd eaten? Dr. Williams had been going to ask Cherry. Perhaps she should ask her. If he'd felt it was important, then maybe she should find out what it was.

Cherry was still pale, but she seemed to be more or less fully recovered. She had her appetite back, at any rate: she'd had three bowls of cereal for breakfast, and was already hungry.

'I'll make you a cream cheese bagel,' Stacy said. 'But can I ask you a question first?'

'But I'm *starving*.'

'Hello, Starving,' Dan said, from across the room. 'I'm Dad. Nice to meet you.'

'Daaaad!' Cherry said. 'Stop it!'

'Sorry, Starving. I'll stop.'

'One quick question?' Stacy said. 'Then a bagel?'

Cherry nodded. 'What?'

'Thank you, Starving,' Stacy said. 'Here it is. Think about it, OK? So, at school before you got sick, did you eat anything or drink anything unusual?'

'Like what?'

'Like a mushroom? From the playground?'

'No, Mom!' Cherry laughed. 'I don't even like mushrooms!'

'Anything else?'

'Kingsley gave me some candy.'

'Kingsley?'

'He's in my class.'

'What kind of candy?'

'I don't know. Little ones. They looked like chocolate. I never had it before.'

'Did Kingsley have it?'

She shook her head. 'He's allergic. He's allergic to everything.'

'Did he give it to any other kids?'

She nodded. 'Ella. He had four, and he gave one to me and one to Ella. Can I see Ella? I want to play with her.'

Stacy blinked away tears. She fought to control her voice. 'Later,' she said. 'Who else did he give them to?'

'Some boys. I can't remember.'

'Bren? Was he one of them?'

Cherry smiled. 'Yes! It was Bren. And his friend, Nathan.'

'OK,' Stacy said. 'Thanks. Now, time for that bagel, Starving.'

2

Stacy called the hospital. She wanted to speak to the man who had called to tell her about Dr. Williams's suicide. She had googled COO and the name of the hospital, and he had come up. Sandy Price.

The switchboard put her on hold. Normally she had no doubt he would not have taken the call of a patient, but as the parent of a child who was the only survivor of the four who had been admitted a few days ago, she still retained a kind of twisted celebrity status.

It worked. Moments later he was on the line.

'Mrs. Evanston. How are you?'

'Good.'

'And Cherry? Is everything OK with her?'

'It seems to be. We're keeping an eye on her, as Dr. Williams suggested.'

'Very good.'

'That's kind of why I'm calling, actually?'

It was clear he didn't understand. 'Oh?'

'It's something Dr. Williams said. He mentioned that he thought Cherry and the others may have eaten or drunk something toxic, which caused their symptoms. The others – according to Dr. Williams – did not vomit, whereas Cherry did, which might explain why she survived.'

'He did discuss this with us,' Price said. 'But Dr. Hall – a liver expert from Portland – was not convinced. It's possible, I suppose.'

'He was going to ask Cherry if she and the others ate anything unusual.'

'It's a shame he won't be able to.'

'It is. But I asked her.'

He paused. 'You did?'

'Yes. And she said they *did* eat something unusual.'

'Really? What was it?'

'Candy.'

'That doesn't sound very unusual, Mrs. Evanston.'

'I know. But she didn't know what kind of candy it was. A boy called Kingsley had it. He'd brought it from home.'

'Candy is hardly a poison.' He gave a low chuckle. 'At least not in small quantities.'

'I agree. But it seems odd that Kingsley had four of them, and he gave them to Cherry, Ella, Bren and Nathan. It's an odd coincidence, don't you think?'

'It is.' He took a deep breath. 'But that's all it is, I'm sure. Candy doesn't cause this kind of illness.'

'You should look into it, though. At least close the loop on it.'

'Of course, Mrs. Evanston. We will follow up on anything that could shed light on these tragic events.'

'Thank you.'

'Is there anything else I can help you with?'

'No,' she said. 'I think – I think that's it.'

'Then have a great rest of your day, and thank you for the call.'

The line went dead. She knew Sandy Price was busy, but why did she feel she'd just been given the brush-off?

And why did she get the feeling Sandy Price knew more than he was letting on?

There was one more call to make. Frances, Kingsley's mom.

It went to voicemail. Stacy left a message, telling her she was Cherry's mom and that she was OK, but she had a question about something she may be able to help with.

Frances called back two minutes later.

'Hi,' she said. 'I got your message. I'm so sorry about what happened to you.'

'Thank you. We're OK now.'

There was a long pause. 'You said you had a question for me?'

'Yes,' Stacy said. 'It's probably nothing, but I'm trying to find out if Cherry ate anything unusual which might have caused the – the illness. She mentioned some candy Kingsley gave to her and the three – the three other kids.'

'Are you suggesting' – her voice hardened – 'are you saying that this is Kingsley's fault?'

'No, not at all,' Stacy said. 'I'm just trying to get to the bottom of what happened to my daughter, and to Ella, Bren and Nathan.'

'I'd like to ask you to leave us alone,' Frances said. 'You need to stop blaming us.'

'I'm not blaming you. I'm just asking—'

'You're doing that doctor's dirty work. He called yesterday with the same questions. I wouldn't speak to him and I'm not going to speak to you. I understand what happened has been traumatic, but that doesn't give you the right to harass other people. Don't call me again.'

She hung up. Stacy stared at her phone. Dr. Williams had called Frances too? Why? What had he heard?

Had he found out something that had pushed him to kill himself?

Or was it even worse?

A chill ran through her as another thought pushed its way to the front of her mind.

Had he killed himself? Or had he found out something that had got him killed?

Varun Miller

They had all worked at the center in Barrow, Maine.

They had all worked in the town where the girl had died. But she had died of an illness, not because someone had killed her.

As far as he knew, anyway.

Maybe there was more to this. He typed her name into Google.

Ella Farmer, death

A similar set of results came up. He scrolled through them, scanning for anything unusual.

Something caught his eye.

The search words were highlighted, but it wasn't those that got his attention. It was the words around them.

Ella Farmer, death . . . two other pupils at the school also died . . . Nathan Carter and Bren Murdoch

He clicked on the link. It was a story from the *Barrow Times Record*.

What it said was shocking. His stomach seized and he had to struggle not to throw up.

Two other pupils also died that night, both of the same mystery illness. Nathan Carter and Bren Murdoch were taken ill and passed away at the Memorial Hospital. One other child – Cherry Evanston – also suffered from the same illness. Fortunately, she survived.

There were two more, and one more who fell ill?

'Hey,' he said. 'I have a question for you. For the pilot. About Ella Farmer.'

The intercom buzzed into life.

'What is it?'

'The girl, Ella Farmer. She died, right? That was what Chip said.'

The pilot's voice was cold. 'She did. She was killed.'

This did not square with the news reports, but he could come back to that later.

'OK. My question – my question to you is, was she the only one who died?'

The pilot paused.

'No. There were more.'

Jill Stearns looked at him, her eyes narrow. She raised an eyebrow questioningly.

'How many?' he said.

'Two more. Two boys.'

'How did they die?

'The same way.'

'So three murders?' he said. 'You think someone here is responsible for three murders?'

'More.'

He sat forward. The news article had not mentioned any others.

243

'How many more?'

'Three,' the pilot said.

'And did they die the same way?'

'No.'

'How did they die?' he asked.

The reply was a long time coming.

Barrow, Maine 2018

Stacy Evanston

Stacy woke up suddenly. She had been in a deep sleep and she realized immediately something was wrong.

Something had woken her. Something had set off a trigger in her subconscious mind and it had flooded her body with adrenaline. She was, immediately, wide awake.

And she knew immediately what it was.

An atavistic, primitive human fear, one of the oldest and most terrible of all.

Fire.

She heard it, first. The crackle and snap of flames eating into their fuel. The pop of wood, dry and old, succumbing to the heat.

And then there was the smell. The acrid smell of paint and Sheetrock and things that shouldn't be on fire.

Burning.

In her house.

Where her baby slept.

She shoved Dan, hard. 'Dan!' she shouted. 'Wake up!'

He opened his eyes slowly, but then the neurons that had snapped her awake did the same for him.

'Fire?' he said. 'Cherry.'

He jumped out of bed, naked, and ran across the room. She followed him out of the door and into the corridor.

Her heart sank. It was an inferno. The glow of the flames washed the walls in red. To the left was Cherry's room; she stepped toward it but the heat was an impenetrable barrier.

To the right, the stairs were a glowing maw. There was no way down.

'Oh, God,' Dan said. 'Go out of our bedroom window. I'll get Cherry.'

'I'll come,' she said. 'I'll help.'

He shook his head. 'No. Get out. And get the trampoline. Drag it under her window. We'll jump out.'

'Dan. I want to—'

'No! Go, now!'

He pointed to their bedroom, his expression hard.

'Stacy. Now. Before this gets worse.' He took a step down the corridor, holding his hands up against the heat, then pushed Cherry's door open and stepped inside.

Stacy went to the bedroom. It was cooler in there, less smoky, and she sucked in lungfuls of air. The fire would be consuming the oxygen; in her military training she'd done a course on firefighting and knew that was what killed most people in a fire. Not the heat; the asphyxiation.

The window was a sash window large enough for a person to climb through. Beneath it was a pitched roof above a dining nook that jutted out from the kitchen. She climbed out and put her feet on the roof tiles. They were cool against her bare soles. She sat down and braced herself against her hands, sliding down inch by inch.

When she reached the edge of the roof her right foot hit something – a patch of moss, maybe – and she slipped off the edge. She twisted to her right, grasping at the tiles for something to hold on to. Her fingers scrabbled uselessly on the roof, and she fell, spinning in the warm air.

246

She thudded on to the ground, the breath knocked from her lungs. For a moment she was winded, then she remembered what the situation was and forced herself up onto her elbows. She had to help Dan. She had to help Cherry.

She grabbed the rail of the trampoline and dragged it toward Cherry's window. There was a sharp pain in her ribs; something was broken, but she could deal with that later.

She shoved the trampoline against the wall.

'Dan!' she shouted. 'Dan!' She looked up at the window, willing it to open. Behind it she saw the red glow of the fire, and she knew no one in there could have survived.

But she was not going to give in. She ran to the back door and pushed it open. They – like many people in small-town Maine – did not lock their doors. She stepped inside, and her worst fears were confirmed.

The heart of the house – her home – was a furnace. The heat pushed her back. There was no way she could get upstairs; there was no way she could get even another six feet inside the house.

'No,' she said. 'No.'

How had this happened? How did a fire start in a house like this? They had a wood stove but that was not running. A gas leak from the propane tank? Had they left a stove top on? How did something like this happen?

Dimly, she thought of the doctor, and the question that had come to mind.

Had he killed himself?

Was this an accident?

She heard sirens, and backed out of the house. Dan and Cherry were gone, there was no doubt about that, and suddenly she was sure of one thing: she did not want anyone to know she had escaped.

She ran, barefoot, to the back corner of the yard and crouched by a maple tree. A fire engine pulled up outside

247

the house, followed by another, then another. Yellow-suited figures swarmed out of them and ran toward the house.

A firefighter appeared by the trampoline. He shoved it out of the way and a second firefighter swung a ladder against the wall. He scrambled up and prised the window open with an axe.

He leaned back against the heat and shook his head.

A shake of the head that said everything. She lowered her eyes.

When she looked back, the firefighters were dousing her home with water and foam. Gallons and gallons spewed from the hoses in thick white ribbons, landing with a hiss on the place she had raised her family.

No one could have survived.

But she had to be sure. When the blaze was extinguished, her house a smoldering wreck, she watched as the firefighters, masks on their faces and oxygen on their backs, hacked a path into the house.

When they emerged, they were not carrying the coughing bodies of Cherry and Dan.

They were trudging, defeated and empty-handed into the same future as her. But for them, it contained their families.

For her, she was alone.

Barefoot, in her nightgown, she walked silently into the woods.

PART TWO

Stacy Evanston

She walked all night through forest trails until, as dawn approached, she returned to her home.

Her former home.

She wanted to see it one more time.

She sat by the maple tree. She heard Cherry's voice echo from the summer before.

Can we get maple syrup from it, Mom?

Sure. Why not?

Dan's laughter. *Maybe feed a mouse or two with what we get from one tree, but it's worth a try.*

They had tapped it and hung a bucket from the tap. When the sap had run the bucket had half-filled. Dan had taken it and showed it to Cherry.

Looks like we got us some maple syrup.

Can I eat it?

I have to boil it up, first.

The next day he had come into the kitchen with a mason jar full of dark brown maple syrup. *Here it is. Cherry's Maple Syrup.*

He had bought it from the store and poured it into the jar; wasn't even real maple syrup, but the cheap stuff you put on pancakes. Cherry loved it. She told everyone she had made it.

She looked up at her house.

What was left of it.

It was a burned-out shell. A skeleton of charred bones. An empty, blackened mess.

It was the perfect metaphor for her life.

She had watched it burn. She had watched her family and her house – her entire life – be devoured by the flames.

Documents, photos, books. Clothes.

Everything was gone.

Everyone was gone. Nobody had come out of the house. No Dan. No Cherry. And nobody could have survived in there.

They were gone, too. Her husband and her daughter. Ashes to ashes, Dust to dust.

She shuddered at the thought of them in the house, the flames all around them. How had it happened? Was Cherry dead when Dan got into her room? Or had he tried to rescue her, but been unable to beat the fire? Perhaps they had died together, in each other's arms.

She wished she had been there. She should have gone with him. It would be better than this. Anything would be better than this. She was numb with the shock, but already she knew that when it hit, the pain would be like nothing she had ever experienced. Like nothing she had ever imagined.

She groaned, her rib cracked or broken. She welcomed the pain. She deserved it. She should not have let them die. She should have done something.

But what? What could she have done? It didn't matter. She should have done something, instead of sitting in the backyard, watching.

Even if it cost her life, she should have done something.

What next?

Her life was over. It was done. There was no way she could move forward, not after this.

Her hand fluttered down to her stomach. There was Baby Two to think about. Could she kill herself when there was Baby Two?

She wasn't sure. But she wasn't sure how she could live, either.

Dawn was softening the edges of the night. A new day was starting. A day without Dan or Cherry.

The first of many.

A sob racked her body. Pain from her rib shot through her chest. Another sob followed, then another. She fell forward and beat her hands on the dew-wet grass.

'Hello?'

She heard the voice from a distance, but it didn't register.

'Is anyone here?' It was louder now. She recognized the voice. Molly. She knew what came next. A hand on her shoulder. A cool hand on the back of her head. Molly telling her how sorry she was.

She didn't want that. She didn't want anything.

She fell silent and got to her feet. She slid back into the shadows. She watched as Molly appeared at the side of the burned-out shell that had been her home. For the first time she truly understood what it meant to call a place a home. It was so much more than the physical structure, than the timber and Sheetrock and nails and furniture that had been turned to ashes. It was the memories, the laughter, the love, and the promise of more to come. That was what had been taken from her.

And she did not want to see or talk to anyone.

Because right now no one knew she was alive. They'd assume she was in the house, her body so destroyed by flame that it was unrecognizable. A fire that destructive would make it impossible to count the bodies, so the only way they would know who was there was by DNA testing.

And why would they do that? If she was not outside the house, then she was inside.

And, for now, at least, she was happy for them to think that way.

2

She sat in a diner on the outskirts of Barrow, a cap pulled down low over her forehead. She was wearing some workout clothes she had left in her car. They were musty with the smell of sweat, but she didn't care. There were some twenties in the bag too. Not much, but enough for a few days.

She cradled a mug of coffee in her hands. She'd taken a sip, but she didn't want any more. It felt wrong to eat or drink, like her body was not her own. She was disconnected from herself. What was a body? How was a body the same as a person? Was Cherry gone because her body had been destroyed? Was Dan? Or would she see them when her body ceased to function?

She didn't know. But she wanted to find out. The best case was they were reunited. The worst was oblivion.

Although perhaps that was the best.

She looked at her legs. A pair of gray spandex leggings. That was all she had left.

She had nothing of her own.

It was all gone.

The waitress came and gestured with the coffee pot.

'Some more?'

255

She shook her head. 'I'm good. Thank you.'

Even now, politeness was a reflex.

'Let me know if you need anything,' she said.

'My rib hurts.'

The waitress gave her an odd look. 'Would you like some ibuprofen?'

She had just been saying it. She had felt the pain in her rib and had said it hurt. She didn't want anything. What would she want?

'Sure,' she said. 'That would be great.'

'I'll bring some.'

As she left, Stacy winced.

It wasn't. This was something different. An ache in her stomach, a twisting, pulling sensation. It was like getting a period.

She felt a wetness between her legs.

She knew immediately what it was. She half-ran to the diner bathroom and sat on the toilet.

Blood. And not a period.

She had been pregnant. Not any more.

After all this, a miscarriage.

She was, now, truly alone.

December 23rd, 2022

The Pilot

'There were three more killed,' she said into the headset. 'One was a suicide – faked to look like a suicide, anyway.' She took a deep breath and looked out over the ocean. Dusk was coming. The sky was darkening ahead. 'The other two died in a fire,' she said. 'A fire in their house.'

She checked the instruments. The fuel was reaching the point where they would have to turn back, or they would no longer have the option.

And she was now sure it was going to come to that. None of them were going to confess. She was disappointed. She had come so close.

'Who were they?' A man's voice. 'The one in the fire?'

'Their names were Cherry and Dan. Cherry and Dan Evanston. Which makes six. Six people killed. Six people murdered. Four children, two adults.'

She paused.

'So now you see how serious I am. And it is time to come clean. One of you is responsible. And you have – still – time to confess. But we are soon going to run out of fuel. It will soon be too late for us to turn back.'

'Can I say something?' A woman, this time. Jill Stearns, she thought.

'Go ahead.'

'These are just names. They mean nothing to any of us on the plane.'

'That's not true. They mean something to one of you. They mean *everything* to one of you.'

'Can you help? Give us more context?'

The pilot thought for a moment.

'I will,' she said. 'I will tell you where all these murders happened.'

'Where?'

'Barrow, Maine.' She paused. 'Where you all worked at the time they were taking place.'

Varun Miller

He typed the new names into Google.

Dan Evanston and Cherry Evanston. He added *house fire* and hit search.

It came up immediately. A house fire in Barrow, Maine. He opened the news story.

TRAGIC FIRE CLAIMS THREE VICTIMS

A house in Barrow, Maine burned to the ground last night, killing all three inhabitants. Fire Chief Eric Chandler said that although three fire crews attended the blaze, nothing could be done to help the victims.

'This was one of the most ferocious fires we have seen,' he said. 'It started and spread with incredible speed and the occupants of the home had no chance of escape.'

The victims were Stacy and Dan Evanston, 36 and 37, and their daughter, Cherry.

Miller froze.

Cherry. He recognized the name. He had read it in the

earlier news story, about the kids dying of the mysterious illness. But she couldn't have died of both.

He went back to the other story.

> Two other pupils also died that night, both of the same mystery illness. Nathan Carter and Bren Murdoch were taken ill and passed away at the Memorial Hospital. One other child – Cherry Evanston – survived.

So Cherry had survived the illness, only to die along with her mother and father. But the pilot had said only two people had died in the fire, and that was three.

Maybe she had it wrong. He could hardly ask without giving up the fact he had a connection. He took a piece of paper and wrote a note to Jill.

> *The three kids died of a mystery illness. There was one other kid who got sick, but she survived. She was called Cherry. She died in the fire, along with her parents. Then there's the suicide. That makes seven deaths, not six. She's probably just mistaken.*

He beckoned to Jill and handed her the note. Jeff Ramos started to say something, but Miller put a finger to his lips.

Jill read the note. Her eyes widened in shock and she turned to stare at him. The shock in her eyes was quickly replaced by something else – almost disbelief – and then, to Miller's surprise, fear.

Then her expression hardened and she wrote on the paper:

> *How do you know all this?*

He wrote his reply and handed it back.

I have a connection. Hacked the router. I called for help. Should be on its way.

Jill nodded and gave him the thumbs up. She wrote something.

Got it. I'll talk to her.

Jill Stearns

'Are you listening?' she said. Her tone was serious and businesslike, flat, emotion at a minimum. 'I'd like to talk.'

There was a pause and then the pilot responded, her voice muffled by the intercom.

'I'm listening. But all I want to know is which of you did it.'

'That's what I want to talk about.'

'Then I'm listening.'

'I don't think you're going to like what I have to say.'

'I'll be the judge of that.'

She watched as the note Miller had written was passed around the cabin, saw the hope light up her colleagues' faces as they read that help was coming. Marcia wrote something and he held it up for her to read.

KEEP HER TALKING. HELP IS ON THE WAY

Jill nodded.

'I remember the events you are talking about,' she said. 'I was in Barrow at the time. It was not a story you could miss. The sudden illnesses and deaths of three children, and the fire.

But you are mistaken if you think any of us had anything to do with them. It's simply not the case.'

The pilot laughed. There was no humor in it. 'Of course not.'

'Yes, we were working there, but so were many others. If there was any link, it would have come to light at the time. These kind of things are investigated.'

'Then what did happen?' the pilot said.

'Nothing,' Jill replied, 'other than the events themselves. You're looking for a conspiracy, for someone to blame. But there's no one there. There's only the tragic, terrible events.'

'No. You're lying.'

'I'm not lying,' Jill said. 'I don't lie. There's no murder here. There's no conspiracy. And we can end it all, right now. Take us home and I promise we will not involve the police.'

'I don't care about the police,' the pilot said. 'And we're not going home. We're not going anywhere.' She paused. 'We have about ten minutes before it's too late. Don't speak to me again. Don't ask any more questions. Don't say anything, unless it's a confession. Understood?'

'Understood,' Jill said. 'But one more thing. I remember there being three victims in that house fire. You only mentioned two?'

There was a long silence. When she spoke, the pilot's voice was tinged with suspicion. 'You remember that?'

Jill had to tread carefully. 'Like I said, it was a big story. I remember thinking how sad it was that an entire family died.'

'You remember correctly. The press reported three victims.'

'Reported?' Stearns said.

'Reported. But that wasn't what happened at all. There were only two.'

Jill felt a chill spread up her spine.

'What happened to the third one?'

263

'She escaped the fire. Everyone assumed she was killed, but they were mistaken.'

'Why?' Jill said. 'Why did she let people think she was dead?'

'Because she was. Inside. But she started a new life.' She laughed again. 'She had a background in the US Air Force, so she became a pilot, in case you were wondering what she did with herself.'

Stearns looked from face to face. So now they knew who was flying their plane.

'Anyway,' the pilot said. 'You have ten minutes.'

Varun Miller

There was no doubt now that this was going to happen.

This woman had lost everything, and she believed it was someone on this plane who had done it. She was prepared to kill them all to get what she wanted, and she was prepared to die.

The only way out – the only way he'd get to see Ari and Susheela again – was if the person who had killed those people confessed.

But what if the pilot was wrong? What if it was just some theory she had cooked up in her grief?

Then they were all doomed.

The thought left him feeling hollow, although – despite it all – he was quite calm. He had often wondered how he would confront death, and now he knew.

To his right, Mary Jo was sitting by Chip, holding his hand. He was gray, his skin waxy. It was not good, but at least they had the nurse on board.

'Listen,' she said. 'I don't know what you all think. But she's willing to do this. This is no bluff. And I don't know you, or if one of you had a hand in this, and I don't want to. But if what she says is true, one of you had better step forward, or we all die.'

'I do know these people,' Jill said. 'And none of them did this.'

'Yeah?' Kevin Anderson said. 'You think? Most of you would sell your own grandmother – or grandfather, gotta be inclusive these days, right? – if it got you the next promotion. So let's not pretend otherwise.'

'Speak for yourself, Kevin,' Jill said. 'Or was that a confession?'

'No, it wasn't,' he said. 'But if I change my mind, I'll be sure to let you know, Ms. Stearns.'

'Thank you.'

Mary Jo stood up. 'We have less than ten minutes,' she said. 'Please, if one of you can stop this, then I beg that you do. I know that I am innocent. I do not deserve this.'

She didn't. He felt bad for her. She was unlucky to be here.

Mary Jo Fernandez. An innocent bystander, caught up in events beyond her control.

He typed her name into Google. She had a Facebook profile, as well as LinkedIn. He opened it.

She was a nurse in Portland, with her current employer for three years. Before that she had been a unit manager at another hospital.

A hospital in Barrow.

He sat upright. She was in Barrow, working in a hospital, at the time of the deaths.

'Mary Jo,' he said. 'I have a question for you.'

'Of course.'

'Do *you* know Barrow at all?'

She turned to him. 'Why do you ask?'

'Just wondering. Since it seems to be central to all this.'

'I do.'

All eyes swiveled to her.

'In what way?' Varun said.

'Yeah,' Anderson said. 'How do you know Barrow?'

'I worked there,' Mary Jo said.

'As a nurse?' Ramos asked

'Yes.'

'When?'

'2018.'

'That's right,' Miller said. 'You were a nurse at the hospital where the kids died. You didn't think to mention this earlier?'

Barrow, Maine 2018

Stacy Evanston

Bill Standish, with his wife, Frances, and son, Kingsley, lived in a new development on the outskirts of Barrow. She walked through the forest trails, head down in case she passed anyone. She needed to leave town as soon as she could, but before she did there was one thing she had to do.

If the house was occupied, it wouldn't work; she could not be seen. No one could know she had survived the fire. She wasn't sure yet why this was so important, but she knew it was.

Or would be.

Either way, if the house wasn't occupied, she had a plan. She would get in and find the candy her daughter had eaten. Because that was central to what had happened. Dr. Williams had called the Standishes for a reason, and he was dead. She had, too, and she should also be dead.

She approached the development. There were six houses in a clearing in the forest; it had been controversial when it was built, locals preferring to maintain the natural environment, but the need for new housing had been too great.

Only one house had a car outside. It was on the far side

from the Standishes' house, so she darted around the edge of the forest until she was at the corner of their yard.

She walked quickly across the lawn to the back door. It was unlocked – very Maine, and very useful – and she pushed it open.

The house looked empty. She listened for a sound. There was nothing, so she stepped into the kitchen.

There was something wrong. She looked around. There were no pictures on the wall, nothing stuck with magnets to the fridge.

Through the glass window in the hatch she could see there was nothing in that, either.

She opened a cupboard.

Empty.

She entered the living room. There were two bookshelves, neither of which contained a single book. She ran her fingers over the dust that had settled on the edges. Not big readers, apparently.

She knew now that the occupants weren't at work.

They had left.

Two hours later she sat at a computer terminal in the library in Auburn. No one knew her here.

She had searched for Bill Standish and Frances Standish on Facebook, Instagram, Twitter, and LinkedIn.

There was nothing. If they had ever had any social media profiles, they were gone now. They had left town and erased all trace of themselves from the internet.

All except one.

There was an article from the *Barrow Times Record* a year ago. Bill Standish had attended a fund-raiser for the Barrow Educational Fund. He had given a speech as the representative of a major donor.

His employer, the food company that had its research center in Barrow.

A research center where he was head of Research and Development.

2

She had no option but to call from a phone booth. There were very few of them left but she found one by the bus station. It was old and scratched and for a moment she wondered whether it would take her coins, but they dropped into the slot and the credit flashed up on the screen.

There was something going on here, something that had ended up with Ella and Bren and Nathan and her daughter and husband dead.

She wondered at how she was feeling. Broken, raw, hollow. But not hopeless. Stronger, almost.

And then there was the doctor. He had – apparently – committed suicide, but the more she thought about it, the more she wondered whether something else – something altogether more sinister had happened.

She thought she knew what it was.

She looked at the slip of paper in her hand. She had written down the number of the hospital, intending to call Sandy Price again.

She paused. She knew how this would sound. She knew that it came across like a mad conspiracy theory. There were all kinds of ridiculous examples out there, from the moon

271

landings being faked to Area 51 to Paul McCartney being dead to shadowy cabals running world governments.

But then there were the real ones. Companies hiding evidence that smoking was bad for you or polluting rivers or mis-selling mortgages.

And this was one of those, she was sure of it.

What if Kingsley's dad, Bill, had given the kids some kind of new candy that turned out not to be ready yet? That turned out to be poisonous? And then his company decided to cover it up.

What would that cover-up look like?

If there was a nosy doctor asking too many questions – well, he'd be silenced. And if it could be made to look like suicide, so much the better. Another doctor would need to certify the deaths as the result of a virus or infection.

And if there was a survivor, they would have to be cleaned up.

It was hard to believe that it was what had happened, but she had to find out.

And she had a way to do so.

She dialed the hospital.

3

'Sandy Price.' He sounded serious, cold and unwelcoming.

'Mr. Price?' She raised the pitch of her voice by a tone and inflected it with a Southern drawl. 'I was wonderin' whether I could have a few minutes of your time.'

'You're a reporter?'

'That's right.' She had told the switchboard she was calling from a Boston internet news site in the hope he would take her call. 'Matty Prine. From Treetop News in Boston.'

'You're not from Boston originally?'

'No sir. I grew up in Georgia, but I always wanted to be near the snow, so I headed up here a few years ago.'

'How can I help you?'

'I wanted to ask some questions about Dr. Neal Williams? Apparently he committed suicide?'

'He did. Tragic. It's a huge loss for the hospital.'

'Can you share any details why he might have taken that step?'

'No. I'm afraid I can't.' He paused. 'Why, if I may ask, are you interested? Dr. Williams was a fine doctor, but I don't see how his death, however untimely, is of interest to a Boston news site.'

'Well,' she said. 'I also heard that there was an outbreak of a mysterious illness? That killed three children and left another very ill, and I wondered whether the two were connected.'

'You mean, whether he was tipped over the edge by the stress of that case? It's certainly possible, but—'

'No, sir, I don't mean that. You see, I heard that those children may have been exposed to something that caused them to become sick, and Dr. Williams was trying to find out what it was. And maybe—'

'That's preposterous,' Price said. 'Dr. Hill – who is a very eminent physician – also worked on the case and he was quite sure it was a tragic, inexplicable illness. Unfortunately, Ms. Prine, despite all the advances in medical science there are still many things we do not yet know, and from time to time these kind of events will occur. If you are looking for anything else then you are barking up the wrong tree. I would add that, if you publish anything suggesting that the hospital is engaged in any activities that are not one hundred percent – and I mean *one hundred percent* – above board and compliant with all laws and regulations, you and your company will be defending your claims in court.'

'I don't know, Mr. Price—'

'This interview is over. I am happy to discuss any and all reasonable questions with you, but these outrageous accusations are unacceptable.'

'Sorry, Mr. Price. One more. What about the fire?'

He paused for a long time.

'Excuse me?'

'The fire that killed the *other* girl. And her parents? Isn't it convenient that she died?'

'What are you *saying*?'

'I'm just askin' questions, sir. And I noticed that Mr. Bill Standish – whose son was at school with the kids who got sick – has left town.'

274

'Where are you getting this information?' Price said.

'Are you sayin' it's true?'

'No! I am not saying that in the slightest! And if you print anything to the contrary you'll regret it! I am asking who is feeding you those lies!'

'I could tell you,' she said. 'If you'd like to meet.'

4

Stacy had suggested the hospital as a meeting place; Price said no. He did not want to be seen with her at his workplace, so they'd have to meet elsewhere.

This was all the proof she needed. If there was nothing to this, he wouldn't have agreed to meet her. He had no incentive to. She was just a nuisance he could safely ignore. But if there *was* something to this, then he would want to know what she knew and where she was getting her information.

And he could not let her go free.

He had suggested a diner a mile from the hospital. He told her to wait for him in the car park at 6 p.m.

She arrived thirty minutes early, on foot. There was a high picket fence at the rear of the car park, behind which were the grounds of a church. She walked around to the gate, and let herself in. The church was unlit and empty. She skirted the fence, searching for a gap. When she found one, she sat on the ground, and waited.

At ten minutes to six, a black Chevy Suburban pulled into the car park and rolled slowly to the rear. The driver backed into the parking space to Stacy's right, and killed the engine.

No one left the vehicle.

Her skin prickled.

At two minutes past six, a Mercedes Benz – something gray and sleek – entered the car park. It moved silently across the tarmac, coming to a halt a few spaces away from the Suburban.

She could see the driver. He had short, dark hair and round glasses. He looked around the car park, clearly expecting someone.

It was Price, she had no doubt.

He was here, waiting for her.

But she had no intention whatsoever of talking to him. That was not her plan at all. She wanted something else entirely.

She waited as the minutes passed. At six ten the door to the Mercedes opened and Price got out. He walked around the car park, looking into the other cars.

He did not check the Suburban.

When he was satisfied they were empty, he headed for the diner; perhaps Matty Prine was in there, eating pie and drinking a mimosa.

A few minutes later he was back, his face set in a deep frown. He got back in his car, and folded his arms.

At six twenty-five, he climbed out, and walked over to the Suburban. The window came down.

'What time did you arrive?' he snapped.

She could just make out the reply. 'Ten minutes before six. Like you said.'

'Did you see her?'

'No. She wasn't here and she hasn't arrived.'

'Fuck!' Price slammed his hand against the Suburban. He took his phone from his pocket. 'Little bitch. I'll teach her to mess with me.'

'What you doin?'

'Calling her boss. You guys can leave.'

Stacy stifled a laugh as the Suburban pulled out. Price's frown darkened as, she assumed, he searched for Matty Prine and Treetop News.

Neither existed.

She took a great deal of pleasure in watching him realize he'd been played.

And she took even more pleasure in the way he looked: he was worried.

December 23rd, 2022

Kevin Anderson

'Well, there it is,' he said. 'You and your' – he put on a mocking tone – '*my husband's dying and I want to see him. I'm just an innocent little nurse*, and all along you were hiding your dirty little secret. It was *you*.'

'Kevin, shut up,' Ramos said.

'Why? Isn't it obvious? We've all been on this plane how many times? And the one time she's on it, this happens. I don't think so. So you shut up, Jeff.' He turned to the nurse. 'Anything to say?'

'I worked there,' she said. 'But I wasn't in ER.'

'And I suppose you never heard of these kids who died?'

'I did. Everyone did. But it wasn't in my area.'

'Very convenient.'

'Not really,' she said. 'I was in the NICU.'

'The what?'

'The NICU,' she said. 'Neo-natal intensive care unit.'

'Whatever the fuck that is.'

'Are you a father?' she said.

'No.'

'That is probably for the best,' Mary Jo said. 'But if you were, you would know what the NICU is. You'd have heard

279

of someone whose kid was in there. It's where we treat newborns with serious illnesses. Heart problems, organ failure, difficulty breathing or keeping food down. We take them from their parents and try to keep them alive. Some of them don't make it. It's the kind of job that doesn't leave much room for anything else. You tend to get absorbed in what's going on around you.'

'Just like your dying husband,' he said. 'Convenient. I don't like to be a cynic, but we can all see what's going on here.'

The nurse held his gaze for a few seconds, her eyes hard and glittering. There was an edge to her that he had not expected, which simply confirmed what he was thinking.

'What is that, exactly?' she said.

'You killed them. Some kind of "Angel of Mercy" deal. In your head, anyway. But you're just another psychopath, and this fucking pilot somehow found out you'd be on this plane. How, I have no idea. But the thing is, you're not the person you say you are.'

'No,' she said. 'I'm not.'

'Yeah,' Kevin said. He smiled. 'Here it comes. The confession.'

'You think I'm kind and tender-hearted. A nurse, friendly and caring, in a profession I love which gives me the satisfaction I need. But I'm not. I'm cynical and bitter. And exhausted. Have you got any idea what the last few years have been like?' She looked around the plane. 'Any of you? Yes, you read about it in the news, but I – and my colleagues – *lived* it. The endless parade of patients, fading and dying, unable to see their loved ones to say goodbye, the days spent sweating in swathes of protective clothing, the shifts bleeding into one another. It was hell on earth.'

She gave a dry, humorless laugh.

'And you give us a million-dollar check. Less than your annual bonus. It's an insult. A tiny fee to assuage your conscience. How is it that teachers and nurses and meat-packers got to risk their lives to keep the world moving, while you worked from your home offices, looking out over a view of the ocean? Yet it was you who made millions, while they were paid a pittance, just one medical bill from losing their house, or having to choose between clothes and food.'

She made a sweeping gesture, taking in the jet.

'Have you any idea how *gross* this is? How unjust? That you fly around in a private jet, convinced it's because you're better and more talented and more deserving than the rest of us? You're *worse*. You're selfish and greedy and back-stabbing. I've dedicated my career to helping others; you've dedicated yours to getting rich.'

'Seems to me you'd be quite happy to crash us into the ocean.' Kevin folded his arms. 'Dying husband? Nothing left to live for? Why not take down the people you hate? Is that it? Are you working with the pilot?'

'I feel sorry for you,' she said. 'But I forgive you. If these really are my last few minutes, I don't plan to spend them on someone like you.'

She closed her eyes and clasped her hands in her lap, her mouth moving in a silent prayer.

Marcia Fournier

She had a headache, and she wanted a drink. It was all she could think of. She was empty, a shell. There was nothing left.

Jeff Ramos walked past her and crouched by Chip Markham. Jill put a hand on his shoulder.

'What are you doing?' she said.

'Talking to Chip. Maybe he knows something.'

'He's in no state to talk. You might cause him more stress. Make it worse.'

'I have to try. And it makes no difference now anyway. It's not like this could get any worse.'

Jill nodded, and Ramos knelt close to him.

'Chip,' he said. 'Can you hear me?'

Chip's eyes were closed, his breathing shallow and slow. He seemed to have aged twenty years; his skin was gray and waxy. In truth, he looked half-dead already.

Marcia did not think he'd make it whatever happened.

'Chip,' Jeff said. He put his hand on Chip's wrist. 'I hope you're OK, man. You're going to be.'

Marcia was surprised to see that Ramos was concerned, or at least giving the impression that he was. She had met him on his first day with the company – nearly two decades ago – but had no idea who he really was. All she knew was that he had joined after a distinguished military career, was not married and had no kids, but other than that his private life was a mystery to her – and, as far as she knew – to everyone else.

She had tried flirting with him once, at a conference in Miami. It was the perfect opportunity for a fling: far away from home, no one to see it, her practiced in adultery, him single. What was there to lose? The anticipation was delicious, and then she had made a move, a subtle hint that she was available. A hand on his elbow and a meaningful look, holding his gaze just a moment too long.

He had looked at her as though she was some kind of animal. As though she was worthless, as though the thought of what she was offering was utterly disgusting. There was no emotion in his eyes, just a cold dismissal, no trace of humanity.

So it was a surprise to see him behave like this.

'Chip,' he said. 'We're in a shit situation here. I need your help, if you can give it. Can you remember anything about the girl that died? Ella? You knew her name. Do you remember anything else?'

Chip's breathing sped up, and his lips parted.

'Go on, Chip,' Jeff said. 'You can do it.'

Chip's breathing slowed again, as though the effort was too great.

'Chip,' Jeff said. 'Do you know how the girl died?'

Chip rocked forward. His eyes opened, and he caught Jeff's gaze. 'Matty,' he said.

'Matty?' Ramos replied. 'Who's Matty?'

'M-M-' – Chip was almost panting, his cheeks moist with sweat – 'M-My son.' Every word was punctuated by a wheezing breath. 'Matthew. Tell him. Tell him I love him. And I'm sorry.'

283

He sat back, his breathing gradually slowing until it stopped altogether.

Jeff felt for a pulse.

'Shit,' he said. 'He's gone.'

'What?' Marcia said. 'What did you say?'

This was impossible. Chip could not be dead. He was a – what? Friend? Colleague? Former lover?

All of them. But mainly he was *there*. She could hardly conceive of a world without Chip, but it had arrived.

And it was going to arrive for her family. They were going to get a call telling them she was dead, and their worlds would change forever.

'He's dead,' Ramos said. 'Fuck.'

'Well,' Kevin Anderson said. 'That's fucking wonderful. If it was Chip, then we're screwed, because he'll never say another word.'

She turned to look at him.

'Have some respect,' she said. 'Please.'

'For Chip? I'll give it a miss.'

'You know,' she said, 'I think you're protesting too much, trying too hard to cast blame on others. Is there something you want to tell us, Kevin?'

He let out a long, harsh laugh. 'You're accusing me?'

'Why not? You were in Barrow at the time. You could have been involved.'

'Involved in what, exactly? Some kids got sick and a house got burned down. Big deal. Happens all the time.'

'I don't know,' Marcia said. 'But someone seems to think they're linked, and you seem very keen to suggest it's other people who are the reason why.'

'You still got some hidden booze?' he said. 'If you do have some more, feel free to share.'

'No. I'm done drinking.'

'Really? Once a drunk, always a drunk. Isn't that what

they say?' He pursed his lips. 'How many nights did you black out when you were in Barrow? Plenty, I'd say.'

'You'd be right.'

'Do anything on those nights you shouldn't have?'

She almost laughed. She did *nothing* on those nights. That was the point. She drank until everything went away and she could sleep a dreamless sleep, at least until four o'clock in the morning, when she woke up with a dull headache and a raging thirst and a promise that this was the last time.

Those 4 a.m. promises didn't seem to stick, though.

Jeff Ramos stood up. 'Can you shut the fuck up, Kevin?' he said. 'We'd all appreciate it.'

'Yeah,' Miller said. 'Seconded.'

Kevin Anderson glared at Jeff, then turned to Miller. 'Fuck you, you useless brown bastard.'

Marcia gasped. 'You can't say that.'

'Can't I? It's true though, isn't it? We all know it. He's a useless bastard who only got his job so Jill can fill her fucking quota.' He grinned. 'We're all going to die, so we may as well tell the truth! And I want that asshole to know we all see through him. Make that your dying thought, Miller.'

She watched Ramos's face darken. He took a step forward.

Miller shook his head. 'Don't,' he said. 'I have a better idea.'

Varun Miller

He realized that they thought he was being noble, showing a heroic restraint in the face of unthinkable provocation.

It was nothing of the sort.

He had always known that Kevin Anderson didn't like him, which was fine. They were colleagues. They didn't have to like each other. They just had to be professional and work together.

The thing was, Kevin Anderson didn't *rate* him.

And that pissed him off. He had a degree from a more prestigious school, he had broader and more relevant experience, his career trajectory was steeper, and he was harder-working and better liked.

But despite all that, Kevin Anderson thought Varun had his job for one reason, and one reason only. Because of the color of his skin.

The degree, the experience, the hours of dedication, the hard-won respect of his peers; none of that mattered to Kevin. It was his skin color that had got him the job.

He was a brown bastard, and Kevin wanted him to know.

Well, there were some things he wanted to tell Kevin.

The outsourcing contract they'd worked together in 2017 when he'd spotted a career-ending mistake in Anderson's work and corrected it for him? He'd kept the records.

The time Anderson had shown up late for an arraignment, stinking of whiskey and Miller had sent him home, explained he was sick, and covered for him?

He had the records of that, too.

And there were others. Plenty of them.

But that was all a waste of time. He needed a way to get his message across in a more succinct manner.

And he had just the method.

He unclipped his seat belt and stood up.

'You,' he said, 'are a fucking idiot.'

'Fuck you, Miller,' Kevin replied, rolling his eyes. 'You—'

Miller reached out and grabbed his injured wrist. He twisted it a fraction of an inch.

Anderson's eyes bulged in his eye sockets. He opened his mouth but all that came out was a high whine.

Miller twisted a little more. He felt bones grinding under the skin. It was very satisfying.

Anderson shook his head. 'No,' he gasped. 'Stop. Please. No. It hurts.'

'I was wondering,' Miller said. 'How I could make it clear to you how you make me feel. I was looking for a clear and unambiguous method of communicating to you what happens when I have to be in your presence. And then it came to me.'

He twisted further and Anderson groaned, his face slick with sweat.

'It was obvious, really.' He twisted again. 'This, Kevin, is the effect you have on me, and probably others.'

He let go and Anderson slumped into his seat.

'Got it?'

Anderson didn't reply.

'I'm sure you do. I think I made myself clear.' He leaned down and whispered into Anderson's ear. 'And don't ever call me a brown bastard again, understand? Or it won't be your wrist I twist off.'

Stacy Evanston

There they all were.

She looked at the list. She had pieced it together from the company website, news releases, LinkedIn profiles.

She had created a new account for herself to search for them. They would see that Lindsey Sandbrook, Recruitment Executive, had been checking out their profiles. No doubt they would get a thrill: a headhunter, looking at them!

If they knew the truth, the thrill would fade quickly.

Because there was a headhunter in their lives, but it was not the kind of headhunter you welcomed.

She read the names:

> Jill Stearns, chief executive officer
> Chip Markham, chief financial officer
> Jeff Ramos, chief technology officer
> Marcia Fournier, chief marketing officer
> Varun Miller, chief legal officer
> Kevin Anderson, chief operating officer

One of them – or more – but at least one, knew what had happened. Maybe they had been involved; maybe they were just informed. But something had killed Ella, Nathan and Bren, and there had been a cover-up.

And as part of the cover-up, her husband and daughter had been killed.

She knew better than to go to the police. The authorities wouldn't listen to her. Even if they did, the company would get to them somehow. A commissioner, or senator, or some other person with influence and power would quietly shut down any investigation.

And then she would have an accident. Maybe her brakes would fail. Or she'd have a fall when hiking. Or suicide, a bereaved mother destroyed by grief.

Or maybe she'd simply disappear one night. Who would come looking for her? Who was left?

So no: she would not be going to the police. She would deal with this on her own. How, she didn't know. But she would.

She tucked the list into her pocket. It was her reason to live. There was nothing else: without it, she would kill herself, that was for sure.

But with it, she had a purpose.

I am a headhunter, she thought. *I like that.*

2

She sat at the bar. She had dyed her hair a metallic red. She was wearing tight jeans and a crop top. A bit slutty. She figured Kevin Anderson for the kind of guy who might like that.

She'd soon find out. Next to her, he was reading his phone.

She had found his address online and made her way to Portland to take a look. His apartment was downtown; she sat on a bench and waited. Just after 6 p.m. a taxi had pulled up and a man in chinos and an expensive shirt had got out. He had dropped his bag in the hall, then walked toward the center of Portland, and into a bar.

And now she was next to him, sipping a glass of white wine. She glanced over and he looked up. She smiled and lifted her glass.

'Slainte.'

'You Irish?' he said.

'Aren't we all?'

He shook his head. 'I'm not.'

'Shame. I like the Irish.'

He grinned. 'Allow me to introduce myself. Patrick O'Guinness.'

She laughed. 'Very good. I'm Tara.'

'Kevin.'

'You live nearby?'

'Up the road. I just got back from work.'

'Where do you work?'

'Well, today I was in New York.'

She raised an eyebrow. 'Quite the trip.'

He shrugged. 'I'm lucky. I get to take the company plane.'

She widened her eyes. 'Like a private jet?'

He nodded and sipped his cocktail. 'Like a private jet.'

'Wow. You must be a mover and a shaker.'

'In a way.'

'You fly a lot?'

'Quite often.' He gestured to her glass. 'Another?'

She looked around. 'Maybe go someplace else? A bit less stuffy?'

He grinned, his eyes lighting up at the prospect of an easy conquest. 'Sounds good. I'll get these.'

He took his wallet from the inside pocket of his jacket and placed a hundred-dollar bill on the bar. He slid his wallet back into his jacket and stood up. 'Bathroom. I'll be right back.'

She smiled a warm, encouraging smile and watched him disappear to the back of the bar. Then she slipped her hand into his pocket and pulled out his wallet. She palmed it, got to her feet, and left.

He had seven hundred and fifty dollars in cash, plus a bunch of credit cards and his ID. She took the cash and threw his wallet into the Casco Bay.

It was a start. Next she needed ID; that was easy enough. Find someone who looks like you and take theirs. It would be good enough to get her on a bus to Boston.

And once she was there, a thousand dollars would get you a social security number in whatever name you wanted.

291

In the Air Force she had taken a course on identity theft. She had never thought it would come in so useful.

And once she had her new identity, she quite liked the idea of becoming a pilot.

The Pilot

Commercial aircraft had no radar tracking other planes so the first she knew of the jets was when she saw them.

She jumped in her seat; they shot past the private jet, one on the left, one on the right. She braced herself for the noise that would follow.

It came seconds later, a deafening roar that shook the small plane.

The jets circled back, one going high, one low. She lost sight of them, but she didn't mind. They'd be back.

How had they known where she was? There were no communications on the plane.

Unless there were. Somehow the passengers had got a message out. Maybe one of them had a satellite phone, or some other satellite device. Dan had had one; he had solo hiked the Hundred Mile Wilderness in Maine the summer before he died. It was a rugged, remote stretch of the Appalachian Trail and there was no way of communicating with a normal phone, so he had bought a Garmin inReach, a lightweight device that allowed him to send text messages, as well as his location, if there was an emergency.

He had not needed it, other than to tell her each night that he loved her and Cherry.

It was possible one of these guys had something similar. It was the kind of thing they'd buy – a gadget designed for the wilderness that they would never use, but which would make them feel tough and outdoorsy. They probably kept it with their climbing magazines.

The jets appeared, level with her, one on each side. She could see the pilots. The one on the right glanced at her. He tapped his microphone.

Let's talk.

She nodded and opened the channel. His voice was crackly in her earpiece.

'You need to return to your approved flight path,' he said.

'I don't intend to do that.'

'You need to deviate to an airport. If you're low on fuel, we can help you find one. Otherwise, Portland is ready to receive you at any time.'

She looked at the pilot and shook her head.

'I'm afraid not,' she said, and cut the communication.

So the jets were here to escort them home. It was pointless. What could they do? Shoot her out of the sky? What good would that do? They would all die anyway, which was not a problem for her. And they weren't a threat to any civilians; they were over the ocean.

She closed her eyes. She was exhausted. This was nearly over now. Pretty soon they would be past the point where they could make it back to land, past the point where there were any decisions left to be made.

And she welcomed it. She'd had enough.

It was over. And she was glad.

Varun Miller

He had emailed Sharon asking for the organizational charts from when he was in Barrow.

He studied it. They were all there: Jill, him, Chip, Kevin, Jeff, Marcia. Then there were the other people, local to the research facility in Barrow. Tom Higgins, Susie Clarke, Dimitri Hodge, Bill Standish.

He looked them up in the corporate directory. Higgins and Clarke were still in Barrow. Hodge was in the Boston office.

There was no sign of Bill Standish. He remembered him – he was a wry, serious man who ran the research team. He wasn't much older than Miller.

He googled him.

Nothing. No Facebook, no Twitter, no news stories, no LinkedIn.

It was weird. There was no sign of him at the company, and if he'd left he'd still be in the workforce. He'd have some kind of online profile.

He IM'd Sharon.

Do you remember Bill
Standish?

> Yes. He was friends with my
> cousin, Janet.

What happened to him?

> He left. Took early retire-
> ment.

Early retirement? At what? Forty-five?

Very early! When did he leave?

> 2018. June, I think. I can
> check?

No, it's fine.

> How are things on the
> plane?

How did you answer that? Things were unbelievably awful,
a terrifying shit-show to end all shit-shows.

Not good. But no space
here to dwell on it.

He went back to the news stories and checked the dates.
June 9th and June 11th. Just before Standish had taken
early retirement, and not just retired, but – seemingly –
vanished.

Miller's neck prickled. There was something going on here.

Something that explained why the pilot was doing what she was doing.

Because maybe she was right.

He typed a message to Sharon.

This is urgent. Ask Marc Tanner to check the email archives for June 7–9, 2018 and see if there was any correspondence from Bill Standish to Jill Stearns, me, Chip, Jeff Ramos, Marcia or Kevin. I need this asap.

On it.

He was waiting for her to reply when something exploded. There was a noise like sheet metal being crumpled, or torn apart. He looked around, expecting to see half the plane missing, but it was still there.

Maybe it was thunder. He checked the window; nothing but blue skies.

'What the fuck was that?' Ramos said. They all turned to their windows, but there was nothing to see.

And then, out of nowhere, two military jets appeared, one on each side of the plane.

A white star, and the words *US Air Force*.

The cavalry had arrived.

Behind him, Marcia Fournier gave a little cheer. 'They're here,' she said. 'Finally.'

'Yeah.' Kevin Anderson was bent over in his seat, cradling his wrist with his uninjured hand. 'But what good's it going to do?'

'They can escort us to an airfield,' Marcia said.

'How? Threaten to blow us out of the sky unless the pilot does what they say? That's what she wants.' He shook his head. 'We're no better off than we were before.'

Anderson was right. Miller's stomach contracted. They were going to die. They really were.

The Pilot

She thought about Cherry, pictured her as a seven-year-old, as an eight-year-old, a nine-year-old. Imagined kissing her goodbye on her first day of junior high, holding her as she cried after her first heartbreak, telling her about Dan and how they had met.

Cheering as she graduated from high school.

Crying as she left her at college, the eighteen years of having her at home too short, but knowing that she had to grow up. Had to become an adult, so that, in turn she would be a grandmother.

She thought about Dan and the father he would have been. Steady, warm, loving. Not perfect, but not far off.

And not only to Cherry. To Baby Two. And maybe Three and Four.

But all that had been taken from her. And she wanted two things.

She wanted to know why. And she wanted justice. And this was how she was going to get it.

And if it didn't work?

She'd get the next best thing.

Revenge.

Jill Stearns

Anderson was wrong. They were better off. The arrival of the jets changed plenty. It didn't make things perfect, but it made them better. It gave them a chance they did not have before.

She leaned forward and beckoned to Jeff, Marcia, Mary Jo and Miller. Chip and Anderson were no use for what she had in mind.

'Listen,' she said in a low whisper. There was no time for passing notes. 'I have an idea.'

'What is it?' Jeff said.

'We break into the cabin.'

Jeff again. 'Kevin tried that. It didn't do much good.'

'I know. But he used brute force. If we can get a lever, then we might be able to open it.'

'We still need her to fly the plane,' Marcia said. 'She'll just crash it.'

This was what had changed when the jets arrived. 'Maybe not,' Jill said. 'We can overpower her – quickly – and the Air Force pilots can talk us through how to bring it down on water, as close to land as we can get. Then they can pick us up from the water. Get a Coast Guard vessel or something.'

'So we crash the plane? That's what she wants,' Ramos said.

'No. We land it on water.' She shrugged. 'It's not perfect, but it's the best we have.'

'It won't work,' Ramos said. 'It'll just piss her off. She'll slam this thing into the ocean.'

'Why so cynical?' Jill said. 'It's all we've got.'

'OK,' Marcia said. 'Let's assume we can. What's next?'

'We need a lever. Like a crowbar.'

'I didn't bring mine,' Jeff Ramos said. 'Left it at home.'

'What about the fridge?' Mary Jo said. 'It's bolted to the floor with a metal bracket.'

Jill knelt and looked at it. She gave a thumbs up. 'We need some way of undoing it. A tool kit. Is there anything on board?'

'Left my tool kit at home as well,' Ramos said.

'I have something.' Mary Jo reached into her bag. 'I have this. It's Ray's Christmas present for our son-in-law. I picked it up yesterday.'

Jill stared at her. She was holding a brand-new Leatherman. 'It's perfect,' she whispered.

The Leatherman opened out into a set of pliers. Jill knelt on the floor and squeezed hard on the first bolt and tried to turn it.

The jaws of the pliers slipped.

She squeezed harder and tried again.

The bolt turned a fraction of an inch. The next turn was easier, and, within a few seconds it was turning freely. The next two bolts were the same. She worked them free and slid the bracket out.

A slim, strong piece of metal.

A lever.

There was only one question left to answer. If this fit in the gap between the door and the frame, it might just work.

She walked slowly to the front of the plane, and slid it into the gap.

It fit perfectly.

301

The Pilot

What the hell was going on?

The sound of metallic scraping was coming from the door. She looked over her shoulder. It was bending outwards by the lock, as though it was being pulled hard.

As though someone was levering it open.

They would not get through. The doors were made to resist this kind of assault.

The scraping sound continued. The bend in the door deepened.

Then it stopped, and the door returned to normal.

She waited.

They would not have given up.

And then it came again, louder than before.

The door bent.

The lock strained.

She had no idea how they were doing this, but it looked like it was going to work.

She braced herself.

They would not get what they wanted.

Not now, not ever.

Varun Miller

Sharon's reply appeared on the screen.

> There are no emails at all from Bill Standish in that date range.

The alarm bell that had been threatening to sound at the back of his mind went off full bore.

It was *impossible*; there were no emails. There were always emails. The only way they were gone was if they had been deleted. It was possible there were other ways of getting to them – maybe there were some backups somewhere and, given time, someone would have been able to retrieve them.

But he did not have time.

What it told him, though, was that something *had* happened back then, and the evidence had been covered up.

With no proof, though, there was nothing he could do. He paused. Was there anything else he could look for? Phone records? Notes.

Instant Messages.

Of course: emails weren't the only way people send messages. He typed a note to Sharon.

Ask about IMs.

People thought instant messages were fleeting, less permanent than emails, and they were right. But they were not
impermanent. They were all stored, if you knew where to look.

A few minutes later, an email arrived. It contained three
instant message records.

They were from Bill Standish.

There's been an incident. Some kids got sick.

The reply was from an employee ID, and not a name. He
copied it and sent it to Sharon.

Who is this?

The reply was time-stamped one minute after the original
message.

What happened?

> I don't know. Only that four
> kids were taken to the
> hospital with some kind of
> organ failure. Maybe liver.

What's this got to do with
us?

> My son got hold of some
> product. He gave it to them.

What product?

Not yet on the market. We
were testing it and the
results weren't great.

OK. Say nothing to anyone.
Understood?

Miller's whole body went cold. This was it. This was the
smoking gun. The company had killed those kids. In error,
yes, but it was still their fault.

The fire was no error, though. It was a cover-up.

It was *murder*.

His IM flashed. It was Sharon.

Surprised you don't know that employee ID. It's Jill.

He stared up at Jill Stearns. She was standing by the cockpit
door, straining to force it open. Behind her, Jeff Ramos
watched, arms folded.

She had done this.

Oh, God. She had done this. He had to say something.

Before he could, there was a loud pop, then a bang as the
cockpit door swung violently open.

Jill Stearns

Jill pushed the door open hard and stepped through into the cockpit. Ramos stumbled and banged into her back; it knocked her off balance, but she recovered, ready to spring at the pilot.

She froze. The pilot was facing her, a gun pointed directly at Jill's chest.

It was a shock; she had never seen a gun before, much less had one pointed at her.

'Sit back down,' the pilot said. 'Both of you. Or I'll shoot you in the knee. And him.'

'No,' Jill said. 'I won't.'

'You will.' She tapped the fuel gauge. 'And it's nearly too late anyway,' she said.

'You're really going to do this?' Jill said.

'Yes.'

'What if you're wrong?'

'I'm not.'

'You are.'

The pilot shook her head. 'He said, she said. I know what happened.'

'It was a series of terrible accidents,' Jill said. 'Nothing more.'

'No,' the pilot said. 'Something poisoned the kids. Something Bill Standish's son, Kingsley, gave them at school. Something your company made. And you covered it up. My daughter survived, so you killed her. You thought I was dead, but I wasn't. And one of you knows what happened. That's all I want. The truth, and for justice to be done.'

'You've been waiting all this time?' Jill said. 'For this moment?'

'Waiting and planning,' the pilot said.

'What's your name? Not Sarah, right.'

'Stacy.'

Jill remembered the name. She paused. 'I feel for you. You've built your life around this. It's what gave you meaning after the loss of your husband and daughter. But it's all in your head, Stacy.'

'No. No, it isn't.'

'It is. And if you stop this now – while there's still time, just – I will personally make sure you get the help you need. You will not be punished. You will be helped.'

'No.'

'It's time, Stacy. You know I'm telling the truth.'

'You're lying. You're a liar.'

'It's painful to hear this, I know. But it's time to accept it and move on.'

'It's not true. It can't be.'

Jill reached out a hand. For a split second Jill thought the pilot – Stacy – was going to take it, then she gave a violent shake of her head, and shoved the control column forward.

307

Varun Miller

It was her. It was Jill. Maybe others, too. But definitely her.

He had to speak up, now, before the pilot did something stupid. He got ready to shout out *I know what happened! Stop this!*

He didn't get the chance. He was thrown forward, an invisible hand in his back thrusting him into the seat in front of him. Chip's body slumped against the front bulwark. Anderson squealed in pain from the sudden movement.

They had gone into a steep dive. He let out a shout – aware that somewhere on the plane someone was screaming – and looked out of the window. The blue-gray of the ocean filled his field of vision. It was impossible to say how far away it was, but one thing was clear.

It was getting closer, fast.

The engines whined. This was the end, then. This was his death.

How long did it take to crash a plane? Seconds? Minutes? That was what remained of his life. Scenes from his childhood, his wedding, Ari's birth flashed past him.

It was over. He closed his eyes and awaited the end.

And then the whine of the engines faded and the pitch of

the dive eased and the force in his back lessened and the plane was flying level.

He opened his eyes. Jill Stearns was standing by the main cabin door, looking at her colleagues, her expression set and grim.

'What happened?' Varun said. 'What did you do?'

'I told her the truth,' she said. 'I told her it was me. I did it.'

Barrow, Maine, December 2022

Stacy Evanston

Stacy ran her hand through her hair. It was short and black, and she was wearing green contact lenses. No one would recognize her from a distance; even up close she looked different, her face lean and gaunt.

Still, she looked warily down the street for a familiar face. At midday, it was more or less deserted.

Her house was gone. She'd expected that, of course. She'd watched it burn down three and a half years ago. She hadn't expected a new house to be there in its place. It was nearly finished, a van parked outside, the construction crew presumably finalizing the interior.

A new home, a new family: it was as though she and Cherry and Dan had never existed. They had been removed from the world and left no trace behind.

Except that would change soon enough. Soon enough their existence would matter.

A man in his early thirties in Carhartt pants and a dark T-shirt came out of the house. He opened the door to the van and took out a toolbox. He looked up at Stacy.

'Hi,' he said.

'Nearly done?'

'Couple of weeks.'

'Then onto the next job.'

'After we move in.'

Her throat tightened.

'This is your house?'

'Yeah. Been working on it for a while now.'

'You built it yourself?'

'Me and my brother.'

'Congratulations.'

'Thanks. We're looking forward to moving in. My wife and I have a five-year-old.'

'Boy or girl?'

'Girl.' He smiled. 'Another on the way.'

'Congratulations again.'

'Thanks again. Seems Barrow is a good place to raise kids.'

'It sure is.'

'You live here?'

She shook her head. 'Used to. I moved away a while back. Just here for the day now.'

'Did you enjoy living here?' There was something eager in his question, a need for validation of his choice to live in Barrow.

'I loved it,' she said. 'It was a shame it came to an end.'

'I'm sure you're enjoying where you live now.'

'You know,' she said. 'I can say with complete honesty that I wish we all still lived here.'

'So what brings you back for a day?'

'Just stuff to do. Getting ready for a new phase in life, so I wanted to see some old haunts.'

'Oh,' he said. 'Well, good luck with whatever comes next.'

2

She sat in the diner, coffee on the table in front of her. Next to it was a piece of paper. She unfolded it and read the names:

> Jill Stearns, chief executive officer
> Chip Markham, chief financial officer
> Jeff Ramos, chief technology officer
> Marcia Fournier, chief marketing officer
> Varun Miller, chief legal officer
> Kevin Anderson, chief operating officer

They flew in the company plane a lot. Together, sometimes. Such as after a board meeting, when they would all be returning to Portland.

At first she had pictured doing it just to scare them.

You killed my husband and daughter! And now I'm going to kill you!

But then she had thought, *Why not? Why not kill them? Why not get revenge?* She could explain it all as they went down.

And then she thought, *Why not make them confess? That would be the end of them and the end of the company.*

So she made her plan.

There was no way she could get a job flying the plane, but if she could find out when the flight was scheduled – and that was easy enough – she could hijack it. The hangar was low security, the two pilots complacent and unsuspecting. When she opened the door to their office all they would see was a woman they didn't recognize. She'd smile and hold out a bottle of water, a bottle that concealed the syringes.

A fast-acting sedative. Two syringes, one in each hand. Then she would lock them in, remove the barrel from the handle and get on board.

From there it should be plain sailing.

December 23rd, 2022

The Pilot

Stacy's throat was tight, her eyes wet. Out of the window she could see the white caps. The plane was level.

She had what she wanted. She could scarcely believe it.

I did it, Jill had said. *It was me. I did it.*

Still, she had needed proof.

Did what? Stacy said. The plane was dropping like a stone, the nose tilted down in a steep dive. *What did you do?*

And then it came. The story she had known was true. *Arranged a cover-up. Somehow the four kids got sick from one of our products. We couldn't let it leak so we covered it up.*

And the fire? she said.

Me too.

She had felt deflated. She had expected to feel joy or exultation or validation, but all she felt was tiredness. It was true, but so what? It wouldn't bring Cherry or Dan back.

So she had pushed the plane into a steeper dive.

Hey! It was Ramos. *You made a deal.*

She didn't respond. She gave herself up to the coming oblivion.

You're no better than her. You're a damn liar as well.

But she was not. She grabbed the control column and pulled back on it. The ocean was rushing up to meet them mere hundreds of feet away.

The plane didn't respond for a few moments, and then, slowly, leveled out.

Marcia Fournier

Marcia listened to Jill Stearns in the main cabin.

'What happened?' Varun said. 'What did you do?'

'I told her the truth,' she said. 'I told her it was me. I did it.'

'Jesus,' Jeff Ramos said. 'What the fuck, Jill?'

'What was I supposed to do?' she snapped at him. 'Let it come out? They were about to discover what happened and I had to stop it.'

Marcia stared at her. She had been pretty sure this was all a misunderstanding, and that Jill had been right – the pilot had it all wrong. Maybe it would be ironed out and they would make it home, or maybe the pilot, deranged and determined to gain revenge would kill them. But she had not thought it was real. Not for a moment.

And not Jill. Maybe Anderson, or Chip. Ramos, possibly. But not Jill.

'No way,' she said. 'It can't be true.'

'It is. I'm sorry.'

Marcia looked around the plane. Chip was dead, Jill had confessed to the murders of six people, Anderson had a broken wrist, and they were flying about a hundred feet over the surface of the ocean.

It was an unbelievable mess.

The pilot's voice came over the intercom. She sounded flat, more tired than anything else.

'Please take a seat. We're heading back.' She paused. 'We have barely enough fuel. But I think we can make it. I guess we'll find out.'

Jill walked back into the main cabin. Her face was fixed, her lips pressed together. Jeff followed her, and slumped into his seat.

The plane banked left and began to rise.

'So Jill,' Marcia said. 'What the fuck did you do?'

Kevin Anderson

Well, what the fuck. There was going to be a major shitstorm, but all that could wait. The good news was that it looked like he was going to get back for a weekend with Katie after all. He was going to get this wrist fixed up and in a cast and then invite her round to his apartment with a bottle of champagne and some coke and he was going to party all night long.

And then he was done with this shitty company. He was going to resign – they'd fire him anyway, after what he'd said, although given what was to come it made no difference, and it'd be bankrupt soon enough – and live it up for a few months, before finding some other gig.

It wasn't clear who he'd resign to, though. Until a few minutes ago it would have been Jill, but not now. She was fucked, well and truly fucked, and he was glad to see it. That bitch had never liked him and he had never liked her. Was it because he didn't like having a woman as a boss? Possibly. Probably, even, but the solution was simple enough. Work for a man next time.

He had to give her credit though. He was impressed she had the balls to pull off this kind of shit. Metaphorically, of course. He watched her sit down. She looked broken. He found it thrilling.

'So Jill,' Marcia said. 'What the fuck did you do?'

She didn't reply for a long time. Anderson wondered if she ever would, and then she spoke.

'I did what she said. What I just outlined.'

'Any more details, Jill?' Ramos asked.

'We were working on a new product. A synthetic sugar. Super dense, super cheap, easy to store and transport. It preserved food for longer, too. Kind of a magic bullet for our industry: we'd have better, cheaper, tastier products. We could have patented it, too, so if anyone wanted to compete they'd have to pay us for the rights to it.

'It was perfect,' she continued. 'Only it failed some early tests. It caused liver failure in mice, so we dropped it. Like many others.'

'I think I see where this is going,' Ramos said. 'So how did it get to those kids?'

'It was too valuable a product to give up, so a small group continued to research it. The group was led by Bill Standish. It was all off the books. Only me, Chip and the team knew. Standish was getting ready to test it again. He had some pellets ready to give to the mice. Somehow his son got hold of them and decided they were candy, and four of his friends might like to eat it.'

She took a deep breath.

'Then they started dying. Standish told me and I knew right away we couldn't let it get out. It would have torched the company, destroyed our reputation. So we covered it up. Got a doctor to say it was an inexplicable accident. Except one kid survived, and told her parents about the candy.'

'Jesus,' Ramos said. 'And Chip knew about this?'

'The product, yes. And the death of the kids.'

'The cover-up?'

319

She shook her head. 'I told him we had proof it wasn't the product after all, and so there was no problem. He wouldn't have gone for a cover-up, so I had to cut him out.'

'And the fire?' Ramos said.

'I paid for it,' Stearns replied, her eyes hard and hollow. 'I didn't know who did it – I just said I wanted it done and provided the money. Fifty thousand dollars. Not that much to remove a problem that could have cost us hundreds of millions, even billions.'

Kevin shook his head. Was it that easy? Was the country that corrupt? He'd always kind of thought so, but it was thrilling to discover it actually was. It opened all sorts of doors.

'The fire chief made sure there was no mention of arson. Just a tragic accident. He got a nice new Grady White boat out of it. And that was that. Problem solved. The girl and her parents were gone.'

'Except they weren't,' Marcia said. 'One of them survived the fire.'

'That's right,' Jill said. 'One of them did.'

The Pilot

It was hard to see through the tears.

Years of them, all at once. She had cried plenty in the months after the fire, but at some point the tears had stopped, replaced by an empty, unfeeling determination to get justice for her daughter and husband.

And now that moment had arrived.

She listened to Stearns – she could barely face even thinking her name – explain what had happened. She was so matter-of-fact, so *businesslike*. The company was going to have an expensive problem, so she got rid of it.

That was what her daughter and her husband were worth.

To her they were everything; to that woman they were close to nothing.

She had read that psychopaths were much more common than people thought – maybe one percent of the population met the definition. Remorseless, lacking empathy, focused only on getting what they wanted: was it any wonder that many of that one percent ended up as CEOs and CFOs and other business leaders?

Maybe it was a requirement: if you cared about other people even a little, how could you do what was needed?

Profit over people: that was designed into the system from the start, and she was just another example of it.

Well, this time Jill Stearns would not get what she wanted. Stacy would: she would have justice for Cherry and Dan and Ella and Dr. Williams and the two boys.

And then what?

What would she do with her life afterwards?

She didn't know. She didn't care. All she cared about was that her daughter and husband were not meaningless, and the world knew it. She would tell their story and the world would listen.

'Excuse me?'

There was a woman standing behind her. She was kind, grandmotherly, almost.

'Yes?'

'I'm Marcia Fournier.'

'I recognize the name.'

'Are you OK?'

She bit back the sob.

'Fine.'

'OK. This must be very hard.'

'Not as hard as the last few years.'

'No. I suppose not.' She hesitated. 'I was wondering whether we could have the Wi-Fi back on? I'd like to contact my husband. Tell him we're OK.'

Stacy was about to say *no, you can wait* but she paused. Why not? What harm could it do now?

'That's fine,' she said, and switched it on.

Marcia Fournier

She emailed Mike.

> Hey. You won't believe what happened. We should
> be OK now, but we'll have something to talk about
> when I get home. More than something! We kind of
> got hijacked. Love you.

So what happened now?

Chip was dead, and Jill was history. It was going to be a
rough time. Lawsuits, bad publicity, plummeting stock price,
difficulty raising capital. It was all to come.

The company would need leadership.

Someone established and trustworthy. A steady hand to
get them through.

Kevin Anderson was a joke, Miller was too young and
she was going to refocus on other things, not that she was
in the running anyway.

That left only one option. Ramos. He would bide his time,
let the board come to the right conclusion on their own.

There was a vibration from the engine and the plane
lurched down and to the left. She braced herself against her

seat. There was a high whine, and then the hum of the engines faded.

Perhaps she had emailed Mike too soon.

The intercom clicked on.

'We have a problem,' the pilot said. 'We're out of fuel.'

The two US Air Force jets disappeared out of view, rising above the plane. Except they weren't rising at all.

The plane was falling.

'Not now,' Marcia said. 'Not after all this.'

'Out of fuel?' Kevin Anderson said. 'What does that mean?'

The engines coughed, and spluttered, and died.

'That's what it means,' the pilot said. 'We're not far. But I don't think we'll make it.'

'And?' Marcia said. 'What then?'

'We ditch in the ocean. Everybody, take a seat, now! Make sure you're buckled up. Prepare for impact.'

Her phone pinged. It was a group text from Jill. Marcia didn't want to read it, didn't want anything to do with Jill. She had given her life to the company, and she felt nothing but disgust for what Jill had done.

Then she glanced at the message, and she understood what Jill had done.

This was not over yet. Not at all.

None of this was what it seemed.

The Pilot

She watched the islands of the Casco Bay pass by: Peaks Island, Great Diamond, Little Diamond. Portland Harbor was about a mile in the distance.

They were not going to make it.

They were going to ditch in the ocean. She adjusted the flaps to try and maintain altitude, but the plane slowed; she trimmed them to try to find the optimal balance.

The ocean came ever closer, the water black and lethal, roiling beneath them.

'Brace! Brace!' she shouted, and then they hit the water, hard. The plane slowed to a near immediate stop, water a far better brake than anything mechanical, and she was flung hard into the wall of the cockpit. The impact caused her to lose her bearings and it took a few moments before she was sure where she was and what was happening.

The plane was still, and silent, and then she heard a sound which reminded her of childhood days spent on the lake: the lapping of waves against a hull.

Except this was not a hull. This was the fuselage of an aircraft.

She clicked the radio on. It was dead, but they knew the

plane was here. It was just a matter of how quickly they could get there.

She looked out of the cockpit window. To the right was an island, the summer homes shuttered for the winter, the marina empty. No one left boats in year-round; the risk of storms or frozen seas was too great.

She measured the distance to the island. Maybe four hundred yards. Portland – where there were boats and people and warmth – was maybe a mile. So, if they had to swim, then the question was whether they could all make it that distance. She thought she could. She was a strong swimmer, but even so she was not sure. The water temperature at this time of the year would be what? Forty-eight degrees Fahrenheit? Less, maybe. That gave you about twenty minutes before hypothermia, and eventually death, set in.

Could they swim that far in that time? She had no idea.

What she knew was that they could not rely on the plane to float. If it was undamaged, it could – in theory – stay above the water for some time, but there was almost certainly damage. Hitting water at that speed was better than hitting the ground, but it still subjected the plane to massive stresses. There would be holes and cracks and they would only get worse.

So they had to get off the plane.

She reached for her life vest and got to her feet. The floor pitched and rolled as she walked back to the main cabin. It was an unnerving sensation, which underlined how much danger they were in.

The passengers stared up at her.

'Life vests on,' she said. 'We have to deplane.'

'Can't we stay on?' Jill Stearns said.

'No. If it starts to go under it could happen very quickly. We'll be trapped. So we get out. I'll go first.'

326

2

She had no idea what the temperature was, but as she slid into the ocean from the plane door it took her breath away. She waited a few moments for her body to adjust – as much as it was going to – and then took a few strokes away from the plane.

Kevin Anderson was next off, followed by Mary Jo and the others. There was a pause, and then Jill Stearns appeared. She gasped as she entered the water.

'We'll swim to the island,' Stacy said. 'It's the closest land.'

'I can't,' Kevin Anderson said. 'You broke my fucking wrist.'

Stacy did not feel like apologizing. 'You'll have to do your best.'

'Maybe we won't need to,' Marcia said. She was facing Portland. 'Look.'

In the distance two boats were moving rapidly toward them. One was a little ahead. At the speed it was moving it would be there in minutes.

Stacy watched it approach. It was a coastguard vessel, a large rib that could outrun anything else in the Casco Bay. The coastguard were very proud of it; whenever she had talked to them when she was in the Air Force, they had been sure to mention it. As it neared them, it slowed, then came to a halt a few feet from them. Two figures in all-weather suits leaned over the gunwale. One of them gave a thumbs up.

'Swim over,' he said. 'We'll pull you aboard.'

Stacy went last. Two hands gripped each of her wrists and hauled her over the side and onto the deck. The other passengers were already in a small cabin, wrapped in blankets.

The two coastguard officers looked at her. She read their names. Fred Coffin and Truman Kentley. Coffin handed her a blanket.

'Is there anyone else on the plane?' he said.

She nodded.

'How many?'

She held up one finger.

'Are they in good condition?'

She shook her head.

'Alive?'

Another shake of the head. Before Coffin could respond there was the wrenching sound of tearing metal. She turned to the plane. It was lower in the water. The sound came again, and it moved lower still, water rushing through the open door.

Slowly, it disappeared beneath the waves.

Kentley glanced at Coffin. 'We need to get these guys back asap,' he said.

Stacy pointed at the cabin. Jill Stearns was looking out at the spot where the plane had been.

'L-l-let me t-t-tell you,' she stammered. 'She's a m-m-murderer.'

Kentley nodded. 'Yes, ma'am. You can explain it all when we get back to shore.'

Marcia Fournier

Marcia waited in the entryway of the police station. Mike was on his way; he'd be there in minutes.

The return boat journey had been quick. They were met at the dock by what looked like a small army of police officers and hustled into a police cruiser each – they were warm, thankfully – and taken to the station.

She had been handed some dry clothes and coffee and then given her statement, outlining what had taken place. The police officer – a woman called Cindy – had smiled, and told her she was free to go, should watch for signs of hypothermia, and await a call from the police who would likely have further questions.

As she waited, Mary Jo Fernandez walked into the lobby. She smiled and came over to Marcia.

'OK?' she said.

'More or less. Not sure I'll sleep all that well, but – hey, just glad we're alive.'

'Same here. I didn't think we'd make it. Waiting for a ride?'

'My husband Mike's coming,' Marcia said. 'You?'

'Taxi. Ray's not up to driving.'

'Oh. Of course. We can pay,' Marcia said. 'For the cab.'

Mary Jo shook her head. 'That's OK. Looks like it's here.'

A yellow cab pulled up. The driver climbed out. 'Bags?' he said.

'Don't have any,' Mary Jo replied. 'Bye, Marcia.'

Marcia raised a hand. 'Bye. And good luck.'

The Pilot

The cars the others were in left immediately. She sat in the back of hers, blanket around her shoulders, waiting.

The door opened, and a man in a dark suit climbed in. He was holding handcuffs.

'Do I need these?' he said.

She shook her head.

'Good. Let's talk. Seems you hijacked a plane?'

'I can explain.'

'I'd hope so.' He held his hands palms up. 'You don't deny it, though?'

'How can I?'

'Good point. So?'

'I had no choice. She – Jill Stearns – is a murderer.'

He raised an eyebrow. 'She is?'

'Yes. She killed six people. One was my daughter.'

'And this was your revenge?'

'No. This was my way to get a confession. To get justice.'

'And you got the confession?'

Stacy nodded. 'I did.'

The man put his hand on the door handle. 'I'll be back. We can discuss this more at the station.'

331

He left and she smiled to herself as she thought of Stearns. They would soon be telling her they knew what she had done. Maybe even at that moment, Stearns would be understanding what had happened, coming to terms with the seriousness of it, accepting what the future held for her.

Disgrace, and a prison cell.

No doubt the stock price of the company would plummet, but none of that mattered to her. That was not – and had never been – her motivation. Her motivation was Cherry and Dan, and them alone.

No doubt also that she would be in a whole heap of trouble herself. She thought she would be OK, though, in the end. Once the story was public there would be an outpouring of sympathy for her; yes, technically she had done something wrong, but the morality – the overall morality – was clear.

And if the judge didn't see it that way, she was fine with that, too.

Most of all, she was simply exhausted. If they put her in a cell she would sleep for days. The last few years she had existed in a state of nervous tension, constantly on edge. It was only now, when this was finished, that she realized what it had taken from her.

The exhaustion overwhelmed her. Her eyelids were heavy; she let them close, and then, the quiet of sleep.

She was woken by the car door opening. A uniformed officer sat next to her. He did not speak. The car pulled away and headed for Portland. She watched the streets go by, calm and content with how this had ended.

It was what she had wanted. Whatever the consequences for her, this was what she had chosen.

The car reached the police station. They waited to turn into a parking lot. Outside, people walked along the streets, illuminated by the streetlights.

In front of the station, Marcia Fournier was hugging someone – presumably her husband. Her life would be different, the company she worked for in the media spotlight, but she'd be OK.

And then another figure she recognized appeared in the entrance'.

It was Jill Stearns.

She looked left, then right, then headed toward the city center.

Something was wrong here. Something was very wrong. Why was she walking away? Why hadn't she been arrested?

Her throat constricted.

What had she told them? What lies had she made up?

She tried the door; it was locked. The officer put his hand on her forearm.

'Don't,' he said. 'You're in enough trouble as it is.'

PART THREE

December 23rd, 2022

Stacy Evanston

The interview room was about ten feet by ten feet and windowless. She was sitting on a hard plastic chair on one side of a wooden table. There was an unopened bottle of orange juice in front of her. On the other side were two chairs.

She'd been here about half an hour. On arrival they had taken her prints and driving license and booked her in.

She was trying to remain calm, telling herself this would work out as she had planned, but she kept catching herself drumming a pattern on the table with the tips of her fingers.

Because she was nervous. This was not what should be happening. No one – up to now – would listen. She had tried to explain but her words went unheeded. She wanted to scream: after all these years with no voice, it seemed nothing had changed.

Yet. Yes, Stearns was free, but not for long. Eventually she would get to tell her story and this would all be set right. She had all the proof she needed.

But still, she was confused, and that made her uneasy.

The door opened. A woman – about her age – in a dark suit walked in, followed by a tall, shaven-headed man in his thirties. She pulled out a chair and sat down. The man remained standing.

'Stacy Evanston?' she said. 'My name's Annie Mitchell. This is my partner, Oscar Strand. You've been read your rights?'

'Yes.'

'And you don't want a lawyer?'

'I don't need one.'

'Sure?'

'Sure. Once I explain you'll understand.'

'As you wish. I just want it on record that this was done by the book.' She held up a driving license. 'They took this when they booked you in.' She read the name. 'Sarah Daniels. You gave the name Stacy Evanston when we booked you in. I take it you're not Sarah Daniels?'

'No, ma'am.'

'You're Stacy Evanston?'

'I am.'

'The same Stacy Evanston presumed killed in a house fire in 2018?'

'Correct.'

'Which means you weren't killed in a house fire after all?'

'No,' Stacy said. 'I wasn't.'

'Want to explain what happened?'

'I got out. My husband and daughter didn't.'

'I'm sorry about that.'

Stacy shrugged. 'Don't be.'

'And then you disappeared?'

'Yes.'

'Why?'

'Because I realized what had happened.'

'Which was?'

'They had made the kids sick somehow, and three of them had died. The doctor figured it out, so they killed him. Then

338

they came after me, Dan and Cherry because we knew their dirty little secret.'

Mitchell glanced at her partner. He raised an eyebrow.

'Who is *they*?' Strand said, his tone skeptical.

'Jill Stearns. Maybe others in her company.'

Strand folded his arms. 'Ms. Stearns mentioned you might say this.'

'Of course she did. I told her on the plane.'

'And you believe this to be true?' Mitchell asked.

'I know it is.'

'You understand how far-fetched this sounds?' Mitchell said.

Stacy nodded. 'That's the reason I had to do what I did. Who was going to believe me? So I had to get the truth another way.'

'And that way was?'

'I knew one of them had the answers. So I had to put them in a position where they had no choice other than to come clean.'

'And that way was to threaten them with crashing the plane unless they did so?' Strand said.

'Correct. And it worked. Stearns confessed.'

'Right,' Mitchell said. 'Except there's no evidence for what you're claiming. The fire was an accident – the fire department report confirms that – the doctor committed suicide – the medical records confirm that – and the three children who died had nothing to do with any company. It was just a tragic accident. It's clear.'

It was as though they had not heard what she said about the confession.

'The records were falsified, and the people who created them were paid off. She said that.'

'Do you have any evidence of that?' Strand said.

'No. But I bet it's there, if you look. That's the whole point: no one would look unless I forced them to.'

'This kind of stuff doesn't happen,' Mitchell said. 'Outside of conspiracy theories.'

'It did in this case. But didn't you hear what I said? She confessed. Jill Stearns confessed to it all.'

Mitchell's gaze flicked to Strand. He leaned forward.

'She confessed to *nothing*,' he said.

'She confessed to *everything*. All the other passengers heard her.'

'Not according to her. Or them.'

So that was her story. Stacy had seen it coming: get on land and say she never said it. No doubt the others were backing her up. Why wouldn't they? They had stocks in the company; a scandal would cost them a lot of money.

Which was why she had made a recording. They had taken her phone when they booked her in, but she had insurance.

She reached into the watch pocket of her jeans and pulled out a small, silver bullet-shaped device. She put it on the table.

'Listen,' she said.

2

It was me. I did it.

It was faint, but audible, and definitely Stearns. Stacy stopped the recording. 'That's her. Jill Stearns.' She pressed the play button. 'There's more.'

Stearns's words came from the small recorder.

We were working on a new product . . . Kind of a magic bullet for our industry . . . we'd have better, cheaper, tastier products . . . only it failed some early tests . . . a small group continued to research it . . . Somehow his son got hold of them and decided they were candy, and four of his friends might like to eat it.

'You see?' Stacy said. 'You see now what happened?'

Then they started dying . . . So we covered it up . . . I just said I wanted it done and provided the money. Fifty thousand dollars. Not that much to remove a problem that could have cost us hundreds of millions, even billions . . . And that was that. Problem solved. The girl and her parents were gone.

She looked at Mitchell. 'Except I survived. And here I am.'

'And you did all this?' Strand said. 'Stole a plane, kidnapped seven people, potentially caused one to have a fatal heart attack?'

'I didn't mean for that to happen.'

'You don't deny it, though?'

'How can I?'

'And the pilots who were supposed to fly the plane? You locked them in an office?'

'They'll be fine.'

'Maybe. But what you did is a felony, nonetheless. They got out and told us what had happened. By then you were gone, of course. But we can add that to the list of crimes.'

Stacy held up her hands. 'Listen, I don't mind what you put on the list. This was the only way I could get justice for my husband and daughter. You think I care about what you think? About going to prison? My life was over the night they died. All I care about is seeing Jill Stearns pay the price for what she did.' She tapped the recorder. 'And she will.'

Strand looked at Mitchell. 'You want to tell her? Or should I?'

'I will.' Mitchell folded her arms. 'It gives me no pleasure to do this,' she said. 'I feel for you. I can't imagine what you've gone through. But you have invented all of this to make yourself feel better about what was a tragic accident.'

'No. I have not.'

'It's quite common. People want meaning. It's hard to accept that the universe is cruel, so they look for a villain. But there's nothing here.'

Stacy's voice rose. 'I have a CONFESSION!'

'You have nothing. This confession is worthless. Stearns made it to stop you crashing the plane. She told us this already. One of the other passengers tried a false confession, but you knew she was lying because she didn't know the details. But you gave enough details when you told them what your theory was – the deaths, the cover-up, the fire – so that she was able to convincingly confess to it. But she was lying, Ms. Evanston.'

342

Stacy's skin tightened and crawled.

'No,' she said. 'She's just saying that now. She *confessed*. You heard it.'

'She faked it, to get you to stop.'

'No. NO!' Stacy banged her fists on the desk. 'You can't let her get away with this!'

'There's no evidence,' Strand said. 'There's no evidence any of this happened. There wasn't then, and there isn't now.'

'You have to investigate!'

'We have to have something *to* investigate,' Mitchell said. 'And there's nothing here.'

'Is she paying you too?' Stacy shouted. 'Is that what's happening?'

Mitchell shook her head. 'I don't have to listen to this. If you want my advice, get yourself a good lawyer. Other than that, this interview is over.'

December 24th, 2022

Kevin Anderson

DRAMATIC PLANE KIDNAP ENDS IN TRAGEDY

A plane was stolen yesterday and the passengers kidnapped, in what appears to be a senseless and random crime.

A woman, Stacy Evanston, 40, managed to lock the pilots in an office in the hangar where the private jet was parked. She posed as a pilot, then, when the plane was in the air, headed off the flight path and threatened to crash the plane for reasons that remain unclear.

One of the passengers was able to alert the authorities, who sent two air force planes to escort the jet to a safe landing at a military base.

Tragically, one of the passengers, whose identity has not yet been released, suffered a fatal heart attack.

Ms. Evanston is currently in custody, facing a suite of charges. Her motivation – if she has one – is not yet known, and may never be.

Kevin Anderson's wrist was in a cast as of this morning, but it was still fucking painful, despite the opiates he had taken in numbers much higher than suggested by the rubric on the side of the pill bottle. That said, he had drunk most of a bottle of champagne and the opiate / alcohol buzz was a thing of great beauty, like Katie, who had come to meet him at the hospital with a worried frown and a promise to take care of him.

And she had, as soon as they got back to his apartment. *Does it hurt?* she said. *Is there anything I can do to help? Yeah,* he replied. *There's one thing.*

I'll be gentle, she said.

That – and the pills and booze – had worked wonders. Yes, even through the haze he could feel the pain in his wrist, but that would pass.

This had been a great start to the rest of his life.

Because that was the other thing. He was fucking done with Stearns and the rest of them. She'd claimed it was a bullshit confession – he wasn't so sure, it was exactly what he would have done, if he'd had the balls, which, if he was honest he wasn't sure he would have, Stearns was a hard bitch, she really was – so she was still the CEO, and after what he'd said on the plane it was walk or be forced to walk.

So he'd walked. He told her as they got off the boat.

She said, *I'm not sorry to see you go, but stay in touch, Kev, OK? In fact, maybe don't bother.* And he'd said, *Fuck you too, you sarcastic bitch,* and she'd said, *Where was that character the last fifteen years, huh?* which had kind of hurt, he had to admit.

But not that much. He was glad to be gone and glad he'd said what he did to that little fucker Miller. He'd get another job – a better one – and until then he had plenty of money. That was the dirty secret – they paid you so much you were invulnerable. Fire me; have at it. Doesn't make a blind bit of difference.

And it left him free to enjoy himself with Katie. Maybe it was his money that attracted her, but he didn't care. Just *look* at her. She was fucking sensational.

He tapped her on the ass.

'Read this.' He passed her his iPad. 'Made it to the *Globe*.'

She propped herself up on her elbow.

'Let me see.' She read the story. 'They're not saying everything, huh? Her motivation is not yet known? You said she wanted justice. I think it was revenge.'

'They're not going to print that. Stearns wouldn't let them.'

'You think she did it? Had them killed?'

'Wouldn't surprise me. But we'll never know.'

'I can't *believe* you went through that.'

'I know.'

'At least you tried something, unlike the others.'

He'd made sure to emphasize his heroic attempt to storm the cockpit, and the agonizing result.

'Yeah. I couldn't just sit there.' He looked at the clock. Nearly 2 p.m. He was due another pill in four hours. He opened the bottle and shook two out. 'One for you, one for me.' He swallowed it, and swigged some champagne to wash it down. He handed her the bottle. 'I made it, though. Let's celebrate.'

She popped the pill. 'If she did it,' she said. 'You could get your job back. Tell her you know the truth and unless she agrees you'll tell everyone.'

It was such an absurd suggestion that he burst out laughing.

'Yeah?' he said. 'You think so? If I did, I'd be next. You don't know Jill Stearns. She's got this locked down, and there's no way she's ever letting go.' He reached over and put his hand on her thigh. 'I'm done with all that, and I'm glad. All the more time to spend with you.'

She kissed him and ran her hand up his leg. 'Again?' she said. 'Already?'

He needed the bathroom. 'Give me a minute.'

He walked to the bathroom and stood in front of the toilet. He scrolled through his messages. There was one from Laura.

346

How've you been? Let's catch up soon.

He was done with her. He had Katie.
But still. She was attractive enough, and available.
And it would be fun to have sex with both of them in one day. He could tell Katie he needed to go into the office to get his stuff, meet Laura for an hour, and be back in time for a late dinner.

Yeah! Sorry – been busy. Are you free around five? I've got some work stuff later but could swing by for an hour or so then?

Dots scrolled along the bottom of the screen before the reply appeared.

Going out with the girls in a bit but that sounds good. See you then. My place?

Yes, her place. He could hardly have her here while Katie was around, although there was a thought.
Fuck, retirement was fun.

Jill Stearns

Mila sat on the couch, her head on Jill's shoulder. It had been years since she'd done that. Jill tried to recall the last time; she thought it was probably when she was seventeen and Clark, the handsome, athletic son of a billionaire hedge fund manager, had dumped her for a girl who ran track, had a 4.0 GPA and was hellbent on a career in finance.

Mila had got over it quickly enough, but Jill had always thought of Clark as the one who got away. He was certainly better than Archie, who had cried for a good half an hour after she got home the night before.

I'm just so glad you're OK, Mrs. Stearns. I can't stop thinking about what you went through and how awful it must have been.

The worst part was how Mila had looked at him as he spewed this drivel. Her expression was pride – at what, Jill could only guess, but she assumed it was his sensitive, emotional side.

She told him not to worry. It hadn't lasted long and she was fine. He just shook his head. This was evidently too good an opportunity to feel another's pain not to be fully exploited, and he exploited it to the maximum.

He was still at it in the morning. He was sitting opposite them wearing an awful, caring smile. 'Can I get you something? Coffee? Water?'

'Water, please,' Jill said. He might as well make himself useful. 'Seltzer, if we have some.'

'Sure. Mila, darling?'

'No thanks.' Mila sat upright. 'So,' she said. 'I know you've had the worst time, but we do have some news.'

Of course. The news. It had crossed Jill's mind on the flight up to Portland, but she hadn't asked. She'd hoped it might have gone away.

'Yes,' she said, and smiled. 'We were going to have dinner last night. You were paying, if I remember?'

'We could go for brunch,' Mila said.

'I think I'd rather stay here for now,' Jill said. 'And anyway, I can't wait any longer.' Her eyes flicked to Mila's stomach and she raised an eyebrow. 'What's the news?'

Mila laughed. 'Not that,' she said. 'Not yet, anyway.' She beckoned Archie to come over. He sat on the edge of the couch, his hand on Mila's knee.

Oh shit. It was obvious what this was.

'I want to ask you for something,' Archie said. 'The most precious thing you have.'

'My diamond Rolex?' Jill said. 'It's probably too small for you.'

He laughed, although not with his eyes. His big moment was not a matter for joking.

'Not that,' he said. 'Something infinitely more valuable. I want to ask for your permission to marry your daughter.'

No, she thought. *No fucking way. Maybe I should say that. Tell him he doesn't have my permission. But then what? They'd get married anyway, which was why, apart from the fact she didn't want her daughter to marry this half-baked loser, this was a fucking stupid situation.*

'Well,' she said. 'You don't have to ask my permission. It's not up to me.'

'I would like it,' Archie said. 'It means a lot to me to get your blessing.'

There was a long, awkward pause.

'It's really not up to me,' she said.

'Maybe,' Archie replied, 'but we'd like to know you fully support our union.'

'I do. I fully support it.'

It was an outrageous lie, but what was she supposed to say?

'Thank you.' His eyes filled with tears. 'This means everything to me.'

She forced herself to smile. 'I just hope she says yes.'

'Mom!' Mila said. 'Of course I'll say yes!'

'In that case' – Archie got down on one knee and pulled a small ring box from his jeans pocket, which he opened to show a really quite pathetic diamond – 'would you do me the honor, Mila Stearns, of agreeing to be my wife?'

It was a sickening display.

'Yes!' Mila said. 'Yes, yes, yes!'

She jumped up and hugged him, then kissed him for a long time. Jill looked away; when she looked back they were staring at her, expectantly.

She stood up and put a hand on each of their shoulders.

'I'm *so* pleased,' she said. 'I know you'll make each other very happy. Congratulations.'

Archie knelt again and took out the ring. Mila extended her hand and he slipped it onto her finger.

'Could I see it?' Jill said. She held her daughter's hand and pretended to examine it. 'It's beautiful. Perfect.'

She kissed Mila. This was a disaster, but at least it wasn't a baby. They were permanent, unlike the Archies of this world.

'Congratulations, Mila,' she said. 'I love you.'

And she did, in a way, which was why this wedding was never going to happen. She didn't know how she was going to stop it, yet, but she would.

She would get what she wanted. She always did. She couldn't rest if she didn't, it would eat away at her, keep her awake. It was as though the universe was out of alignment and she could not settle.

It was like that with the sick kids in Barrow. She'd felt bad, of course – she wasn't heartless – but she'd had no choice. If she hadn't acted, it would have ruined everything. She had to stop them, and there was only one way.

And when you thought about it, it made sense. For the families it was a tragedy, but what was that when counted against the alternative? The demise of a huge company, massive job losses, disruption to the food supply? That would cause misery for tens or hundreds of thousands of people, so yes, the death of a few children was sad, but surely it was preferable to the suffering of all those people?

It was a tough decision, but that was what she was paid to do. Take tough decisions, see the bigger picture. And that left her with only one real option.

She had not counted on Evanston, though. She admired her. She had done amazingly well to get as far as she did, but sadly for her she had fallen at the last fence. Jill had seen the path to put this to bed once and for all – a confession, then a retraction.

She had had to time it well – if she had confessed earlier, she would have been like Marcia, so she had needed to wait until Evanston had given her enough information, and the situation had become critical enough that Evanston would believe she was cracking under pressure, and then it was time.

And, in the end, as always, she had got what she wanted.

351

As she would with Mila. Archie would not be marrying her daughter. She didn't know what would happen to stop it – an affair, under-age porn on his computer, a gambling problem – but she would come up with something that would look very convincing.

It would be fun. Something to keep her occupied.

She smiled at Archie. 'Congratulations,' she said. 'Welcome to the family.'

Marcia Fournier

Lunchtime, on Christmas Eve. Perfect time for a drink. She stood by the fridge, her hand on the door.

There was a bottle of white wine in there, calling to her.

The night before, Mike had picked her up from the police station and brought her home. Her car was in the lot but he had insisted. On the way back she had studied his face in the lights of the freeway. She knew it so well, every detail as familiar as the detail of her own body. The tufting eyebrows, the slight purse of the bottom lip, the bend where he had broken his nose in college: she had seen all of them thousands of times.

And yet this time was different. This time she felt she was looking at someone unfamiliar, but it was not him who had changed. It was her.

When they arrived home he opened the fridge.

Drink? You must need one?

She did, but not in the way he meant. She needed it in a much deeper, much worse way. She needed it in a cellular way, she needed it to rebalance her body's chemistry to a state in which she was comfortable.

But she had decided that was all over. The drinking was done. She had changed.

Had she, though? Because she couldn't stop the voice in her head telling her that one wouldn't hurt. Especially after the day she'd had. She could start quitting tomorrow.

Like she had before. She had decided to quit tomorrow many, many times, but it seemed tomorrow never came.

And she hadn't told anyone other than the people on the plane. She could carry on drinking if she wanted. She'd made no promises, other than the ones she'd made to herself, and she'd broken so many of those they were now meaningless.

So had she changed? Had she really?

Why not try, she thought. *Say no, and deal with tomorrow, tomorrow.*

Yes, she said. *That would be great.*

She drank most of the bottle, and sneaked in a vodka too. Quitting could wait until tomorrow.

Well, tomorrow was today. She opened the fridge door. The bottle was there, crisp and cold. Her mouth filled with saliva.

'Bit early, isn't it?' Mike was in the doorway.

'Christmas Eve,' she said. 'Why not?'

'Not for me. I have to go and see Mom. She won't know who I am, but you know.'

She felt a thrill run through her. When he was gone she could drink as much as she liked. Just two glasses of wine so there was half a bottle left in the fridge when he came back, but then there was the rest: vodka on ice, perhaps a little tequila. She could sink into her drunkenness undisturbed.

She'd made no promises. It would be different if she had, if she'd got home and declared to Mike she was an alcoholic and she was never drinking again. Then she'd have to stop. But she hadn't done that.

So she'd get drunk, and wake up with a hangover and a feeling of self-loathing.

Nothing had changed, really. It felt that way on the plane, but now she was home, nothing had changed at all. He would leave and she would get drunk, on her own, and for no reason other than that she had no choice.

That was her life. Struggle through the workday, come home, get drunk. She used to play tennis in the evenings, go to the theater, meet a friend for gelatos. She did none of that now. She couldn't go out at 8 p.m. to play tennis, because she couldn't stay sober until then. She should go and visit her mother-in-law but no: that would mean she missed an opportunity to drink free and undisturbed.

She knew this. She knew all this. She sat there knowing what she was going to do, and she was powerless to stop it.

'Everything OK?' Mike said. 'You look lost in thought.'

'Nothing.'

'OK. I'll be back by three. Love you.'

This was it. This was the moment. This was her chance to say *I'll come with you* and leave the house and get away from the drink. But she had faced this moment many times, and it had always ended the same way.

'See you later,' she said. 'Give her a kiss from me.'

2

She heard the key in the lock. The bottle was on the table in front of the couch, the corkscrew and glass next to it.

He came into the room and put his jacket on the arm of the couch.

'It's cold out,' he said.

'How was your mom?'

'Same.' He sighed. 'It's hard. She has no idea who I am. She can get quite belligerent.'

'I'm sorry.'

'You have a good afternoon?'

'It was.'

'What did you do?'

'Not much.'

He sat next to her, and looked at the bottle. He ran his finger down the side. 'That's getting warm. It's better in the fridge.'

'I got it out when you left. It's been there a few hours. I've been here, looking at it.'

'Right.' He drew the word out. 'Marcia, you want to tell me you've been staring at a bottle of wine for most of the afternoon.' He tapped the neck of the bottle. 'An *unopened* bottle of wine?'

'Mike,' she said. 'I have a problem.'

As she said the words it was as though she started to float, a weight gone from her shoulders.

'What is it?' he said.

'I'm an alcoholic,' she said. 'And I need help.'

December 25th, 2022

Varun Miller

Father Christmas had been kind to Ari, and to Susheela. Varun felt some guilt – well, a lot – at how much time he spent at work, so he tried to make up for it by spending lots of money on presents. He knew it was a cliché, but he didn't care. If he wanted to spoil Ari, he would, and in any case he wasn't sure he could stop himself.

Not that Ari knew. As far as he was concerned the presents were just more plastic trucks and cars and animals; after they'd opened a few with him, he'd reverted to his favorite toy, a stuffed leopard Susheela's mom had bought him. Varun wondered why he kept going back to that one – perhaps it was the smell, or the familiarity.

Either way, he didn't care. He was simply happy to be alive, happy to be with his family.

Which Stacy Evanston wasn't.

Her daughter and husband were dead.

He pushed the thought away. It was a house fire, tragic and heartbreaking, but an accident. It could have happened to anyone. It had been investigated, and the proper authorities had determined that was all it was.

There was no way Jill Stearns was responsible. He heard her words again.

Fifty thousand dollars. Not that much to remove a problem that could have cost us hundreds of millions, even billions. The fire chief made sure there was no mention of arson. Just a tragic accident.

She had only said it to convince the pilot to stop. Nothing she said – nothing anyone said – in those circumstances could be relied on. He was a lawyer, he knew that no court in the country would admit a confession obtained in that way.

And as for the idea she had somehow covered up that the cause of the three kids' deaths had been caused by some experimental product – that was ludicrous.

At least, in the absence of other evidence it was.

Evidence like a message from Bill Standish to Jill linking the product to the deaths.

And if an investigator had *that*. Well, they might start digging, and then what would they find? *Was* the doctor's suicide a suicide? *Did* the fire chief really get a new boat around that time? Cover-ups depended on leads not being followed, on trails going cold, questions not being asked, but if people who knew how and had the means – lawyers, say – started digging, then the truth would be there to be found, and it would come out. If Stearns had made sure these leads went dead, the evidence would be there.

And if – just suppose – a lawyer was in possession of that evidence but didn't bring it forward, what then? Would that lawyer be complicit?

The answer was obvious. That lawyer would be both breaking the law, and worse, crossing a clear moral line.

It would, though, destroy the company, and take his career – and the millions he had in stock and options – with it.

Who would employ him after that, even if he was innocent? No company would want the taint attached to them.

And he *could* just keep quiet. No one would ever know. Sharon would, but he could smooth that over. Tell her it was all part of how they got off the plane. This would all fade away, and it wasn't like doing anything would bring back the people who had died.

He looked at Ari. Susheela was kneeling next to him, brushing her nose on his then peeling away, both of them giggling uncontrollably.

Stacy Evanston had had this. And it had been taken from her.

Three others had suffered the same fate.

'Babe,' he said. 'Can we talk?'

2

'What is it?' Susheela put her hand on his bicep. 'You look worried? Are you – did something happen? Are you ill?'

He shook his head. 'No. I'm fine. But' – he took a deep breath – 'on the plane I learned something. Something important.'

'OK?'

'You remember that Jill made a false confession? To stop the pilot?'

'Right.'

'What if it wasn't false?'

'You said it was.'

'What if it wasn't?'

'I don't understand. Jill didn't do it. She *wouldn't*. There's no reason to think she did. It's a tragic accident.' She put her hand on his shoulder. 'I know it's hard to accept, but accidents happen. And she said it was a false confession.'

'If it wasn't, though? What then?'

'Why would it not be? There's no evidence otherwise.'

'Maybe there is.'

Susheela stepped back from him.

'What do you mean, exactly?' she said.

361

This was the moment. 'I found something. Before she confessed. I was going to tell the pilot, but then there was no need.'
'What did you find?'
'A message.' He picked up his iPad. 'Here. Take a look.' He called up the message, and showed it to her.

There's been an incident.
Some kids got sick.

What happened?

I don't know. Only that four kids were taken to the hospital with some kind of organ failure. Maybe liver.

What's this got to do with us?

My son got hold of some product. He gave it to them.

What product?

Not yet on the market. We were testing it and the results weren't great.

OK. Say nothing to anyone. Understood?

Susheela stared at him. 'Who's Bill Standish?'
'The guy who ran the research center in Barrow.'

'And the other person? There's no name. Just an ID.'

'I checked it out. That's Jill.'

Susheela didn't reply. Her jaw clenched and unclenched and she rocked back and forth on the balls of her feet.

'I see,' she said. 'That complicates things.'

'I know.'

'And you said nothing?'

He shook his head. 'I was going to, on the plane, but then she confessed.'

'And if she did that, then' – Susheela stared at him. 'She did the fire too.'

'I know,' Varun said quietly. 'I know.'

Susheela gave a small shake of her head. 'This can't be happening.'

'I know. But if it is? What do you think I should do?'

She folded her arms. 'I don't think you need me to give you an answer. I think you know, which is why you told me this in the first place.'

'I look at Ari,' he said. 'And I think that if it was him and you in that fire, I'd never get over it. I'd want justice to be done.' He held her gaze. 'So what now?'

She smiled. 'You know. There's only one option, Varun.'

3

He needed to discuss this with someone, and someone he could trust. Someone who had been around for a while and who had a spotless record. A man of honor. A veteran.

Ramos picked up on the second ring.

'Jeff,' he said. 'Hope I'm not bothering you. And Merry Christmas, by the way.'

'No bother at all. Same to you. Just another day to me. How's the family?'

'Great. It's wonderful to be back together. I wasn't sure we would be.'

'No. It was a close-run thing in the end.'

'I'll be processing it for a while,' Varun said. 'It'll stay with me, for sure.'

'No doubt. So. What's up? You don't call me on Christmas Day for no reason.'

'Right. Well, something came to light, on the plane.'

'You sound on edge, Varun.'

'I am.'

'Why?'

This was it. 'I think she did it, Jeff.'

Ramos paused. 'You'll have to be more specific. Who are we talking about, and what did she do?'

'Jill. We're talking about Jill.'

Ramos laughed, loud and long. 'Have you been drinking already? Jill made all that up. She said so.'

'I have reason to believe she didn't,' Varun said. 'Are you at your computer?'

'I can be.'

'Then I'll send it. Call me back when it arrives.'

It was twenty minutes before Ramos called. His tone was grim.

'Sorry it took so long,' he said. 'I had to log in and then I had to read it a few times before it sunk in. You realize that this is fucking dynamite?'

'I know.'

'At the very least it will trigger an investigation, which will leak, and that alone will be bad news for the company.'

'We still have to bring it forward.'

'No doubt about that,' Jeff said. 'But we have to be careful.'

'What do you mean? It seems clear to me. We have to tell the proper authorities.'

'I know we do. I'm not suggesting otherwise. What I'm saying is we have to be careful how we do that. If we get it wrong, Jill will find a way out, and we'll have missed the opportunity.'

'I still don't get it.'

'The problem is we don't have enough evidence. She can simply say that the message was about something else, or spin another story. Or maybe there's a procedural problem with how it came into your possession, and her lawyers squash it. Or she says it wasn't her at all? This is a start, but it won't cut it. We need more. We need a smoking gun. It needs to be irrefutable.'

'I think it's enough.'

'It's nowhere near enough. It's enough for you, but not a court, not against her team of lawyers. All she needs is reasonable doubt. We need to take that away. And remember, she's ruthless. If she finds out we're poking around, we'll be next to have an accident. This has to be cut and dried.'

'You're saying we?' Varun said.

'Yes,' Jeff replied. 'We. If she truly did this, she needs to pay the price. I can't stand by and let an injustice of this magnitude pass. So yes, we. It'll cause chaos, but that's how it has to be. We get more evidence.'

'And how do we do that?'

'The fire is the key. Get proof she ordered that and it's over.'

'Sounds good. But now can I point out a problem?'

'Shoot.'

'How? How do I do that?'

'I don't know. But it starts with the pilot, Evanston. She was there. She knows what happened. We need her.'

'She's in a cell.'

'Then get her out. Get her a bail hearing and get her out. Then bring her to me and we'll decide what the hell we do.'

'Bail?' Varun said. 'There's no chance she'll get bail.'

'We'll need another solution, then.'

'Like what?'

'I don't know. But it won't be easy.'

December 27th, 2022

Stacy Evanston

The cop stood in the doorway.

'Your lawyers are here to see you.'

She frowned. She had not been expecting this.

'I didn't ask for lawyers,' she said.

'That's what he said you'd say. They said to give their names and see if that changed your mind.'

'Oh? What are they?'

'Miller. Varun Miller. And Jeff Ramos.'

Miller? He was the last person she would have expected, and Ramos wasn't even a lawyer.

So what the hell were they doing here?

'Send them in,' she said.

A few minutes later, Miller and Ramos came into the interview room. Miller was wearing a smart suit; Ramos was in a leather jacket.

'Ms. Evanston,' Miller said. 'Thank you for seeing me.' He gestured to the officer in the door to leave. 'I'd like to be alone with my client, please.'

'I'm not your client. And I don't want a lawyer,' she said. 'Least of all you.'

He ran his hands through his hair. 'I understand why you feel like that. But this is not what it seems. I have something that will help you.' He looked around the interview room. 'I don't want to talk about it here. But appoint me as your attorney, I can explain, and then, if you don't like what I have to say you'll never hear from me again.'

'Why should I trust you?'

Varun held his hands out, palms up. 'I'm not asking you to. I'm just asking you to give me a chance. And at least you'll be out.'

She studied him. He worked for the woman who had killed her husband and daughter, who had covered up three other deaths and faked a suicide. There was no way she was going to do what he said, none.

And he knew that. Which raised a question: why were they here? If this wasn't in some way genuine, why were they bothering?

'OK,' she said. 'Tell me more.'

He closed his eyes for a moment and took a deep breath. He opened his notebook and began to write.

I don't want to talk aloud. I know Stearns did it. I have proof, but not enough. I need your help.

She read the message, her skin crawling, and wrote a reply.

Really? What kind of proof?

Messages she thought were deleted.

'So,' Ramos said in a loud voice. 'Here's the plan.'

She nodded and looked at Ramos. 'Tell me.'

'We get a bail hearing,' Ramos said. 'They grant it, we post it, and we're out of here. Then we work on your defense.'

'Will I get bail? How does it work?'

'Well,' Varun said. 'Bail is a constitutional right for anyone accused of a criminal offense.'

'Does everyone get it?' Stacy said. She shrugged on the jacket.

'Not in all cases,' Varun said. 'But I think you have a reasonable case. And it'll be set at a high level. Very high.'

'How high?'

'Half a million?' Varun said. 'A million?'

'And who pays? I don't have that kind of money.'

'Me and Ramos. If you abscond, it'll cost us a lot of cash.'

He wrote a note and passed it to her.

This is how we get Stearns. You have to trust us. So?

She hesitated. Why should she trust them? There was every chance that once she was out of here they'd take her to some remote location, kill her and dump her body. Nobody would miss her. Nobody would come looking.

She didn't have to take that chance, though. Once she was outside she could disappear. They knew that, too. But they were prepared to take that chance.

But then this would be over, and Stearns would be free. If they did have evidence, she wanted to see it.

So whether she trusted them or not, this was her only chance.

'OK,' she said. 'I agree.'

Varun stood up. 'Well, Ms. Evanston,' he said. 'We have what we need. You can let the officers know you've appointed me to be your lawyer.'

2

Miller – or Ramos – must have pulled some strings. Not long afterwards they were in front of a judge.

Bail was set right in the middle of the range Varun had estimated. Seven hundred and fifty thousand dollars.

Varun smiled and shook her hand.

'Jeff has gone to post the bail. Wait here.'

'I want to leave now.'

He hesitated. 'It's better if you wait for us.'

'No. I'll meet you.'

She could see him wondering whether she would simply vanish. His name would be part of the record. If she disappeared, he would be caught up in any fallout.

'OK,' he said finally. 'We'll meet you on the top floor of the Casco Bay parking garage, east corner.'

She nodded, and walked away, wondering whether she could trust them, after all.

She waited on the top floor of the garage. There was a brand-new Audi parked in the bay by the east corner; she assumed it belonged to Miller or Ramos. It was certainly the kind of thing they would drive.

She was not waiting there. She was concealed behind a Chevy Suburban on the other side. She had no guarantees it would be them who turned up and not some hired thugs, or even the cops, although why they would spring her from the police just to hand her back, she had no idea.

But it was always better to take nothing for granted.

She glanced at her watch. It had been five minutes. They should be here by now. Her pulse quickened. She would give them five more, and then she was leaving.

She would deal with Jill Stearns in her own way, if necessary.

She shifted into a more comfortable position, and then she heard voices echoing around the garage.

Footsteps. Clicks, like someone wearing brogues.

They were coming from the stairs. She turned to see who it was.

The voices grew louder, and then there they were.

Miller and Ramos.

They walked to the Audi. Miller took some keys from his pocket and pressed a button to unlock it. He looked around.

'Stacy?' he called.

She stayed hidden. What if this was a trap?

If it was a trap, it was a very public way to do it, if that was their plan. They were on the court records.

And what did she have to lose? She'd been prepared to die to get justice for Dan and Cherry, a prospect which – until Varun had shown up – was further away than ever. This was, whether she trusted him or not, the only chance she had.

So yes, she could walk away now, but then so would Stearns.

She stood up.

'I'm here,' she said.

They stood by the Audi.

'What's the proof?' she said.

'A message. But we need more,' Miller said.

She pointed at Ramos. 'Why's he here?'

'I told him what's happening. You can trust him. It was his idea to get you out.'

'Why would he want *more* evidence?'

'He wants to help. I promise. So. Are you in?'

She ran through it all again, and arrived at the same conclusion. What options did she have? But she would not share everything with them. She would find a way to keep control, somehow. She nodded. 'OK.'

'Thank you, Ms. Evanston,' Ramos said. 'I have to say I wasn't hoping our paths would cross again, but it seems they will.'

'Me too,' Stacy said. 'I'd say I'm sorry, but I don't want to start off with a lie.'

'I'm sorry for what happened to you,' Ramos said. 'That's not a lie. And if it was Jill Stearns – or anyone associated with the company – I want to see them brought to justice. If you need a token of my sincerity, how about this: when this gets out, the company's stock price will plummet, and that will cost me tens of millions of dollars. But that's a price I'm prepared to pay.'

'Me too,' Varun said. 'I couldn't live with myself otherwise.'

Varun seemed sincere; with Ramos she couldn't be sure.

'What do we do?' she said.

'Find more evidence,' Ramos said. 'We need to hear everything from you – exactly what happened, when, who was involved, everything you remember, and then we decide where to dig.'

That would not be a problem. It was burned into her memory. 'I remember it all,' she said.

'So tell us. All of it. Then we can find the loose ends and start to unravel it. And – for your safety – I suggest you find someone independent, a lawyer, or journalist, who you can share this with.'

'We can follow the money,' Varun said. 'The new boat, if it exists. Then there are nurses and doctors. Someone knows something. And we need to find out what that is.'

'And when we have enough,' Ramos said. 'We go to the right people.'

'Who are?' Stacy said.

'Not sure. Maybe the press. I know some journalists. We need to get it out there.' He paused. 'But let me warn you: this is dangerous. Since the moment you stepped out of the courthouse you've been on borrowed time. The police will have figured out you're not there by now. And you can bet Jill Stearns knows.'

She glanced at Varun. 'Why?'

'Because if someone was keeping an eye on you, they'll know you're out.'

'So what do we do?'

'Hide,' Ramos said. 'And right away.'

Stacy almost laughed. 'Where do we hide?' she said. 'I don't have a place to go.'

'No,' Ramos said. 'But I do. We can meet there.'

'Where is it?' Stacy said.

'In Western Maine. A couple of hours from here, in the Carrabassett Valley. It's way up on the side of a hill, on the east side. The other side has the ski resort, but my place is very remote. Very quiet. And no one will think I'm involved.'

'I know it well. I used to ski there.' Stacy glanced at Varun's wedding ring. 'Your wife OK with this?'

'She's safe,' Varun said. 'My son, too.'

'What next?' Stacy said.

'You two get a rental car,' Ramos replied. 'Send the details to me, and no one else. That way I'll know what car to expect.'

'What do you think's going to happen?' Varun said. His hands were shaking.

'I don't know,' Jeff said. 'I only know that if someone *is* watching, and they find out you're with Ms. Evanston, then who knows what they'll do? They'll know something is going on, and they'll want to stop it.'

Stacy looked at Varun. He was staring out of the garage, his jaw clenched.

'What's the address?' she said.

Ramos told them. 'After you give me the details of the rental car, no more phone calls or messages,' he said. 'Get there as soon as you can.'

He pressed a button and a car a few bays down beeped. 'I'll go right away. I'll be waiting.' He walked down to the car. As he climbed in, he turned to them.

'Good luck,' he said.

Stacy watched the car pull away.

'Go home,' she said. 'Maybe see your wife and son, then meet me at the car rental place. There's one downtown. That's better than the airport. Then we put an end to this, once and for all.'

3

Stacy sat in the rental car – a black Corolla, rented using a license in the name of Andi Stevens – and waited fifty yards up the road from the rental office. A car with an Uber sign pulled up and Varun got out. He looked around nervously, scanning the area for anything out of the ordinary.

She flashed her lights, and he froze.

She flashed them again, and then opened the window. She put her head out and beckoned him toward her.

'Jesus,' he said. 'I wondered who you were. I was thinking we'd hardly even got started and someone was already on to us.'

'Just me,' she said.

'You got the car?'

'I got *a* car.'

He frowned. 'What do you mean?'

'I have to go and do something before we meet Ramos.'

'I don't understand.' His nervous expression returned. 'Is there something wrong?'

'Plenty,' she said. 'But nothing new.'

'Then what is it?'

'It's personal.'

'I don't mind what you do,' he said. 'I'm happy to come along.'

She shook her head. This was her insurance, her way of keeping control. 'I'd rather be alone.'

He paused, then nodded. 'OK. So what's the plan?'

She pulled out a Maine atlas she had bought at a gas station and opened it to the page she had bookmarked. She tapped it.

'This is Ramos's house. It's past the ski resort, Sugarloaf, on the way to Eustis. Like I said, I used to ski up there and it's very remote. Almost totally empty. Just a winding, remote road that runs beside the river. There's a right turn off the main road, then the house is about half a mile further along. Let's meet at that turn-off and go in one car.'

'Why not meet somewhere else?' He looked at the map. 'Kingfield, maybe?'

'I think it's better nearer the house. It could be good to have a second car, if we need it.'

'Why would we need it?'

She shrugged. 'I don't know. But we might, and at least we'll have the option.'

For a second he looked like he was about to cry, but he swallowed and inhaled sharply through his nose.

'OK,' he said. 'We meet there. What time?'

'It's about three hours from here,' she said. 'My detour will take around an hour. So head straight there and wait for me. If you take your time, I shouldn't be far behind you.'

'I'll tell Jeff to expect us.'

She nodded. 'But only your car. Don't mention this one.'

'Why? You don't trust him?'

'I don't trust anyone,' she said. 'You included.'

He pursed his lips. 'I suppose that's to be expected.'

'Go and get your car,' she said. 'I'll wait here so I know what you're driving.'

He headed to the car rental office. She waited, noting which cars passed, which parked or lingered in places they could see her. There was nothing suspicious; at least nothing she could see.

Ten minutes later a blue RAV4 appeared at the entrance. Varun was behind the wheel. He glanced in her direction, just long enough to see she was there, and pulled into the traffic.

She pulled out her phone, and opened Craigslist.

4

An hour later she parked her car by the train station. The sign outside hadn't changed.

Welcome to Barrow

She got out and pulled her cap low over her head, then started walking. She had no need of a map. She knew every street in this town. Her destination was a small, white cape on a large lot. There was a Prius and a Highlander parked in the driveway; on the grass in the corner of the lot was an old blue Ford Ranger.

She knocked on the door. A man in his fifties opened it. He was wearing a red flannel shirt and had white, tufty eyebrows.

'Priscilla?' he said. 'I'm Rusty.'

She'd sent a message through Craigslist in a false name. Rusty had replied immediately, saying he was home and she could come at any time.

'Yes. Thank you for replying so quickly.'

He shrugged. 'Nothing else to do. Winter goes slow. You want to see the truck?'

'I'd love to.'

He had the keys in his hand and he gestured to the Ranger.

'She goes good. Bit temperamental, but runs nice.'

'How many miles?'

'Two fifty.'

Stacy nodded thoughtfully.

'That's a lot.'

'Plenty more in her. Treat her right, that is. I was keeping hold of her for my daughter. She's driving now, but she don't want an old truck. Seems it's not cool enough.'

'I would have loved this when I was sixteen,' Stacy said.

'That's what I was hopin'. But I got it wrong, I guess.' He handed her the keys. 'Here. Start her up.'

The truck was unlocked. Stacy climbed in the driver's seat and put the key in the ignition. The engine turned over once, twice, then coughed into life. She listened for a moment, then revved the engine. It sounded fine.

'Take her out,' Jeff said. 'I trust you'll be back.'

'You know,' she said. 'That won't be necessary. I think I've seen enough.'

'Not for you, huh?' he said. 'Too old?'

'Not at all.' Stacy smiled. 'I love it. You said two thousand in the listing? Would you take fifteen hundred?'

'Seventeen fifty,' he said. 'I'll fill in the paperwork, and she's yours.'

'Got it,' Stacy said. 'You have a deal.'

5

The Ranger was old and creaky and would need some new shocks soon enough, but it ran, and it wasn't the rented Corolla, which meant it was untraceable. The Corolla was parked in a corner lot near the train station, just another commuter vehicle left for a few days. Even if it was found, it wouldn't tell anyone where she was, only that she had been to Barrow. It was as likely she had taken the train to Boston as bought another vehicle and driven somewhere new. If the last few years had taught Stacy anything it was that you couldn't be careful enough. She enjoyed invisibility, and she had no intention of giving it up.

In the truck, cap on her head, she could have been anyone, man or woman.

She headed out of town, west toward the Carrabassett Valley, but there was one more stop she needed to make before she left.

The cemetery was on the road out of Barrow. She parked against the fence, and grabbed her coat. It was getting dark, and Maine's winter cold was biting.

She walked along the path between the graves until she reached her destination.

Cherry and Dan, side by side.

Her grave to the left of Cherry's. A daughter taking her eternal rest between her loving parents.

She had seen it before but it never failed to send a shiver along her spine.

She split the flowers she had bought at the gas station into two bunches and placed them on the graves.

Her daughter, and her husband.

The pain of their loss was as great now as it had ever been. It would never go away. Maybe – maybe – it would lessen over the years, but she doubted it. If anything, it got worse, the sense of what she had had taken from her sharpening as time went by. Cherry would be nine now. Four years of her daughter's life had been stolen from her. In a decade that would be fourteen. The more that had been taken, the worse the pain.

So she was pretty sure the wound would always be there, like a missing limb, its very absence a reminder it was gone.

She had stood here many times over the years, placed many bunches of flowers on the graves. She wondered whether anybody had noticed them and asked themselves who was bringing them. Perhaps she had been spotted, but she didn't think so. She came at quiet times, always when it was darkening, and she was careful to make sure no one was around. Once she had been startled by a couple turning into the row she was on, and she had looked down and covered her face as though crying.

She knelt and placed her hand on Cherry's gravestone.

'I think I'm getting close,' she whispered. 'To getting justice for you. But it's dangerous, so maybe I'll be joining you soon. I'd love that.'

She pressed her cheek to Dan's gravestone. It was ice cold. 'I miss you,' she said. 'Every day, all day. I love you.'

There was no reply. Just the quiet of the graveyard, and the pain of the cold stone on her cheek.

She got to her feet and headed for the truck, wiping the tears from her cheeks as she went.

6

Stacy knew the area reasonably well. Before Cherry was born she and Dan had spent a lot of cold and icy winter weekends skiing. They had friends with a ski condo at Sugarloaf Ski Resort so they had a place to crash for the night; those friends had rented it to them for a week in the February before Cherry and Dan were killed.

As she approached Kingfield – the last town before the ski resort – she couldn't help remembering driving this route with the two of them ahead of one of the best weeks they had had as a family.

Cherry had been in ski school from nine to three each day, leaving her and Dan with precious hours to spend together. They had spent a lot of them skiing, although most days they had taken advantage of the empty condo to work on a sibling for Cherry. Then at three they had picked up their daughter, a miniature skier waiting in a group of class-mates for their parents to come and collect them.

On the first day Stacy had been worried she would not enjoy herself and that they would struggle to persuade her to go back the next day.

How was it? she asked.

Cherry beamed. *I love it!*

Stacy hugged her. *That's great!*

The instructor, a woman in her late fifties, patted Cherry on the shoulder.

She's wonderful, she said. *And such a great skier, for her first day!*

Let me show you, Mommy, Cherry said. *I'm really good.*

Cherry followed her down the bunny slope, her heart bursting with pride and joy at the sight of her daughter wobbling along on unsteady legs, then collapsing in a heap when she wanted to stop.

By the end of the week she was a fully-fledged skier. Dan had shaken his head in disbelief.

They change in front of your eyes, he said. *It's hard to believe.*

What would Cherry have been doing now, aged nine? The black diamonds and double black diamonds? Maybe. It was another thing that had been stolen from her.

She pushed the thought away. She needed to be clear-headed. She needed to remember what they were doing here.

Varun had proof that Jill Stearns knew about a cover-up of a toxic product, a cover-up which had included arson.

A cover-up which had included murder.

But they only had proof of the first part, and they needed more. They needed to get off the grid and build their case.

Anger could come later.

In Kingfield she pulled into a gas station. She needed fuel for the truck and fuel for herself. The pump was card or pre-pay cash, so she headed into the store.

'Fifty bucks,' she said. She wasn't sure how much the tank held, but it was empty, and with gas at nearly four bucks a gallon it would easily take fifty dollars' worth. She picked up some Gatorade and a bag of beef jerky and put them on the counter.

Close by, sirens sounded. A fire truck, then an ambulance sped past the gas station, headed toward the ski resort.

'Someone's had an accident,' the man behind the counter said. 'Probably a drunk skimobiler. Or a heart attack on the slopes.'

'Probably,' she said. She handed over three twenties and the man counted out some change.

'Enjoy the skiing,' he said. 'Supposed to be good right now. Cold, but some decent snow.'

'Thanks,' she said. 'I will.'

As she climbed in the Ranger another fire truck went past, sirens blaring, lights flashing, followed by a police car.

She pulled out behind it and headed toward the mountains.

7

The road ran alongside a wide river. It was mostly frozen, only the occasional pool of water glistening in the moonlight where the current was strongest. For the first few miles the road was alongside the river, but as the road went up the valley it rose until there was a steep drop to the icy water below.

She kept to the speed limit; most cars passed her on the narrow road in their haste to get to the ski resort, but the old Ranger started to rattle and wheeze if she pushed it too hard, so she trundled along, happy to take her time.

There were houses and driveways on the left of the road, but the mountains on the other side of the river were unlit. At one point she saw a house high on the hill; there was a narrow bridge over the river leading to it. Ramos's place was probably similar, but even further up the valley.

After she passed the turn-off for the ski resort – a huge blue sign saying SUGARLOAF – the houses thinned out and the cars became even more scarce. There was about another five miles to go before the bridge where Varun would be waiting. She looked at the clock. At this speed it would take six or seven minutes.

That was nothing. Her back and neck tensed.

This was the moment.

The road curved to the right in a long, slow bend. As she came out of it, she saw a red glow up ahead. For a moment she thought it was a fire, but then she realized it was the lights of multiple emergency vehicles that had gone by her in Kingfield.

She slowed as she approached them. Two fire trucks were parked on the road, blocking her side. The police car was on the verge, and the ambulance was in a small lay-by.

A group of EMTs, cops and firefighters was standing by the barrier, looking down into the valley below.

A cop turned to look at her and waved her on. She tried to see what was in the valley, but the drop was too steep. It wasn't until she reached the next bend that she could get a good look.

There was a car upside down in the river, the wheels still spinning. She stared, trying to make out what it was but it was impossible to tell.

Her head spun. From here it looked like a RAV4. She felt like she was going to vomit.

Was that Varun? Was he the latest victim? She couldn't tell, but she had to find out. She pulled onto the side of the road and switched off the lights.

She waited for a few minutes to see if any of the emergency responders had noticed she had stopped. None of them came over, so she got out of the truck and climbed over the barrier. The cliff was steep and she picked her way down carefully, moving from rock to rock, each time making sure of her footing. When she was halfway down, she got a clear view of the car.

It was a RAV4.

A blue RAV4.

Her heart sped up. She had little doubt now, but she had to be sure. There were plenty of RAV4s in Maine.

She inched further down the slope, squinting until she could make out the plates.

She recognized them and her heart rose into her mouth.
All doubt was gone.
It was Varun's car.

8

She crawled up the rocks, feeling very exposed and very alone.

Varun was dead, that was certain. He hadn't survived that fall; no one could have. And if – by some miracle – he was alive, she was pretty sure that whoever had caused this would have seen to it that he perished.

Because this was no accident.

Yes, it was possible for someone to make an error on these narrow, windy roads, but that was not what had happened here. It was too much of a coincidence.

And it was all clear to her now.

Ramos inviting them up here, and asking for the details of the car. He was in this as much as Stearns was. Presumably he had told Stearns that Varun had found a link to the poisonings and they had come up with this plan. Get him and Stacy up to his remote mountain lodge and arrange an accident on the way. No doubt he would ensure that the local police department recorded it as such, too.

She was utterly deflated. She'd been a fool. It had been stupid to even try. They would stop at nothing and nothing would stop them: not the police, the regulators, the lawyers. They were above it all, and they knew everything.

Except there was one thing they didn't know. Unless Varun had said something – and she hoped to God he hadn't – they thought she'd died with him.

But she hadn't. She was here, on the side of this ravine, alive.

Very much alive.

And now she knew she was truly out of options.

Except for one.

She felt the great relief of clarity.

She knew exactly what she had to do.

Jeff Ramos

Jeff Ramos sat by the stone fireplace, the heat from the blaze in the hearth reddening his cheeks. He sipped his Talisker Malt – eighteen years old – and got to his feet. He wasn't sure he really liked it – he kind of preferred Jack Daniels, if he was honest – but it was expensive, and that alone gave him pleasure.

He walked over to the large picture window that looked down over the Carrabassett Valley. The valley was dark and quiet. His house was past the ski resort, which was where most of the visitors turned off the road. Very few came as far as this.

Somewhere down there Varun Miller and Stacy Evanston were making their way up the winding road, ready to put the final pieces in the puzzle of the downfall of Jill Stearns.

They too would not make it.

In the distance he saw lights between the trees. It was not Miller and Evanston. There were too many lights for one car, and they were too bright. They were also flashing red and blue.

Emergency vehicles.

He turned to the armchair by the fire and smiled. His guest raised a questioning eyebrow.

'Looks like some kind of an accident,' he said, and shook his head, a wry smile on his lips. 'Tragic. I'd hate for someone to have had an accident of any kind.'

Jill Stearns raised the glass of water in her hand in a toast.

'It seems it worked.' She sipped her water. 'You got rid of them. Now let's hope this thing is behind us for good. What did Miller say, exactly?'

'He said he had the instant message between you and Bill.'

'Anything else?'

'No. That was enough, though. If that had got out it would have caused no end of problems.'

'And had he told anyone else?'

'His wife, maybe.'

Stearns folded her arms. 'If he's dead in an accident it'll raise questions if something happens to her as well.'

'Doesn't matter,' Ramos said. 'As long as there's no trail. We can arrange something. And we'll need to do it soon. Before she finds out what happened to her husband.'

'So maybe tonight.'

'Maybe tonight.'

'And Sharon?' Stearns said. 'It was her who gave him the message, correct?'

'Correct. She'll be dealt with tomorrow.'

'OK.' Stearns held his gaze. 'So with Evanston, Miller, his wife and Sharon dead, there's no one else?'

Ramos smiled. 'Not a soul.'

'Could someone else find the message Miller found? It must still be there. And how did he get it? Someone must have helped him.'

'If they went looking, maybe. But I'll get it sorted tomorrow. It'll be gone for good.'

She nodded. 'Do it.'

He gestured at the lights in the valley. 'I'll call and ask what it is. Confirm it's Miller and the woman.'

'Before you do, there's one other thing.'

'Which is?'

'Standish. Where's he now?'

'In Florida. Spending the generous early retirement package we gave him.'

'He knows, too.'

'He also knows what will happen if he tells anyone. To his retirement funds, yes, but also to his daughter. She's a very attractive girl. At the time I explained to him how it would be a real shame if a group of men decided to give her more' – he paused – '*attention* then she would like. He understood what I meant.'

'Still,' Stearns said. 'He's a loose end. And I'm sick of loose ends.'

Ramos sipped his whiskey. 'Are you saying what I think you're saying?'

'Yes.'

'I'm not sure that's necessary.'

'Really?' Stearns said. 'That's nice to hear, Jeff. But forgive me if I'm rude when I say I don't give a fuck what you think. I just give a fuck that you do what I tell you. Is that clear?'

'Yes,' Ramos said. 'It's clear.'

'Then get it done.'

He raised his glass in a sarcastic toast, then put his glass down and dialed a number on his phone. It was answered immediately.

'Chief Fleming.'

'Chief Fleming,' he said. 'This is Jeff Ramos.'

'Jeff. Can I call you back? I'm a bit tied up.'

'Anything to do with the emergency vehicles I can see down in the valley?'

'Yeah, it is. Nasty accident. Someone ran off the road and went down into the river.'

'It's steep there. And a long way down.'

392

'Sure is.'

'I hate to ask, Chief, but are we talking a fatal accident?'

'We are,' the police chief said. 'It's a hell of a fall. We sent a guy down to look. There were no survivors.'

'Did you recover the bodies?'

'Body,' Fleming said. 'We recovered the body.'

'Body? There was only one?'

'That's right. There was one occupant.'

Jeff paused. He glanced at Stearns. 'Are you sure?'

'Hundred percent. Just the one. A guy. Varun Miller. He was in a rental car. Probably not used to these kind of roads. Why do you ask?'

'No reason,' Jeff said, his stomach tightening. He took a large sip of the Talisker. 'Truly tragic. If I can be of any help, you know where to find me.'

'Thanks. I'll let you know.'

The line went dead. Stearns stared at him. 'What is it?'

'There was only one body,' he said.

'Miller? Or the woman?'

'Miller.'

'So where is she?'

'I don't know,' Ramos said. 'I really don't know.'

Stearns rubbed her temples.

'That *fucking* woman,' she said. 'She just won't go away.'

393

Stacy Evanston

She had to move quickly.

She accepted that this was the worst case scenario: Ramos knew about the accident because he had caused it, and he knew by now that she was not in the car. He was also aware that she had his address, because he had given it to her in Portland. So he would assume she was coming.

What he didn't know was why she wasn't in the car or where she was.

So whatever she did, she had to do it quickly.

She started the Ranger, and with the lights off, headed up the road. She kept an eye out for other cars approaching from behind or from the other direction. She would either pull off and wait for them to pass, or, if that was impossible, turn on her lights for just as long as it took for them to go by.

No one came, and in a few minutes she was at the turn for the bridge.

She parked, the tires crunching on the snow, and opened the door. She wrapped her coat tight around her and pulled her wool hat low over her face.

It was freezing, a bitter wind whistling up the valley. Snow swirled in her face.

She moved quickly up the road, trying to keep warm. When the house came into view she left the road and skirted the edge of the property. As soon as she was about a hundred feet from the house, she ducked into the shade of a maple tree.

Like the one in her yard in Barrow.

She pushed the thought away. She needed a clear head.

It was a large, wood-cabin-style lodge. To the rear was a shed; to the front were views over the valley. There were two cars parked in the driveway.

Two. So Ramos had guests.

She looked around. Walking in snow was hard, but worse, it was noisy. To her left there was a trail some animal had made, heading around the back of the shed. From the shed to the house someone had made a path with a snowblower; if she could get there it would be much easier.

She followed the animal trail, placing her feet carefully in the animal's footprints, until she was by the shed, hidden in the pitch darkness of the night.

The house was well lit. Under the corner soffits she could see exterior lights. She wanted to get closer to see who was in there, but the lights were more than likely motion sensitive, so she would have to keep away from them.

She studied the house. She could see into the kitchen, but there was no one there.

And then she saw him.

Ramos walked to the sink and turned on the faucet. He filled a glass of water and drank it down in one. He turned, as though speaking to someone, then took another glass and filled it and held it out, offering it to someone.

The recipient came and took it. Stacy stifled a gasp.

It was Stearns.

Now it really was all clear. Varun had called Ramos and confided in him, thinking he was an ally, but Ramos had betrayed them to Jill Stearns.

She'd told him what to do. Get them up here, and kill them. Maybe she'd given him the name of someone who would run them off the road, or maybe he already had it.

They had brought them here to kill them and put an end to anyone who knew about the message. Which included Varun's wife. Would they kill her, too?

She knew the answer. They'd kill her, and leave Varun's son an orphan.

No. She could not let that happen.

The past fell away. The future was yet to come.

None of that mattered. All that mattered was that she was here. And they were here.

And she was going to end this, once and for all.

She slid along the front of the shed, her back to the door. She tried the handle. Would people up here bother locking a wood shed? There was unlikely to be much crime, other than the stuff Ramos brought himself.

She tried the handle. It turned, and the door opened.

2

The shed contained the usual detritus. Shovels, gardening tools, a lawn mower, a snow blower. A gas grill, and a box containing the grilling implements: scraper, tongs, lighter.

Two gas cans.

Two large green jerry cans. She picked them up to assess how much was in there.

They were both empty. There may have been some gas in the machines, but they didn't hold a great deal. Certainly not enough to cause much damage.

But there was plenty in the truck. Just a bit less than fifty dollars' worth. Over ten gallons of gas.

She knew what else she needed now. She put the flashlight on her phone and shaded the beam with her hand. She scanned the shed.

There it was. A garden hose, hanging in a coil on a nail. She tugged one end until she had a short length, then picked up a pair of shears and snipped it off.

She picked up the jerry cans and the lighter and headed back to the truck. She had never siphoned gas from a tank before, but she knew the theory: you put the hose in until it was in the liquid then sucked until it started flowing. The pressure of the gas was greater at the tank end and it forced the liquid to keep flowing, until you pulled the hose out.

She unscrewed the gas cap and slid the hose down into the tank. Then she opened the first jerry can and put her mouth over the hose and started to suck.

It took a few seconds for the gas to reach her mouth. It was disgusting, a fierce, acid taste. She spat it onto the ground, then shoved the hose in the mouth of the jerry can. It made a rushing sound as it filled the can.

When it was full she moved the hose to the other can. She estimated they were roughly five gallons each, so when the second one was about half full, she pulled the hose from the gas tank. She needed some left in the truck.

She put the cans in the passenger seat and climbed behind the wheel.

3

Stacy started the engine and drove slowly up the road. The Ranger's engine knocked and rattled so she kept it as quiet as she could, but she was aware that anyone listening would hear her well before she got to the house.

It was not a stealth truck. There was no way to make a surprise approach to the house. If they were listening, they would hear her well before she arrived, and then they could react.

She needed them to have no time to react,

Very well, then: make a virtue out of a necessity.

If she couldn't approach slowly, she would approach fast.

Very fast. She pressed the pedal and the old truck started to gather speed.

She turned into the driveway, the wheels skidding on the packed snow. She backed off a little on the throttle; there was no point crashing into a gatepost now.

She straightened up. The house was about two hundred feet away at the end of a long driveway. She sped up, the hood of the truck aimed at the front door.

The Ranger ate up the distance and slammed into the front door.

Wood splintered around her and the truck jarred to a halt. She was thrown against the seat belt, her head slaloming back and forth. She shook the dizziness from her mind, and focused.

Gasoline sloshed from the jerry cans onto the seat; she grabbed them and opened the door, then jumped onto the snow.

She poured gasoline to the left of the front door, then sprinted along the wall of the house, pouring gas against the log walls as she ran. She turned the corner, the jerry can getting lighter and lighter. When it was empty, she threw it away and started to pour gasoline from the second can.

She moved now with a grim determination. She paused at the back door and poured gas all around the frame, then carried on to the far side of the house, where there was a large propane tank.

Perfect.

She emptied the last of the gasoline onto the propane tank, then pulled the lighter from her pocket. She felt in her pocket for something to light; she pulled out the receipt for the gasoline.

She lit it, waited until it was fully aflame, then dropped it onto the tank.

4

The first sound was the whoomph as the gasoline ignited.

She sprinted away from the house and dived behind the shed to seek shelter. She watched as the flames ran around the house, following the trail of gasoline she had left.

It was, after only seconds, already an inferno.

And then, it became a hell.

The propane tank exploded, sending flames high into the night. The wall it was against disintegrated, windows shattering as a ball of fire ripped through the house.

Seconds later, there was another deafening explosion from the other side of the house.

The Ranger.

She turned and ran up the hill behind the house, heading for the safety of a stand of pine trees. She looked down at the house.

It was ablaze, a ring of fire encircling it. The flames rose higher and higher up the walls, consuming the old, dry wood frame of the house as though it was kindling. She could feel the heat on her face even from a distance. Up close it would have been unbearable.

Deadly.

She knew just how deadly. She had felt this kind of heat before, heard the sounds of a fire devouring a house, smelled the wood smoke and the pungent odor of melting paint and burning fabric.

The fire was a wall now, an impassable conflagration. There was a loud groan, then a snap as something gave way and the far wall fell in on the rest of the house. The roof followed, exploding as it hit the ground in a shower of sparks.

They were dead, she was sure of that, but still she waited and watched. Watched for anyone leaving, any figure scuttling away, highlighted against the snow.

There was no one. There could be no one. There was no escape from that inferno.

She sat, snow falling, and watched the house burn, half-expecting Ramos or Stearns to come staggering out of the house, coughing and burned, but alive.

No one came.

It was the second time she had witnessed the death of a house. This was revenge for the first, but she felt strangely empty, strangely unmoved.

They were gone. Stearns and Ramos were dead.

But she was still alone.

She got to her feet and began to walk down the valley. More alone than ever.

5

Stacy sat in the ski condo, the light off, as dawn rose in the valley. She had walked for hours until she arrived at the ski resort, where she looked for an unoccupied condo.

No car outside; no smoke from the chimney. She found a key under the mat by the back door and let herself in.

For a few seconds she had her heart in her mouth as she waited for a voice to call out in the darkness, but there was nothing.

She had grabbed a blanket and huddled on the couch, waiting for the new day.

She read the news on her phone.

TRAGEDY IN CARRABASSETT VALLEY

A fire last night claimed the lives of two people in the Carrabassett Valley. Jeff Ramos, 58, and Jill Stearns, 52, were killed when Mr. Ramos's house caught fire in what appears to have been an arson attack.

A police spokesperson said there were suspicious circumstances but did not reveal any further details.

Ms. Stearns was CEO of a noted food company,

where Mr. Ramos also worked, leading to speculation this is linked to an activist group protesting the use of genetically modified materials in the food supply. A company representative gave no comment.

It was the second fatal incident of the night, after a car left the road and fell into the river, killing its only occupant.

Stacy stopped reading. She had not doubted it, but now she had her proof. Stearns and Ramos were dead. She had one more thing to do, before she ditched her phone for good.

She searched the journalist's name. Mike Taylor. His email came up and she began to type.

Dear Mr. Taylor

My name is Stacy Evanston. I was a pilot in the US Air Force until 2018, when my husband and daughter were killed in a house fire. It was assumed I too was killed, but this was not the case. I disappeared, as I believed the house fire was arson.

My husband and daughter – along with Dr. Neal Williams – were killed as part of a cover-up of a product developed by the company headed by Jill Stearns. This product was toxic and – accidentally – caused the death of three children: Nathan Carter, Ella Farmer, and Bren Murdoch. It also made my daughter seriously ill.

I tried to expose the cover-up by hijacking the company plane Ms. Stearns was on. You can get details from the Portland Police Department. This attempt failed, but Varun Miller – who died last night in the car accident – found evidence of the cover-up and informed me, and Mr. Ramos. It was Ramos who suggested we come here, and he – or Stearns – who arranged Varun's accident, in an attempt at another cover-up.

404

It did not work.

Tragically, Ramos and Stearns suffered an accident of their own. I leave you to decide to what extent this was truly an accident.

Varun's wife has the details, but I have attached the message linking Stearns to the cover-up.

I trust this is enough for you to run with this story. Sadly, I cannot answer any questions as this email will no longer be active.

Yours,

Stacy Evanston

She would track the story as it emerged; everyone would. The demise of Stearns, Ramos and their company would be the biggest story since COVID.

She put her phone in the sink and turned on the water. After a few minutes she took it out and threw it out of the back door into a snow bank.

It was time to leave. The owners could arrive for a day's skiing at any moment. She searched the drawers in the main bedroom; fortunately someone who stayed there was a woman of roughly her size, so she had a change of clothes.

The police would link the truck to Rusty in Barrow pretty quickly. It was possible he was telling them at this moment about the woman, Priscilla, who had bought it.

There weren't that many Priscillas around these days, but it made no difference. They could find all the Priscillas they wanted, but they wouldn't find her.

She had disappeared before, and she could do so again. There would be an unlocked condo, the occupants out skiing for the day, their car keys left carelessly on a table.

She would leave it unharmed, for the police to recover and return to them.

Unharmed, but a long way away. Perhaps on the way to Chicago. Cities were easy to vanish into, easy to get illegal work, easy to get a new identity.

And then what? And then why? Why bother? She had achieved what she had wanted, and now the world was empty for her. There was nothing left. Nothing worth living for.

Except there was. There was a way forward. There was always a way forward. And it started – as everything started – with the first step.

She opened the condo door and walked outside, her boots leaving footprints in the fresh snow.

Acknowledgements

I am always struck by how many people are involved in getting a book from an idea to a draft to a final, published novel. There are many, and I am both grateful to them and in awe of what they do, from copy edit to cover design to marketing. I thank you all from the bottom of my heart.

In particular, thanks to Becky Ritchie, super-agent, for her unerringly brilliant advice on all things writing.

Finally – Kathryn Cheshire and Angel Belsey: it is a wonderful feeling to know that you are in the hands of editors who believe in your work, and whose judgement you can trust. Thank you both.